Dated

Ben Lovejoy

AIRBOOK PUBLISHING

www.airbookpublishing.com

Copyright © Ben Lovejoy 2016

Ben Lovejoy asserted the moral right to
be identified as the author of this work.

First published in Great Britain 2015
by Airbook Publishing.

First edition.

A catalogue record for this book
is available from the British Library.

ISBN 978-0-9931922-3-4

This novel is a work of fiction. The characters and events in it
exist only in the imaginations of its author and readers.

A note on language

I'm a Brit, and the novel is written in British English. Americans can expect to see some unfamiliar spellings which may appear to be typos. Examples include:

- 'ou' instead of 'o' in words like 'colour'
- 're' instead of 'er' in words like 'centre'
- the 'ise' suffix instead of 'ize' in words like 'specialise'
- similarly, 'yse' instead of 'yze' in words like 'analyse'
- 'ogue' instead of 'og' in words like 'catalogue'

English being English, there are also a whole bunch of cases where British English follows or doesn't follow one inconsistent rule, while American English follows or doesn't follow a different inconsistent rule (though American English wins the consistency battle overall).

Dedication

To MPFW, Stephanie.

Acknowledgements

I'd like to thank all the friends who played a role in this novel making the transition from a vague idea to a published novel.

Ingvild Harkes for providing an early and valuable critique of the first chapter.

Birgit Katzer for feedback, encouragement, proofreading and helping to solve a tricky plot problem.

Tania Slavkim for help with chapter 16.

Kathryn Choi for enlightenment in the ways of speed-dating.

Alan Frame for educating me about small children.

Members of Million Monkeys for a conducive writing environment and the impetus to keep going when life got in the way, and those of 13-amp for truly invaluable input.

Candace Mumford, Craig Martelle and others for encouraging me to revisit a novel first written in 2007 and which I'd written-off as my 'practice novel' – and Michael Anderle for creating a supportive group for such endeavours.

Diane Velasquez and Dorene for providing access to beta-readers. Caroline Cole and Henry Cooke Smith for feedback.

Chapter 1

One of the interesting things about being a 36-year-old divorced man who's decided that he's had enough of the casual sex phase, and is now looking for a capital-R relationship, is that your female friends quickly reveal an extensive supply of cute, single, 30-something women friends whose existence had hitherto been kept a closely-guarded secret.

The ease with which said friends are able to recite concise yet comprehensive reviews of vital statistics, career highlights, favourite films and a surprisingly lengthy list of all the things each apparently has in common with me would put a recruitment consultant to shame.

Helen was my closest friend. Thirty-three, 5'6", short black hair, piercing grey eyes and if you asked a random sample of people who know her to describe her, a good 95% of them would begin with the same word: ballsy.

She runs her own PR agency. It's not a profession for wallflowers, and I took an instant liking to her because she is the only person I've ever met who is more opinionated than me, and on a wider range of topics. It genuinely hadn't occurred to me that such a thing was possible.

We met on a marketing training course, and it wasn't a good one. It was led by an academic. That's not necessarily a bad thing. Academics have the freedom to pursue things that are interesting without having to worry about whether they will generate a commercial return (for which I envy them greatly), and that can often lead them to discover things that are both interesting and useful. But not in this case. The course presenter simply didn't understand the nature of the business situations he was attempting to address.

The delegates from the corporates settled for either rolling their eyes at each other discreetly and waiting for it to end, or regressing to their schooldays and huddling in small groups making semi-audible commentaries on the value of the advice being dispensed.

But when it's your own business, and your own money you're spending, you want to see real value from it. So I stood up and, calmly and politely, expressed the view that the situation he was describing didn't generally tend to work the way he thought it worked. He replied that every situation was different, and perhaps my experience wasn't typical.

Which was when Helen stood up and, equally calmly and politely, pointed out that her experience was identical to mine.

At which point he tried to bullshit his way through. This would not have been a good idea with me, and was even less of a good idea with Helen. It wasn't pretty.

So the course ended a little earlier than scheduled, and Helen & I went for a drink afterwards. Drinks led to a dinner, and thus began a close friendship.

I was happily married at the time. While there was admittedly a certain sexual energy between us, it never went any further than a bit of mutually enjoyable recreational flirting.

Now herself happily married, and enjoying her new role of matchmaker, Helen's list of candidates was impressive.

"Why didn't you mention all these friends before?" I asked. "Is it a summer special, or something?"

"Because your interest then was purely recreational."

"Fair point."

The first candidate was Alli, an expat American now living in London. Helen began reeling off the curriculum vitae ...

"31."

"Ok."

"Accountant."

"Hates her job, though, right? All the accountants worth knowing hate their jobs."

"Has a 10-year-old son."

"Hold it righ-"

"... who lives in America with his father."

"Hmmm."

I am not what one might consider natural parent material. I like my life. I like my home. Specifically, I like the fact that neither contains green poo nor is subjected to random episodes of projectile vomiting. If I really have to be woken at 3am, I want it to be by a cute woman who is feeling horny, not by a screaming pink blob who is feeling hungry.

"Do you have a photo of her?"

"Do you carry round photos of your friends?"

Helen can be annoyingly rational at times.

Facebook. Everyone has a Facebook account, right? That would have photos of her, and Helen would have access to her wall.

I hesitated. I didn't want Helen to think me shallow. We have, after all, had many Deeply Meaningful Discussions on a great many subjects. We have discussed politics, philosophy, religion, relationships, literature, art, theatre, Haagen-Daz flavours ... Well, ok, perhaps the ice-cream debates are not strictly relevant here (though anyone who seriously considers black raspberry chip superior to the understated purity of caramel cone must, in my view, be considered a deeply troubled person).

At the same time, men kind of *are* shallow. We're not like women, who seem blessed with the ability to become attracted to someone over time; it tends to be the case that we either fancy someone or we don't.

It's also not that I have movie-star looks myself. I'm sort of averagely handsome. Not a 10, not a 1, somewhere in the middle. I do seem to have the happy knack of batting above my average when it comes to women, but it's not that looks are the most important thing to me or anything, it's simply that sex is part of a relationship, and fancying someone is kind of a prerequisite for the sex part.

"Sports?" I asked, innocently.

6

"If you mean is she fat, no." Helen always could see straight through me.

I decided to turn to logistics. "Where does she work?"

"Woking. She also lives there, and before you do the whole 'outside the M25' number, she does hate her job and is looking for one in London."

"Ok."

"Ok?"

"Ok."

"Good."

"So, um, how does this work? I haven't been on a blind date since I was about 13."

"I give you her phone number, you call her, you start 'Hello, this is Stephen'."

I really have no idea why I'm friends with this woman.

"Hello, this is Stephen."

"Oh, hi. Uh ... Helen's friend, right."

"Right."

"Thought I'd check. Could have been an embarrassing conversation otherwise."

"True. So, you're in Woking?"

I was really showing off my scintillating conversational skills there.

"Yes."

So was she. This would be easier in person. Please god.

"How are you fixed for dinner next Thursday?" she asked.

Alli was clearly not one to hang around. Or, perhaps, like me, she simply had no idea how these calls with total strangers worked, and wanted to get back onto the rather more familiar territory of a conventional date. Anyway, she was friends with Helen, so that had to make her an interesting person. Worst-case we'd have a pleasant dinner with good conversation.

"Sounds good to me," I answered. "You know the town, so you book somewhere and let me know where, ok?"

"I'll meet you at the station. 7pm?"

"7pm it is. Wear a red carnation and meet me under the station clock."

"I think it has several station clocks."

"I'll be wearing a black suit, black shirt."

"How do you know what you'll be wearing in 10 days' time?"

I explained. There are people who can tell exactly what colours go well together, and who can buy a shirt knowing exactly which trousers it will go with. I am not one of those people. I thus have a very simple strategy for matching colours: my entire wardrobe is black.

Additionally, I hate shopping, clothes shopping especially. I have no patience for it. So when I find something I like, I buy at

7

least three of them – including suits. So I had a fairly good idea of what I would be wearing in 10 days' time.

Blind dates carry unexpected complications. You know those times you're trying to find a slot to see a friend and you go through your diaries in that 'Wednesday? Beer with the climbing club guys .. Thursday? Paula's leaving do .. Friday? Got a date' fashion? The date bit, of course, leads to the inevitable questions. The first of which is always 'Who is she?' and the second is always 'How did you meet?'.

Which is when you look shifty and mumble 'Er, we haven't yet, exactly'. I would, to be frank, be glad when it was all over.

At Waterloo, I had time to buy a cup of Earl Grey. I also, it turned out, had time to manage to spill a good 25% down the front of my shirt while attempting to retrieve my ticket from my jacket pocket to show the platform attendant. Just to add insult to injury, after spilling the tea and before managing to extract the ticket, he just waved me past in a bored fashion.

Great, I thought: the only thing worse than heading to a blind date at all is heading to a blind date with tea stains on your shirt. On board the train, I headed straight to the loo to see whether water would remove the evidence, assuming my shirt dried in time. I turned on the tap. A huge jet of water burst forth, splashed up from the sink and managed to spray my jacket, shirt and – oh God, yes – a decidedly strategic area of my trousers.

Thirty seconds previously, I just looked like a bit of a clumsy oaf. Now I looked like a rather unsuccessful Care in the Community case.

I had managed the water-spray disaster once before, but on that occasion was at least in a bathroom with a hot-air hand-dryer. Standing under that for about ten minutes had solved the problem. This time the only thing the loo had to offer was a copious supply of paper towels.

Cheap paper towels, it would appear, as they semi-disintegrated while rubbing them on my trousers, leaving dozens of little white bobbles behind. Attempting to wipe these off with my hands smeared some of them, leaving the crotch of my trousers still visibly wet and with some white-ish stains. This was not going well.

I looked at my watch. I would be arriving in Woking, and my date, in exactly 18 minutes time.

I decided that removing my trousers might at least make it easier to see what I was doing. 17 minutes remained. Attempting to rub off the paper stains wasn't working, so the only thing for it was more water. Carefully, very carefully, I turned on the tap. I succeeded this time in getting a gentle flow of water. I bunched up the crotch area and held it under the tap, soaking it. 16 minutes. I rubbed the fabric against itself and was relieved to see that this was succeeding in removing the paper stains. I carefully inspected my handiwork and found it mercifully free of any traces of paper. 14 minutes, and now I just had the problem of a freshly-soaked crotch.

I briefly considered trying to open the window to wave the trousers in the breeze before vivid visions of the one way in which this situation could deteriorate dissuaded me. I wrang out the water and sort of flapped the trousers around in a half-hearted fashion before putting them back on. 11 minutes. I looked at myself in the mirror. One further advantage of black clothing is that it doesn't show stains very well, and I decided the original stains on my shirt were now faint enough to pass muster if I was careful to keep my jacket on. The water-stained crotch still looked rather obvious.

Oh well, I thought, there was still nine minutes for it to dry sufficiently to avoid me turning up at a blind date looking like I'd just peed my pants.

A loud thumping on the door accompanied by a gruff "What the hell are you doing in there?" seemed to indicate that all I could do now was hope for the best. Emerging from the loo, I opted not to offer any explanation for my extended stay.

Mercifully, my trousers were merely damp by the time the train pulled in, and I figured I could get away with it so long as Alli didn't grab my crotch. And if things were going that well, I could probably tell her the story and laugh it off.

I recognised her straight away. Partly because she really was standing under the clock, but mostly because my suspicions were right.

Alli was, as advertised, 31. About 5'5", average build, long black hair. She had the kind of face that even her mother would have been forced to describe as 'plain', which is one thing, but she was dressed like a woman in her fifties. A mid-calf skirt in a brown check and made of some material that would have been more suited to black-out curtains, and the sort of blouse you'd expect an elderly aunt to wear to church on Sundays. One doesn't like to make snap judgements, but, well, sometimes one just does.

But hey, we were there now, and you can't very well arrange dinner with someone and then change your mind for aesthetic reasons. And just because we weren't going to end up in bed didn't mean we couldn't spend an enjoyable evening chatting. So I flashed her my best smile, gave her a quick peck on the cheek and offered her my arm.

I have a simple philosophy when it comes to getting to know someone: talk about all the topics traditionally banned from the dinner-table. Politics, religion, sex.

Politics was uneventful. In fact, I may have to scrub politics from the list as about 95% of the population appears to share the same view. The Labour Party is now somewhere to the right of Thatcher. The Tories can't position themselves to the right of Labour as that slot is already taken by the BNP, so they have been forced to position themselves about where the LibDems used to be. The LibDems, having been evicted from the centre ground, have had nowhere else to go but to the left. Politicians of all hues are all equally trustworthy, which is to say not at all. We'd pretty much done with politics, in fact, by the time we reached the restaurant.

9

She'd chosen a Bella Pasta somewhere in the middle of the identikit town centre that is Woking.

She left the choice of wine to me. I tend to the view that a first date has enough unknowns without adding wine to the list, so I played it safe with an Australian Cabernet Shiraz I knew to be drinkable in that 'alcoholic Ribena' way the Australians do so well.

Wine to hand and food ordered, I moved things on to topic two.

"So, having exhausted politics, where do you stand on religion?"

"I'm a Baptist."

Ooo-kay. This isn't good. Not only is she a theist and a Christian, but she takes that so much as read that she doesn't even see the need to mention the fact, she just dives straight into the brand. Why the hell didn't Helen know about this? She would surely have warned me if she had? (She informed me afterwards that normal people talk about books and films and music on a first date, they don't jump straight into fundamental belief systems. I asked her where the fun was in that, and she gave me The Look. She also informed me that answering with a specific brand is, in fact, perfectly normal for Americans even if they haven't been to church in 20 years.)

I readily admit that I'm an intellectual snob, and the religion question is partly a disguised IQ test. It's not that I'm looking for some correct answer, more that, whatever someone's position, I need to know it's a considered one. It's been my experience that very few people who answer the question with a specified brand of Christianity meet that criterion.

Though Dawkins describes my position as 'default atheist', I always describe myself as an agnostic. Partly because it seems to me more intellectually honest simply to say that we don't know, and partly because it is difficult to form an opinion about something which has no agreed definition. Anytime anyone asks me whether I believe in God, I begin by asking them to define the term.

"What does a Baptist believe?"

"We believe in the bible."

"As in .. a philosophy of do unto others? .. Metaphors? .. The literal word of God?"

I deliberately left that one 'til last in the hope that she'd laugh and call me silly. She didn't.

"I believe that the bible describes real events, yes."

This was not going well, and the starters hadn't even arrived yet. I decided it was time to segue into something trivial.

"What other books do you enjoy?"

Happily, this diversionary tactic succeeded, and we discovered a mutual admiration of Kate Fox's excellent study of Englishness (actually, mostly a study of middle-class Englishness), Watching The English. I enjoyed it because one defining characteristic of the English is our love of laughing at ourselves. Alli enjoyed it because even after living here for five years, she felt there were many aspects of English society that it's hard for an American to grok.

A highly enjoyable conversation about our respective takes on various countries we'd visited led to discussion of food, cookery, home décor and finally relationship criteria.

Before you jump to any conclusions, I should like to point out that it was Alli and not I who introduced the subject. But by this point, we were getting on well, the wine and conversation flowing equally freely, so when she asked me about mine, I gave a relatively succinct and light-hearted list. I decided to bury physical attractiveness somewhere in the middle.

"Attitude to life is a key one. We all have our cynicisms, of course, but I look for people who have a basically positive 'life is what you make it' approach. Intelligence. I love to discuss and debate, so could never be in a relationship with someone who didn't enjoy that. Physical attraction has to be there, obviously. Enough shared interests to-"

"So do you?" she asked.

"Do I?"

"Find me physically attractive."

That one took me by surprise. It's possible that, with a bit of notice, and perhaps availing myself of the 'Phone a friend' option, I might have come up with a good response. All I could think of immediately was to deflect the question.

"You didn't quiz me about attitude or intellect."

"No."

It wasn't a terribly successful deflection.

Well, it is a blunt question, and you don't ask it that baldly or insistently unless you want an honest response, I guess.

"Um. Sorry. Afraid not. I like you, though," I added brightly.

My cheery addition didn't help. I realised as I answered that the only reason she'd asked the question that directly was because she thought she already knew the answer, and it wasn't that one. Damn!

Things went very quiet. We were only about halfway through the main course and the wine.

At a moment like that, you can either continue the embarrassed silence or take the 'Meet trouble head-on' approach. I hate embarrassed silences.

"You were expecting a different answer."

"Yes."

"Damn. I should have realised that. Sorry! I can be a klutz sometimes."

Nothing.

"It was just, with you asking the question that directly, I didn't know what else to say. I'm a crap liar."

"Right."

Alli resumed eating, so I did the same: it did relieve us of the need for immediate conversation, but also removed the option of taking the easy way out and asking for the bill.

"I'm sorry."

"It's ok."

"I think you're great."

"It's ok."

About a week went by before she put down her knife and fork. I did the same and signalled to the waiter for the bill. It took about a fortnight to arrive. I paid it without looking at it.

"Well, it was good to meet you, anyway."

Oh god, was that really the best I could do? I considered the matter for a moment. For several moments. Yes. Yes, it was. It really was.

Fortunately there was a taxi-rank about two minutes' walk away. What was the etiquette for such a parting? I decided one didn't do the kiss on the cheek thing. And yes, I admit it, I really did repeat the "Nice to meet you" line. Well, it had been, prior to That Question.

A firm resolve was reached that evening. I would never, ever again arrange to meet a blind date for a meal. It would always be for a drink, then any repetition would be mercifully brief.

Helen didn't speak to me for about four days.

Tom, in contrast, found the whole thing hilarious.

"How old are you, Adams? A blind date? You can't be that desperate, mate."

"It seemed like a good idea at the time," I said, weakly.

"It was a bloody stupid idea," he countered. It was hard to argue with that one.

We'd met at Crisis at Christmas ten years ago. We'd each volunteered there on Christmas Day for years. We liked to pretend it was for altruistic reasons, but actually we both had divorced parents, and it avoided the lose-lose question of where you went for the festivities.

Despite being one, I felt I'd never quite got the hang of bloke friendships. The basic deal seemed to be that most of the conversation had to be about trivia, and if you did stray off into areas like relationships, the only acceptable format for this was taking the piss out of each other. The lingua franca of male conversation appeared to be banter.

It wasn't that I minded this, I just quickly bored of it.

Tom was slightly different in that you could, if you persisted, have something approaching a real conversation with him. You just had to get through the ritual banter phase first. Perhaps, I thought, having conceded the stupidity of the blind date, I could cut to the chase.

"So, how does it work, then, this dating stuff. At our age, I mean. I feel a bit old for bar hopping."

I'm not sure why I felt he had any answers. He hadn't had a lasting relationship in all the time I'd known him. I think his record was a little over a year. He mostly seemed happy with the single life. I had been too, for a time.

It had started as a strange sensation, being single again. For 12 years, so many decisions had been joint ones. When even which brand of coffee to buy had been a committee decision, the idea of choosing a house, then decorating and furnishing it, without anyone else to consult felt alien in those first few weeks.

I'd see a particular paint colour and instinctively turn to the empty space next to me to seek agreement.

But within a surprisingly short time, it felt liberating. I could, for the first time in a long while, be utterly selfish. There were only my preferences to consider. Only my tastes to reflect. Only my needs to meet. It was quite thrilling.

I mourned the marriage much less than I'd expected to. I think most of my mourning had already taken place. Helen had given me possibly the single best piece of advice I'd ever received: that I shouldn't end my marriage without first going all-out to save it. Doing that, and failing, meant I really could be sure that ending it was the right thing for both of us.

I'd never been unfaithful, not once. Not that I'd never been tempted, but I did seem to possess the ability to think beyond the immediate moment. I knew how I'd feel in the morning, and I knew how I'd feel the next time I saw Isabel; the temptations were never more than fleeting.

So being single was liberating sexually too. It was like being a teenager again, only without the angst.

The first time with another woman had still felt strange. Not entirely devoid of latent guilt. But that feeling didn't last long, and there followed a phase of hedonistic indulgence I'd expected to last maybe six months before I'd once again feel ready for another relationship.

Six months stretched into two years. But ultimately, it wasn't me. Meaningless sex is fun for a while, but only for a while. Two years in, I didn't want to chase another night of adventure: I wanted to wake up next to someone I loved. I was now officially Dating With Intent.

Tom brought me back to the present with his reply.

"It's easy these days," he said. "Pick an interest, Google it, find some events, wander along, voila, lots of women and you're guaranteed at least one interest in common. Or there's online dating. Even easier: answer a bunch of questions, get presented with a list of women you know are looking. Like shooting fish. Or go perving all your mates' Facebook friends looking for cute single women, and ask for an introduction."

I wasn't going to be doing that one, I decided. I'd had quite enough of fix-ups for now.

I'd never really figured out Tom's attitude to women. His language and tone were quite laddish, he clearly did enjoy bed-hopping, and he really did appear to keep score. But I also knew him as someone who could be thoughtful, and I thought his more sexist comments were more for show than representative of his real attitudes – but I was never entirely sure.

"I think I'll skip the intros," I said. "The activities thing makes sense, though."

"Go for it."

Chapter 2

As it turned out, I hadn't needed to: I met Kathy at Paddington Station. It was perhaps the most clichéd meeting possible: she was struggling to lift her case on board the train, and I offered to help. Whilst I would not claim that her attractiveness passed me by, I would like to point out in my defence that I am equally quick to offer assistance to little old ladies.

I never was any good at guessing ages, but I put her around 30. Long, dark-brown hair that looked impossibly straight. Small, vaguely librarian-ish glasses that should have looked somewhat nerdy and instead somehow added to her attractiveness. A green top with a rust-coloured skirt and purple scarf adding up to a colour combination that ought not to have worked but did. Either no make-up or very subtle make-up. Small ear-rings, no other jewellery. Button nose. I like button noses.

She gave me a delightfully genuine smile of gratitude.

"Thanks."

"A pleasure."

"Nice to see the age of chivalry is not entirely dead."

"One does one's best."

Have you ever found yourself trapped inside one of those conversations where it feels as if the entire exchange was written in advance and you can't quite figure out how to set about departing from the script? I knew how the rest of it went. Where we were each going. Whether it was business or pleasure. Whether we knew the place well. I really didn't want to run through the whole thing, but I wasn't quite sure how to switch into something more meaningful within the 15-20 seconds it would take for one of us to reach our seat.

If it had been a Hollywood movie, the train would have been a glorious old steam train on a journey to some romantic city, and we'd have found that we were sitting opposite each other as the only passengers in one of those delightful compartments in days of old.

Instead, the diesel train was the 09:42 to Swansea and our reserved seats were at opposite ends of the carriage. This was distinctly lacking the Hollywood touch.

We reached her seat first, I put her bag in the space between the seat-backs, she thanked me again and I told her she was welcome, smiled and wandered down to my own seat towards the far end.

Hollywood had failed me. In a Brit film, our cases would have been identical, and there would have been a charming mixup resulting in us opening each other's bags in our hotel rooms only to find that we are staying in the same hotel. We'd laugh about it then go to dinner.

But Brit films were failing me too: her case was an enormous green suitcase and mine was a small black rollerbag.

I'm not a shy person. Most people who know me would describe me as one of the more confident people they know. But I've never been one of those fortunate guys who can smoothly execute a pickup of a perfect stranger in a public place. So for the first few minutes I attempted to formulate a plan. What convincing excuse could I come up with for going to speak with her?

'I just realised, you'll probably need a hand off with your case at the other end – where are you going to?' Way too lame.

'Train journeys are very boring and since we're both travelling alone, care to pass the time with some conversation?' Might have been ok if I'd suggested it at the time, but a bit more desperate-looking if I have to go back five minutes later and that's the best I've been able to come up with.

What would a Hugh Grant character (well, the Hugh Grant character, really) do? Hmm. He'd approach her in a very bumbling fashion and stumble over his words while saying something like "I'm terribly sorry to trouble you, but I don't suppose you'd- No, no, of course you wouldn't. It's just that- No, sorry, I'll, er ... sorry, sorry.' Then he'd sort of half-turn to return to his seat, and she'd find his shyness charming and rescue him with a witty remark, inviting him to join her.

In real life, she'd think I was a bumbling fool and stare at me until I went away. Unless, perhaps, I looked like Hugh Grant. Which I don't.

The movie industry really wasn't proving much help.

Oh sod it. She'll be asleep by the time I think of something. Let's just go for it.

"Hello again, I was just on my way to the buffet car for a tea, and wondered if I could get you anything?" Not exactly going to win whatever the Pulitzer Prize equivalent is for pickup lines, but it was the best I could do at short notice.

"Oh! More chivalry. I had a cup of tea at the station, but thank you anyway."

This was going to be a very short conversation unless I took executive action.

Telling the truth with strangers can be considered either refreshingly endearing or downright weird, depending on one's point of view. I do try to resist completely unprovoked examples; I mean, I don't wander up to complete strangers in the street and attempt to engage them in Deep And Meaningful Conversation. But, under the circumstances ...

"Well, actually, that was the best I could come up with in terms of an excuse to come and talk to you."

"I realised." There was a faint smile there. Amusement? Invitation?

"Did it work?" I always was an optimist.

"Maybe. Have a seat and I'll send you away when I get bored with you."

This girl made me look like an amateur in the candour stakes.

"I'm Stephen."

"Kathy. Do you make a habit of hitting on girls on trains, or am I a special case?"

"Is there a convincing answer to that?"

"We'll see."

We chatted. More briefly than expected, as she was only going as far as Reading, but I wasn't despatched back to my seat in that time, and I was sufficiently interested to ask for her phone number.

She reached into her handbag and gave me a neatly-folded piece of notepaper with her mobile number scribbled on it.

"Do you make a habit of preparing for men on trains to hit on you?"

"I wasn't sure how brave you were going to be; if not, I was going to give it to you as I got off the train."

One of the dating rules I didn't know was how long one was supposed to wait before calling. It would presumably be seen as over-keen if I called too soon, and rude to leave it too long. But what was too soon? What was too long?

I almost called Helen to ask, but thought that seeking dating advice quite so soon after The Woking Incident might be inadvisable – and Tom would probably tell me to 'play it cool, mate.' I settled on two days.

Diary coordination is always a nightmare, and business travel definitely doesn't help. Dinner was going to be about a month away, which seemed silly. Kathy lived in West London, and I was seeing friends in Windsor the following Sunday, so we settled for afternoon tea there.

Afternoon tea is a much under-rated British institution. It has to be done properly, of course. Real china. A generous-sized teapot with separate jug of hot water for replenishment. Sandwiches cut neatly into four triangles. Everything served by a white-haired old lady. If doing the whole cream tea number, the scones must be warm, the whipped cream real and the jam served in little cut-glass bowls.

There is something about the ritualistic nature of it. The clink of china. The embroidered napkins that would be hideous at home but are somehow just perfect in this context. It's almost impossible to savour the experience without a feeling that all is right with the world.

Jacobs was such a tea-shop. My local friends had introduced me to it many years ago, and I swear that nothing had been changed since about 1970. It was a tiny place, and it was a sunny day, so I'd called in on my way to see my friends. Tea-shops do not, of course, offer table reservations, but a cheeky request accompanied by a charming smile can often work wonders, and so it had proven on this occasion. When I arrived back at a few minutes to four, Kathy was already there and sitting at a table with a hand-written Reserved sign. She was wearing a yellow blouse with knee-length red skirt. The effect was quite vivid.

"Good afternoon."

"Hello. They told me this was your table."

"It is, yes."

"That's somehow more impressive than knowing the Maitre'D at the Ritz."

I recalled Helen's words, and we talked inconsequential things.

"What music do you enjoy?" I asked.

"I'm a bit of a jazz buff. Do you like jazz?"

"I love some of it, hate some of it, and would be hard-pressed to tell you what makes the difference."

"What do you love?"

"Well, Nina Simone-"

"That doesn't count; everyone loves Nina Simone."

"I guess the same is true of Billie Holiday, right?"

"Right."

"Does Fats Domino count?"

"I'll let you have that one."

"Thank you. And you were supposed to be telling me about your musical tastes, actually."

"I like Dexter Gordon - heard of him?"

"No."

"Thelonious Monk?"

"Um, no."

"Cannonball Adderley?"

"Uh, so, besides Jazz, what do you like?"

"I always start with jazz because it sounds cool. My other tastes are a little too Radio 2 to admit to straight away."

"Ok, then we can be embarrassed together – I have some very dodgy musical tastes too."

"Such as?"

"You keep throwing my questions back at me."

"Yes."

"Ok. Well, I generally refer to my music collection as 'eclectic' as it sounds more cosmopolitan than 'dodgy'. Everything from Bach to Billie Holiday."

"Neither of those qualify as dodgy - who aren't you admitting to?"

"Well, I grew up in the 70s ..."

Kathy gave me an amused look and raised her eyebrows.

"Well, you know."

"No, do tell."

"Um ... I'd like to point out that, at the time, Fleetwood Mac was very cool."

"Uhuh."

"Though I admit Jeff Buckley probably never was."

"Now the truth is coming out. But I have to confess to that one too."

"Ok, then perhaps I'll let you come back to my place and rifle through my iPod."

"That's the beauty of iPods, you can flick through them anywhere."

"Damn."

We did books and films, too; Helen would have been proud.

This time it was Kathy who shifted things onto more meaningful ground.

"Do you have a plan for your life, or are you just meandering through and seeing what happens?"

"Are those the only two options?"

"As far as I can see, yes."

"Hmm. I'm not sure that I have a plan, in the 'single theory of everything' sense. I have some goals, and I have concrete plans to achieve some of them, but beyond that ... Aside from the sheer number of variables and surprises life throws at us, there's also the fact that what I want from life changes over time. When did you first formulate your plan; I assume you have one?"

"No deflections. Tell me about your goals."

My immediate thought was what an intimate question it was – rather an ironic thought, given my own approach.

My second thought was how difficult it is to describe one's own goals without them sounding trite or superficial on the one hand, or pretentious on the other.

I always thought the idea of taking a deep breath before answering a tricky question was just a saying; apparently not. Kathy looked at me over the top of her glasses in a manner reminiscent of a school-teacher waiting patiently for a child to answer a simple question.

"Well, my business goals are clear: I want to earn more money from the most interesting projects, so that I have to do fewer of the least interesting ones. Perhaps it will sound unambitious, but I have no desire to grow the business, as such. I enjoy being a photographer, and have no wish to become a manager instead. Most of the work is fun, but there's a percentage of it I do only to pay the mortgage – it would be good to lose that."

"Ok, and I guess that's one you have a plan for?"

"I do."

"Ok, next."

"This is like a job interview. Well, like I imagine a job interview would be – I've only ever had one, and that was in a pub."

It was true. I got into photography as a kid, and there came a point where there was no doubt about what I was going to do for a living, only how I was going to get started. I went to university less for an education and more because it seemed like a fun way to spend a few years before knuckling down to work. I'd acquired an overdraft and a wife. At 22, the ink barely dry on my degree, I started phoning round local photographers looking for one who would take me on as an assistant. About the tenth one told me to meet him at his local pub at lunchtime. By the second pint, he'd offered me the job and I'd accepted. I worked with him for a year before setting up on my own.

Kathy smiled, and waited patiently for me to answer.

"I have a rolling list of things I want to experience. As I tick off ones I've done, I add new ones."

"What was the most recent addition?"

"Ah. That's a slightly strange one: to travel from Moscow to Beijing on the Trans-Siberian Railway. I have no idea why, other than I like both cities, and it sounds like a romantic way to travel between them. In reality, it will probably be nine days of stomach bugs from dodgy food and nine nights of fitful sleep on a wooden bunk, but hey ..."

"I like that one."

"Ok, then I can tell you the crazier ones."

"Do."

"I want to climb Everest."

"Seriously?"

"Yes."

"Do you climb?"

"I do. It's within my technical level – Everest is a climb more demanding of stamina than technical ability – but it would require a lot of training and preparation to reach the level of fitness required."

"Do you still have Sherpas these days?"

"Most people join an organised expedition. It's not cheap, but everything is laid on for you, so all you have to worry about is personal preparation." I smiled. "I say 'all' like it's a small thing. It would take some real commitment. Oh, and about thirty grand."

"That's an expensive holiday."

"And you don't even get room service. But I think I've earned the right now to hear your craziest one."

"Ok. I'm going to drive round the world in a VW Camper van."

"Aren't parts of the globe a little damp for driving?"

"It does involve some ferries, but it's surprising how few if you plan your route well."

"What a pair of adventurers we are." I looked around the tea-shop, "Well, armchair adventurers, at least."

It was again Kathy who moved the conversation along. Sorry, I don't mean to keep mentioning that; Helen has made me a bit touchy about the subject.

"Have you been married?"

"12 years."

"You make it sound like a sentence."

I smiled. "No, most of it was good."

"Why did it end?"

That directness again.

In soap operas, the ending of a marriage – returning home early and catching the spouse engaged in extra-curricular activities – is sudden, definite and with a single clearly identifiable cause. The ending of real-life marriages is generally none of these things.

Isabel and I had met when we were 20, moved in together almost immediately, married when we were 22. We married because it was what two young and in-love people did after they'd lived together for a couple of years. I don't mean we did it without thought – we both knew then that the promises were big ones – but we were sufficiently young and romantic to believe the relationship was for life, so expressing that belief in a public fashion didn't seem too great a stretch.

When you separate from your wife, you have to tell a lot of people, and I'd reduced it to a convenient short-hand: "We developed different interests and priorities. What we each wanted from life had become too different."

After a while, the two sentences tripped off my tongue so readily I might almost have had them printed on a laminated card. But what do you tell people? You can't talk them through what happened to each of you over ten years, even if you knew. Social situations demand shorthand, and after a while the shorthand is all you have left.

There was one big reason: The Baby Thing. There are many areas in life where compromise deals are possible; a baby isn't really one of them. There are no trial periods or part-time babies. So when one of you desperately wants one and the other adamantly doesn't, there aren't too many options.

But you can't include that in the shorthand because it raises the obvious question of how the hell you get to be married for ten years with that incompatibility. The truth was mundane: we'd met when I was 20. I was young. I assumed that one day I'd want kids because, well, that's the prevailing assumption. I knew at the time that I didn't want them then, but assumed this would change. It didn't.

I tried the shorthand, not expecting to be allowed to get away with it. To my surprise, Kathy merely nodded.

"And you?"

"Never married."

"Serious relationships?"

"One." The tone and accompanying frown didn't invite further enquiry. Perhaps that was the reason she didn't pry further with me.

"What about after the adventuring?" she asked. "Where do you see yourself living in ten years' time?"

"I'm a classic Londoner, I'm afraid. Other places are fun to visit, but I can't ever see myself living anywhere else. You?"

"I like quite a few places enough to live in them, but London is one of those."

"Kids?"

I had that job interview feeling again, but at least that was an easy one to answer.

"Absolutely not."

"You seem rather definite about that."

"I am."

I gave her the spiel about green poo and projectile vomiting.

"That stage doesn't last long – your thinking on the subject must have got beyond the first couple of months, surely?"

I liked her style.

"Ok, that's the cocktail party one-liner. But I really don't see myself as a parent. I'm too selfish."

"That's another cocktail party cliché."

Well, I quite liked her style.

"True, but it's also the reality. I like my lifestyle. I like the freedom of it. I couldn't live a life where I'd lose that freedom. Having a child is a massive, long-term commitment. Other than photography, I don't know that there's anything I could give quite that much commitment to."

"Including a partner?"

The raised eyebrows and peering over the glasses was beginning to make her look rather like a young Anne Diamond. I was liking her style a bit less.

"That's unfair. But really, several close friends have had kids, and it really is a completely different life. It's fine if you want that life, but I really don't."

"What if you met that one perfect woman, and she wanted kids?"

"Then she wouldn't be that one perfect woman, unfortunately. I take it you want kids?"

Her answer took me completely by surprise.

"No, not necessarily. Not even probably. I think I probably won't ever choose to have them. But I could never have a relationship with a man who was so closed to it."

I tried, and failed, to make sense of that.

"Ok, I think you're going to have to try that in words of one syllable."

"I'll try, but I'm not sure whether a man can really understand it. I don't need kids. Probably don't want them. But I could never be as absolute about it as you are. The possibility of having kids is part of what it is to be female, so rejecting that possibility is like rejecting part of who I am as a woman."

"But if it's a decision made before someone met you, it can't be a rejection of part of you – it's a position reached without even knowing you."

"I know, but you're viewing it from a purely logical perspective, and feelings – especially fundamental ones – aren't logical."

It would have been easy to dismiss this as an irrational quirk on the part of one woman, but I felt I should try my best to grasp this one. A key reason for my divorce was the joint realisation that there was never going to come a time when I would want kids, and I'd made the decision to be 100% up-front about this so that I didn't end up going down the same path again.

I refilled our cups, then poured the jug of water into the tea-pot.

"Ok. I would like to understand it, though, if I can."

"For me, part of the deal of a relationship is being open to the whole of your partner, all that they are or could be."

"I agree with the core of that, but ... none of us are really open to every possibility, are we? I mean, if someone is a city person and they meet someone who wants to live in rural Spain, that's not going to work. If one can be definite about that, why can't one be definite – one way or the other – about the kids issue?"

Kathy sipped her tea while she figured out a way to explain it.

"You have to understand that a lot of who a woman is is biological and hormonal."

"No argument there, and actually, it's just as true of men. We've just had the advantage of defining the baseline for a few centuries, so we defined what our hormones make us as normal and what women's hormones make them as different."

"There may be hope for you yet."

"I'm very enlightened in my chauvinism."

Kathy frowned. Somehow I'd slipped into banter mode by mistake. I think it's partly that I'd spent the last week in an almost wholly male environment, and men communicate with each other almost entirely via banter. Flippant remarks are the lingua franca, and just like returning from a trip overseas, sometimes you have to consciously remind yourself to switch back to English.

"Sorry. I don't mean to be flippant. I do want to get to grips with this."

"It's ok. So even when a woman has made a rational decision that she doesn't intend to have children, it's not like flicking a switch. The decision remains a provisional one. You take the most ardent anti-child woman and let her fall pregnant accidentally, and it's almost certain that she'll agonise over the decision."

I nodded. I did, in fact, know someone who'd done exactly that. She didn't, in the end, have the child, but I was surprised how long it took her to make that decision, a decision that had seemed to me to have been made a long time before.

"It's different for men. You can never face that decision, at least, not in the same way: it's not your body that would have something growing inside it."

"I can understand that, intellectually, at least. But I'm still not sure I understand the idea of rejecting part of you – the generic 'you', that is – simply by stating that I've made a decision not to have kids."

"You can't understand it intellectually. But if you say that to a woman in such a definite fashion, even to one who has, for now, made the decision not to have a child, part of her will be closed to you. Part of her will feel that she can't share the whole of herself with you. And what will limit the kind of relationship you can have with her."

Hmm. I was struggling to fully comprehend what Kathy was telling me, but there was a level at which I did understand. Which presented something of a dilemma.

"Thank you. I think I do get some sense of that. But it leaves me wondering what to do. Realising I didn't want kids was one of the reasons my marriage ended. In a sense, and entirely unintentionally, I misled my wife. I don't want to mislead anyone else. If I soften my stance, that's what I'd be doing. Someone who really, really wants kids may think they can change me, and really, they can't."

Kathy gave me a level look. "I didn't say there was an answer."

We finished our tea.

Afterwards, I sought Helen's input on this. Typically, she had a simple solution: "Stop dating women in their 20s and 30s, and start dating post-menopausal women. Really. It's the only way. You can't predict the biological clock. You can meet a women who's 35 and convinced she doesn't want kids, then she hits 37 and wants to be pregnant by sundown. You can't tell. Really."

This dating-with-intent lark is more complicated than it seems. I hadn't, at that point, realised just how complicated it could get, but I was about to find out ...

Chapter 3

I spend about ten days a month working overseas, photographing newly-built properties. I shoot those 'lifestyle' shots that you see in the property brochures – glamorous-looking couples lounging around in their perfect apartments. The beautiful furniture is there for half a day, the glamorous couples about half an hour. After that, the properties are sold to retired bank managers whose taste in interior décor is on a par with their wives' taste in fashion and coiffure.

There may be worse clients than property developers, just as there may be worse dinner party guests than a couple who have just done their own conveyancing, but in neither case would I be overly keen to have the possibility demonstrated.

Property developers like to get value from their suppliers, so a typical trip involves shooting around 15 properties in five locations spread across three countries. Schedules are drawn up without thought being given to such niceties as eating and sleeping, and the show apartments always seem to be on the top floor of apartment blocks which are scheduled to have power hooked-up to both elevators and air-conditioning systems a few days after the shoot.

Models are booked through local agencies selected by the client. In selecting a suitable agency, a typical commercial client will consider such factors as the number of models on their books, their tearsheets (the publications in which they have been featured), their reputation for reliability, their client list and their fees. A typical property developer will dispense with the first four criteria.

Did I mention that there are some projects I do to pay the mortgage?

I do at least get to fly business class. The combination of changeable schedules and all the gear I have to carry means it's actually cheaper than flying economy given the extra charges I'd end up paying for flight changes and excess baggage.

The less-crowded airline lounges still have something of the feeling of olde-world flying about them. They always feel like the sort of place you could meet someone, everyone having nothing to do but wait, and to avail themselves of the free bar. The reality, of course, is that most of the transient residents spend their entire time on the phone, and I spend most of my time with my head buried in my laptop trying to get the last location's photos Photoshopped before I arrive at the next. And even if you did get chatting to someone interesting, the chances are high that you'd live in different countries.

But just occasionally ...

The BA lounge at Barcelona is large, light and airy. When BA announced a delay to the Heathrow flight due to (what else?) air traffic control problems over London, you could tell who else was on the flight by the ritualistic tutting, muttering of 'Typical!' and that strange half-smile half-grimace expression that is the required British response to such announcements. Two of us also took it as our cue to return to the bar for a top-up.

My fellow pragmatist was an attractive Japanese-looking woman with long, fine, black hair. I'd noticed her earlier, not just because she was attractive, but because she stood out from the sea of black and grey suits by wearing a flowing green skirt with orange blouse and green scarf. On some people, it might have looked out of place in a business setting; on her, it looked elegant and confident.

One of the benefits of adversity, even of the being-forced-to-drink-more-wine-in-a-lounge-for-an-extra-30-minutes variety, is that it becomes socially acceptable to engage complete strangers in conversation. I took advantage of the opportunity to say hello.

Given my self-confessed ineptitude at casual pick-up lines, I decided not to be too ambitious.

"I guess there are worse ways to be delayed."

She smiled. "Yes."

Ok, so it wasn't the most effusive of responses, but her accent was English, and her smile seemed just a touch warmer than a polite smile - and anyway I needed the practice, so I ventured on.

"Is London your final destination?"

"It is. And you?"

"For me too. Business trip?"

"Yes."

"What do you do?"

I hate the question, but I'm English: I have no idea how to relate to someone until I know their occupation.

"I'm a buyer for a department store, here looking at some new ranges of women's clothing."

I decided to skip the obvious line about shopping for a living, but the effort was such that I actually said: "Ah, you must spend half your life travelling."

Ouch. I always respond to that one myself with a slightly strained smile, and here I am inflicting it on someone. But she didn't seem to mind.

"Probably more than half."

"Care to pass the time chatting?"

"Sure."

"Sorry, I should have introduced myself: I'm Stephen."

"Sumi."

I at least managed to resist telling her it was a lovely name. I got my bag from next to my seat and wheeled it over to hers.

You know those times when you get on so well with someone that half an hour whizzes by in an instant but you can't remember afterwards what it was you talked about? I genuinely thought we'd been chatting for about five minutes when the flight was called and I looked at my watch to see it had in fact been forty.

"Where are you sitting?" I asked.

Sumi checked her boarding-pass: "3F."

"I'm 1C – we'll see what we can sort out when everyone is on board."

We were both taking it as read that we wanted to sit together to continue chatting. We walked to the gate together, went on board and had one of those tiny little moments.

I should explain. I grew up in quite an old-fashioned family, with a father who was, well, sexist isn't really the right word. It wasn't that he believed women to be capable of any less than men, but it was simply natural to him that men opened doors for women, carried their cases, held their chairs for them and so forth. The women in my family expected this, and so it never occurred to me that there was anything noteworthy about it; it was just the way of the world.

This was all fine until I hit my early teens. This was the time at which feminism reached the height of its aggressive phase, and suddenly a simple things like opening a door for a woman was considered sexist and patronising. At that age, this was all rather bewildering, and for quite some time I struggled with the conflicting messages I was getting from my upbringing and what had become quite a different world.

It made dating particularly challenging, as one never knew whether such gestures would be seen as charming or insulting. It was a confusing time.

Eventually, of course, things settled down, and my experience today is that most women enjoy a little old-world courtesy. But to this day, there is still a slight hesitancy about it for me.

Anyway, the tiny moment. I placed my bag on my seat and walked back with her. I just assumed she knew I would follow her to lift her bag into the overhead locker, and she did. She put it down on the floor and turned to smile and say "Thank you." It was nothing much, but it just felt good that we were on the same wavelength.

The moment was only slightly tainted by the stern-looking 50-something guy behind me tutting as I apologetically turned around to walk against the flow of passengers to return to my seat.

The cabin attendant closed the door, and I stood up to look back at Sumi's row. Luck was on our side: there was no-one sitting next to her, allowing us to avoid one of those 'Would you mind awfully?' shuffles.

There are some people you just feel immediately comfortable with, and end up revealing quite intimate things about oneself. No, not those kind of things, but stuff like the kind of childhoods we had, those silly little thoughts we have and usually only share with one or two close friends, that sort of thing.

Flying into Heathrow in the early evening virtually guarantees a scenic, if repetitive, aerial tour of Biggin Hill (I have spent so long in Heathrow holding patterns over the years that I can now recognise each of the four main ones by sight), and for once I was welcoming the delay. But you can't even rely on Air Traffic Controllers for consistent delays, it seems: we had a straight-in approach.

We continued chatting as we walked back through passport control, baggage hall and into Arrivals. She was being met by a company car and I had to retrieve mine from the business car-park. I gave her my card, she gave me her mobile number, we arranged that I'd call her the following day to agree a date for dinner and said our farewells.

I have never understood the concept of love at first sight (lust yes, love no), but I was, at least, rather taken with her.

It was as I turned out of the car-park the wrong way and almost drove into a BAA minibus that I decided I'd better temporarily put Sumi from my mind and concentrate on my driving.

"Am I a bit old for a silly crush on a woman I've just met?" I asked Helen in a phone call made almost as soon as I made it safely home.

It's one of the great things about a good friend – you can skip the 'Hello, it's me' and 'How are you?' formalities.

"Is this one post-menopausal?" she asked. She's such an old romantic.

I filled her in on the details.

"Stephen, you don't do silly crushes. You're a pragmatist, not a romantic."

"The two are not mutually incompatible."

"You can be a pragmatist and have a loving relationship, but you can't be a pragmatist and a romantic – they are fundamentally different mindsets. May I remind you of your view on the nature of lifelong relationships? That is not, I would most respectfully suggest, a romantic one."

"I disagree. Pragmatism is an attitude, romance is a process – it's something you create in a relationship."

"Buying flowers?"

"Buying flowers for a first date isn't romantic, it's more .. well, traditional. Buying flowers after 20 years of marriage for no particular reason, that's romantic."

Flowers reminded me that I'd better water my plants. I picked up the mini watering-can from the shelf behind the sink and filled it.

"And believing the 20-year-marriage couple are probably only staying together from laziness is the view of a romantic?"

I decided I needed to come up with a better pitch for that one.

"Ok. There is no such thing as a perfect person, and thus all relationships involve compromise. Fair?"

"I'm listening."

"Even the most devoted couple can still find themselves wishing their partner were different in at least some minor respect or other. True?"

"I'm still listening."

Helen is a hard sell.

"So it's all a matter of degree. We look for some percentage match. If the big stuff is right, we decide the small stuff doesn't matter. Otherwise we'd all be living alone while we waited for the fictitious perfect person to wander into our lives. The one who is telepathic and whose sole aim in life is to make us happy."

There was a brief silence at the other end, and I could picture an amused look on her face.

"What?"

"Stephen, it's not that anything you're saying is unreasonable. I don't disagree with any of it."

"So then why the 'Aww, sweet' attitude?"

"Because it's not what you think that's unromantic, it's how you think. You have an almost mathematical view of relationships. There's nothing wrong with that – it's probably entirely sensible – it's just not an approach that can be considered romantic."

Hmmm.

"Damn," I said, as my watering efforts lost concentration and I managed to spill about half a litre of water on the floor. It's not entirely accidental that I have wooden floors and leather sofas.

"What?" asked Helen.

I explained.

"Men! Completely incapable of multi-tasking, even talking and watering is beyond you."

I considered formulating a rebuttal, then figured that, under the circumstances, this might not prove persuasive.

"Anyway," I said, "I appear to have a most unmathematical crush."

"And yet you phoned me to analyse it rather than phoning her."

"She might not even be home yet."

"You have her mobile number, don't you?"

"Yes."

"So call her."

"It's too early to call. I arranged to call her tomorrow."

"See? Mathematical."

"It's Stephen."

She laughed: "I had a feeling you wouldn't wait until tomorrow."

I felt it best not to mention the circumstances behind this decision.

"Are you home?"

"Yes, just settled in with a large cup of lemon tea."

"As in ... real tea, or herbal?" I tried to keep the suspicion out of my voice.

"Real tea."

"Oh good. I have a bit of a thing about that."

"About tea?"

"Yes, tea is very important. I'm on a one-man mission to inform the world that tea, by definition, is made from the leaves of tea plants. Herbal infusions are not tea. I shall not rest until the phrase 'herb tea' is forever eradicated from our language."

"I do like a man with a clear mission in life."

Tea was a good idea, I decided. My multi-tasking abilities having been demonstrated already, I should perhaps have made it before, rather than during, the conversation, but I figured I'd live dangerously. I filled the kettle, switched it on and put an Earl Grey teabag into a mug.

Some conversations are interesting to relate later to others. Other conversations, however enjoyable they might have been at the time to the parties involved, do not entirely meet the exacting standards for third-party entertainment.

Suffice it to say we discussed, among other things, the worst karaoke evenings we'd endured, the etymology of karaoke ('empty orchestra'), the bizarreness of the cult of celebrity, the weirdest journeys we'd ever made, the differences between male & female perspectives on a range of different cars, great books that had been turned into terrible films, the utter unacceptability of doing a remake of The Italian Job, her love of Asiatic lilies, the- well, actually, I don't suppose the list of topics is any more interesting to relate than the conversation itself, but we talked so effortlessly and enjoyably, there was almost a dreamlike quality to it. Three hours passed and we arranged to meet for dinner in two days' time.

My now-cold kettle of water sat untouched, next to the mug, empty but for the lonely-looking teabag. Multitasking is overrated anyway.

It was a Thursday night. I'd booked a table at the Butlers Wharf Chop House for 7.30pm, and we'd arranged to meet outside Tower Hill tube at 7pm, leaving time for a leisurely walk across Tower Bridge and a drink in the bar. I'd called in at a florist to buy an Asiatic lily, and had asked the restaurant to have an empty vase on the table for it. Helen would no doubt consider it mathematical romanticism.

I got there 10 minutes early and sat on the wall by the steps, being entertained by the guide for a walking tour that started there. Londoners are probably the least-informed people in the world when it comes to our home town because we never do things like go on walking tours. I learned of the Tower's multiple roles over the centuries: fortress, palace, prison, execution spot, armoury, treasury, zoo, mint, public records office, observatory and, of course, home of the Crown Jewels – the latter since 1303, apparently. I felt well-equipped for a pub quiz.

By 7pm, the walking tour had departed and there was no sign of Sumi, but I had a vague recollection that the punctuality rules for dating were that the boy had to be there on time and the girl could be 10 minutes late.

By 7.20pm, there was still no sign of her, and I began to wonder whether there had been a mix-up over the time or place. I called her mobile, which went straight to voicemail, suggesting she was on the tube.

7.30pm arrived, and Sumi hadn't. I called her mobile again. It rang once, then diverted to her voicemail. Odd. I sent a text asking if all was ok, then called the restaurant to let them know my companion was delayed and to ask whether we could make the table 8pm; that was fine.

The text tone sounded while I was on the phone. It was Sumi. A very strange message: 'Sorry! I don't know whether I can do this. I got off the tube early and am sitting crying. Sorry.'

I had absolutely no idea of what to make of it. I tried calling her, and it went straight to voicemail. Communicating via text is less than ideal when one has no idea what is going on. I sent a reply: 'Sumi, whatever it is, just talk to me. No need to go to dinner if you don't want to. Answer the phone, ok?'.

Twenty minutes passed. I phoned the restaurant to let them know there was a problem and I'd have to let the table go and then call them again if my companion made it. I tried Sumi again; voicemail.

I felt concerned for Sumi, but also annoyed at being left in the dark like this, then guilty at feeling annoyed when she was clearly in distress about something.

At 8pm, I tried again. Still voicemail. Concern and irritation doing battle. I didn't want to abandon her, wherever she might be, but I couldn't do anything to help if she wouldn't even answer the phone, and there is a limit to how long one can hang around outside a tube station clutching a flower.

It was another unworthy thought, but there is nothing in the world that signals 'Stood up' so clearly as a man hanging around outside a tube station for an hour with a flower in his hand. I focused on trying to portray via my body language that I'd only just that minute got there and was, in any case, early.

When I concluded that fidgeting wasn't helping, I decided to go for a walk along the river. I texted her to let her know, and that she could call me when she was ready to. I set off towards Tower Bridge.

I tried to formulate theories. Was there something about me she didn't like? That wouldn't explain the tears. Was she in a relationship and intending to have an affair with me, then had second thoughts? That might explain the tears, but she'd told me she wasn't seeing anyone special, and we'd had a three-hour chat when she got home that would hardly have been practical with a partner lurking in the background. And in any case, she'd said she wasn't involved, and I believed her.

My theories grew increasingly elaborate and bizarre. She had six months to live, didn't want to spend it alone but didn't want to hurt anyone by starting a new relationship. She was a secret agent who didn't want to drag anyone into her dark and dangerous world. She was a serial killer who picked up men in airport lounges and- Ok, I didn't quite know how to finish that particular theory.

Walking across Tower Bridge with my flower in hand, it was a bit like a movie scene where the guy has just broken up with the girl and every other person who passes him is part of a couple clearly head over heels in love. I decided it was time to ditch the flower: I left it on the handrail of the bridge. Perhaps someone else would have an unexpected romantic moment by spotting it and handing it to their partner with a flourish. Or perhaps it would spark a terrorist alert as a suspicious spores-dispersal device – who knows, these days.

By 8.30pm, I had walked the path between Tower Bridge and London Bridge twice. I'd decided to give Sumi some space by not calling or texting her again, but I really couldn't hang around all night. Whatever was going on, her behaviour was at least thoughtless. I decided to walk back to Tower Hill, try calling one last time and then, if I still couldn't reach her, text her to say I was going home and she could call me if she wanted to.

Voicemail again. I tapped out the text: 'Sumi, going home now, hope you're ok, call me if you want to talk'.

It was a strange feeling returning home at 9pm, having spent two hours doing nothing but wait and wonder. I couldn't make up my mind whether to be concerned or pissed off, couldn't find a way to do both simultaneously, so compromised by alternating between the two at about five minute intervals. There was a sort of rhythm to it: the more concerned I felt, the more I felt she should realise I'd be worrying about her, and how thoughtless it was of her to leave me feeling that way; the more irritated I felt at her showing such disregard for my feelings, the more guilty I felt at such selfishness when she was so upset, diffusing my anger and replacing it with compassion.

By the time I got home, I'd managed to persuade myself that there was not much point feeling anything at all about it until we'd managed to speak and I'd found out what was going on. I switched on my laptop and downloaded my mail. One mail jumped out at me:

From Sumi Yoshida, Subject: So sorry

I was momentarily confused, as I hadn't recalled giving her my email address, then remembered I'd given her my business card.

Stephen,

I'm so sorry. You must think terribly of me. If you don't want to see or speak to me again, I will understand.

Since my last relationship ended badly, I have been closed to the possibility of another. That must have been somehow obvious in my manner, as it has been some time since anyone has even asked me for a drink. The few who have, I have always said no.

You were so unexpected. We got on so well that I didn't even hesitate to give you my number, and that phone call made it natural that I would have dinner with you.

I was carried away in the feeling. I didn't think. It was only when I was on my way to meet you, on the tube, that suddenly it felt like such a big thing. I am so used to being in my own little world that I was not sure I wanted to leave it. And I felt that, with you, I might.

And my second thought was what if I do want to leave it with you, but you don't want to see me again?

I didn't know which was worse, and the next thing I knew, I was in tears. I just had to get off the tube and walk. I don't even know where I walked to. When you called, I had to divert the call because

32

I couldn't talk. I just sent the text and switched off my phone. I didn't even think about what it must be like for you.

I'm so, so sorry.

Sumi

My earlier torn feelings now felt like a mere dress rehearsal for what I felt at that moment. How could I read that and still feel annoyed? It was impossible not to feel compassion for her.

It was also impossible to avoid hearing the faint sound of alarm bells. I mean, yes, we had got on really well. Incredibly well, in fact. But, looked at objectively, we'd had one enjoyable conversation during an otherwise boring journey, and one enjoyable phone call. Such an extreme reaction was surely out of proportion?

Hmmm. Perhaps Helen was right about my mathematical perspective. But most people, well, most men, at least, would agree there was at least a faint feeling of bunny-boiling about it.

Half of me wanted to reach out to her, and half of me wanted to run away. Both halves agreed that it was time for a glass of wine.

Wine in hand, I distracted myself by dealing with the other emails before returning to stare once again at Sumi's mail.

I didn't know what I wanted to do, but I did at least know that I didn't want her to go to bed without a reply.

Sumi,

Thanks for explaining. Let's talk tomorrow?

Stephen

It allowed me to sleep on it.

Friday morning. I had lots of photo-processing to get through, so dived straight into that. At lunchtime, I checked my email. She had replied at 1am.

Stephen,

I'm glad you're still speaking to me. Yes, I'd like to talk.

Sorry again.

Sumi

I was out with friends that evening, so suggested I call her on Saturday morning. She replied a short time later to say that was good for her.

Saturday morning. I still wasn't quite sure how I felt. I decided to consult my two co-opted dating consultants. I had a feeling the conversation with Tom might be the shorter of the two, and I wasn't wrong.

"Don't walk away, run," he said.

"I know what you mean. But we're all entitled to the occasional wobble, aren't we?"

"Mate, you've known her for ten minutes and on your first date she stood you up and instead spent the time crying. There's nothing more to say. Lose her."

"Ok, thanks."

"You're going to do that, right?"

"Probably," I said. I had to admit his executive summary of events was on the nose. But there was no harm getting Helen's take too.

"What does your gut say?" she asked.

"Well, Tom has a point."

"That's your head talking. What does your gut say?"

"That I should at least talk to her," I answered, without knowing that was what I was going to say.

"There you go, then."

"Hi."

I caught myself. I always greet friends by name, it's always 'Hi whoever', never just 'Hi'. Just 'Hi' means I'm annoyed.

"Hi Stephen."

I wasn't quite sure what to say next. I hadn't formulated a plan for this call.

"Are you ok?" I asked.

Well, better than nothing, I guess.

"Yes. Well, I still feel terrible at standing you up like that. It really wasn't my intention, I just wasn't thinking straight."

"It's ok. I understand."

Did I?

"I don't suppose you'd be willing to give me a second chance?"

It was obvious she was going to ask that question, but I honestly hadn't known how I was going to answer it.

"Of course."

I blinked. I'd said that before I'd even had the chance to consider the question.

"You will? Really?"

I couldn't exactly change my mind at that point, and anyway, I found I didn't want to.

"Really."

"I don't suppose you're free this afternoon? I know it's short notice, well, no notice, but I want to put things right as soon as I can?"

I was. I always try to keep a day free when I get back from a trip as I'm often too exhausted to do anything but read and laze.

"That would be perfect. 3pm?"

Who the hell was that man who kept answering on my behalf?

"When was the last time you went to the Tower of London?"

I thought. "When I was about seven, I think."

"Shall we go?"

"Why not? Ok, I'll meet you at Tower Hill at 3pm."

Arranging to meet at the same place didn't feel ideal, but we were committed now.

There was an unpleasant feeling of deja-vu as I emerged from the tube a few minutes early. I had thought that, if she were truly remorseful, she would have been there half an hour early just to be safe, but no, there was no sign of her. At least this time I was free of flora.

Three o'clock arrived. And departed. I wasn't impressed.

Five past.

I decided this time she was getting ten minutes and that was it.

It was a beautiful day. Clear blue skies, warm, just about perfect. Aside from the fact that I was spending it once again hanging around the same damn tube station.

Eight minutes past. No text. No call. Two more minutes, then I was gone.

I debated whether I was going to call her or just leave. It would feel terribly rude to leave after only ten minutes, but it wasn't ten minutes: it was two hours, one wasted evening and ten minutes.

But it wasn't me, just walking away like that, so I decided I would call.

Ten minutes. I called. It rang for a time then went to voicemail. I tried to keep my tone neutral, but made no attempt at avoiding terseness. "Sumi, it's ten past three, you're not here so I'm leaving." I hit disconnect.

Damn.

Some friends lived about ten minutes' walk from here, so I gave them a call on the off-chance they were in, but they weren't. Now what?

Well, the plan had been to visit the Tower, and while I wasn't entirely in the mood, I was even less inclined to just go home after another wasted journey. I fought my way through the throngs of tourists as I walked through the underpass and round to the ticket booths. Massive queues and crowds. I'd spotted a tourist shop by the tube that sold tickets, so I walked back there to buy one (probably at a premium, I didn't care) then lasered my way through the crowds and in through the main gate.

As I wandered round the Tower, I tried to decide what my response would be when she called. I realised that one of the most annoying feelings in the world is not knowing what to feel. I mean, by rights I am entitled to feel roundly pissed-off as I've been stood-up twice. But there is always a chance that she's laying under a bus somewhere. Or she set off two hours early only to have some Clockwise-style fate befall her.

Ok, if she called from the tube in ten minutes and had a really good reason, I'd meet her; if she called in 30 mins with a lousy excuse, we'd be done. Hmm. Seemed Helen might be on to something with that mathematical business.

She didn't call at all.

I've always admired those people who can completely put something from their mind; they would simply shake it off and immerse themselves in the Tower. I tried my best, but it really wasn't working. By the time I set off home, I was fuming. No email, however heart-rending, was going to work this time. And I wasn't even going to admit to Tom that I'd given her a second chance.

It was another email.

Stephen,

I can't believe I blew it. You gave me a second chance I didn't deserve, and I blew it.

I left my mobile at home. I was in such a rush to get there early. It was only when I got there that I realised. Your number was, of course, in my mobile.

I figured I'd spot you, but it was so crowded. I went back and forth between the ticket booth queues, to the entrance, the gate by the road, the path from the underpass, everywhere I could think of, but there were just so many people. I waited there until after four, and by that time felt sure you would have given up on me.

I got your voicemail when I got home, and wanted to call but you sounded so ... final ... in your message that I knew that was it.

I'm sorry. I know there's no chance now, but I really am sorry.

Sumi

Fuck. I was sure I'd said Tower Hill rather than the Tower. If she'd thought we were meeting at the Tower itself, she would surely have asked where exactly. Though with mobiles, it's not really an issue. If you remember to take the bloody thing with you. Damn her.

Now what? I mean, we've all left our mobiles at home sometime or other, and it's usually on a day when it's guaranteed to cause maximum hassle (the last time I did it, my car broke down in the middle of nowhere and it took me 15 minutes to flag someone down to borrow their phone). But surely nobody in their right mind agrees to a third meeting after they've been let down twice?

I debated the matter with myself. Looked at objectively, she's failed to show twice, and therefore is hopelessly unreliable and absolutely doesn't deserve a third chance. Looked at subjectively, her first reason was .. well, a bit odd, but otherwise hard to fault, and her second reason was just one of those unfortunate things. And we had got on really well.

I decided to follow Helen's advice again. My head was quite clearly saying no, but my gut was, to my surprise, saying yes.

Ok. But I was not risking the slightest chance of hanging around like a stray dog a third time. As I didn't entirely trust myself to be sufficiently stern on the phone, I responded in kind: by email.

Sumi,

I've been debating with myself, and it seems my head lost. So, let's try one last time.

However, my head did succeed in imposing conditions, so here's what I'm offering. I will tell you where I am going to be and at what time. You can be there or not. If you're not, I won't even wait one minute, I'll just go home, delete your details from my phone and we'll be done.

So. Thursday afternoon, I have a corporate shoot with a CEO in Broadgate at 4.15pm. The shoot won't take more than a few mins, so by the time I'm packed up and out of there, it will be 4.30pm. I'll meet you by the huge metal sculpture outside the Broadgate Circle entrance to Liverpool Street (this is the one with the sunglasses shop at the end). It's at the bottom of the steps below the junction of Eldon Street with Blomfield Street

I thought I'd better be 100% clear! I continued:

I know it's still in the working day, but I'm sorry, I'm not willing to wait around so that's the best I can offer.

I apologise for being so hard about this, but I think you can probably understand where I'm coming from after two failed attempts?

You don't even have to let me know whether you will be there: if you are, you are, if not, well, no harm done.

Stephen

I clicked Send before I could change my mind and water it down. She replied almost immediately:

Stephen,

Thank you! I don't deserve it. I will be there. Definitely.

Sumi

CEO headshots are worse than weddings. The whole point of being a CEO, I suppose, is that you can delegate the boring stuff to underlings, but posing for their photo is one task they can't delegate. You typically get a 5-minute slot, usually booked several weeks in advance. They walk in, expect you to take the photo within 30 seconds, are bored within two minutes and have left the room within five. You don't get any second chances, so everything has to be perfect.

I don't leave anything to chance. I arrange with their PA to have the use of the boardroom for an hour prior to the shoot. I identify two places in the room that will work (usually one spot at either end of the table) and set up two identical lighting systems. I have two identical camera bodies with two identical lenses. I agree with the PA that one of the CEO's support staff will be available 40 minutes prior to the shoot so that I can use them for the test-shots, testing both cameras and both sets of lighting. I also agree that the marketing or PR exec will be present to preview the test-shots on my laptop to ensure that they are happy with the result. Then as soon as the CEO arrives, it's just a question of sitting them in one of the two spots, suggesting a few poses and pressing the button. So far, I've never needed any of the backups, but you can guarantee that something would fail the moment I got complacent about it.

At 3.30pm, I was all set up and waiting for the assistant to arrive for the test-shots when my mobile warbled: a text message. Sumi. She was taking no chances and was already there. Great. I switched off my phone (you definitely don't want any interruptions during a shoot).

4.15pm on the dot, the door opened and the CEO walked in. She was unusually chatty and cooperative. I generally have five suggested poses and am happy if they will do two of them; this one did all five. By 4.19pm, we were done. Everyone was pleased. I promised them they'd have the finished photo by lunchtime tomorrow.

I packed up my kit, said my goodbyes and walked the few hundred metres to Richard Serra's dramatic sculpture, Fulcrum. I checked my watch as I got there: 4.29pm. There was no sign of Sumi as I walked down the steps. I walked all around the sculpture. Nothing. I checked the steps all around it. No. I even walked inside the sculpture – she wasn't there either.

It was 4.30pm. I circled around the sculpture once more, checked the steps again, checked the balcony above: she was definitely not there.

That was it. I didn't care what had happened that time, I was not waiting around a third time. We were officially done.

It wasn't until I got home that I remembered my mobile was still switched off. I had a momentary pang of guilt, then decided it made no difference: the deal was very clear, she had to be there at 4.30pm on the dot, and she wasn't.

As I switched it on, I got a text and a voicemail alert. The text was from Sumi, and timed at 4.20pm:

Just need some tissues! Sniffling here. Back in 5 mins.

There were two voicemails, both from Sumi. The first:

Sorry, stuck in a stupidly long queue in Smiths, but just 30 seconds away! Meet me here if I'm not at the statue?

The second:

I guess not.

Then I did feel guilty. But still, the deal was the deal, and she hadn't been there.

Helen had become my co-conspirator. Actually, being happily-married, I think she was getting a vicarious thrill from my dating adventures.

"Am I crazy for not even waiting five minutes?" I asked her. "What if we were perfect for each other?"

Helen has a surprisingly black-and-white view of the world, for a woman. "She's a flake. Maybe a delightful one, but a flake all the same. You and a flake just wouldn't work."

It was hard to disagree. To me, a promise is a promise, even a trivial one. If I say I'll do something, I do it, and I expect the same of those around me. It's perhaps a weakness to set so much store by things that don't matter so much, but I can't help it – it's the way I was raised.

"You know," I said, "it's astonishing the tiny things that might stand between one life path and another. A queue in a newsagents. Maybe we would have been great, and this would be that funny story we'd still be telling in ten years' time."

"True," Helen replied, "but it's equally likely that wasting time with a flake for a few weeks would have you miss out on hooking up with your future partner. You can't second-guess yourself all the time, you can only make your decisions as best you can. Some will be right, some will be wrong, one or two will be disastrous, but that doesn't change no matter whether you choose path A or B. Sheldon Kopp."

'Sheldon Kopp' was shorthand for what Helen knew to be my favourite quotation. Well, 'favourite' isn't quite right, as it's a rather bleak quote in some ways, but it is a quote which I feel very succinctly summarises the nature of life:

I do not mean to imply by this that a man can determine just what his world or his life will be like. A man, after all, is only a man. He stands somewhere between absolute freedom on the one hand, and total helplessness on the other. All of his important decisions must be made on the basis of insufficient data. It is enough if a man accepts his freedom, takes his best shot, does what he can, faces the consequences of his acts, and makes no excuses. It may not be fair that a man gets to have total responsibility for his own life without total control over it, but it seems to me that for good or for bad, that's just the way it is.

It felt particularly poignant at that moment.

Chapter 4

I was, to be frank, sorely tempted to revert to the casual sex stage. It was simple, painless and, all told, not such a bad life for a halfway-presentable 30-something male Londoner. Tom would have fully approved.

I'd always imagined that one had the most sex in one's late teens/early 20s and then things went gradually downhill from there. Returning to the dating scene at the age of 34 had been a revelation to me. It seemed there were few items in greater demand than unattached 30-something men. The Daily Mail had better hope married men never find out or there will be a great many 'Why Oh Why' editorials written on the rocketing divorce rate.

It had been a particular surprise to me given my rather average looks. Helen, of course, had a theory about it.

"Confidence."

"In lieu of devastating good looks?"

"It's the male equivalent. In the same way men are immediately attracted to a long-legged blonde, women are immediately attracted to confident men. It's an effect that tends to increase as you get older. Well, until you're too old, anyway. Though perhaps in these days of Viagra ..."

"I'm not sure I am all that confident in terms of pick-ups."

"Maybe not, but you are confident in life, and that comes across to women."

"So maybe I should stick to the single life."

"You got bored of that, remember?"

"It's looking a bit more attractive after my recent track record in Dating With Intent. Do you realise I've had three dates and haven't had sex with any of them?"

"Shocking."

I sensed her sympathy was waning.

"Anyway, maybe I'll take some time off for good behaviour."

"Don't you mean for bad behaviour?"

"Don't confuse me. I'm easily confused at the moment."

"Who was it who told me it was time again to wake up next to someone he loved?"

"You're in the wrong line of business – you've got that 'taken down in evidence and used against you' routine down pat."

She was right, of course. It was why I'd decided the time had come to move on. But, then again, most relationships just kind of happen, so maybe there was no harm in taking a bit of time out from the hunt?

I was semi-gatecrashing a party on Saturday night. That is, a friend had been invited and as she is single and hates to arrive at these things alone, I was going along to provide the necessary moral support for the interval between knocking at the door and downing the first glass of wine.

Emma was a model I'd met 18 months ago on a corporate office shoot. The client had just moved to ultra-modern headquarters in West London, and they needed some suitably ultra-modern looking models to play the roles of staff in some of the interior shots. By virtue of some skilled clothing, make-up and hairstyle changes, Emma was both the receptionist and a Power Dressed Executive, and I don't think anyone would have realised it was the same person in both shots.

Tom, of course, loves to do the nudge-nudge, wink-wink routine about all the models I work with. I haven't the heart to spoil his fantasies by revealing the litany of reasons models would make lousy dates: most have hulking great boyfriends; many lose much of their lustre the moment they open their mouths; and in any case, the most unprofessional thing a photographer can do is make advances to one of the models. I generally opt for a conspiratorial grin, which keeps his boyish imagination happy and gives me a certain rakish reputation that avoids the need to engage in any macho hobbies.

But I do, of course, get to know a number of the models I work with regularly, and a few have become friends. Emma was one of them. She was a 2nd-year psychology student who did some modelling in her spare time to bridge the substantial gap between a student income and her taste in shoes. She had none of the aforementioned drawbacks, but the age-gap was far too great to make her a realistic relationship prospect.

She did, though, look older than her years, and the stress of my recent dates wasn't playing too heavily on my features, so we didn't look too strange a 'couple' when we arrived.

Perversely, I'd always found parties to be hopeless places to meet women other than for a drunken snog towards the end of the night with someone you'd really rather you hadn't when you sobered up the following day. But the kitchen can usually be counted on for some interesting conversations, and the crap wine can be averted by taking along a couple of drinkable bottles and stashing one out of sight somewhere, so it was as good a plan as any.

I noticed Lucy straight away. As did every other man present: she was absolutely drop-dead gorgeous, with no obvious visible candidate for the role of jealous boyfriend. About 5'9", slender body, long legs revealed by a deliciously short skirt, unfeasibly high heels that made her look even taller, long black hair almost down to her waist and the most amazing dark eyes. My notoriously-unreliable age-estimation program put her at about 25; a little on the young side, but not absurdly so.

It was quite amusing to observe her admirers. There were the attached men there with their partners, sneaking furtive glances whenever they thought their wife or girlfriend wasn't looking, and usually getting a cold hard stare from same as they found they were wrong. The ones getting the darkest looks were those engaging her in deep conversation while pretending to be oblivious to her looks before utterly failing to keep their eyes above hem-level.

Then there were the single men. The younger, drunker ones were mostly gathered in small groups making laddish remarks amongst themselves. The older ones were either looking like they wished they had the courage to approach her, or were simply enjoying the scenery.

I wasn't under any illusions as to my own chances: looks-wise, she was so far out of my league I wouldn't even be allowed to buy a spectator ticket. But I figured I needed the practice, and there was nothing to lose.

Lucy was drinking red wine, so I waited until her glass was nearly empty and she was chatting to only one female friend before approaching with my secretly-stashed bottle of Bin 35. I had the presence of mind to offer to refill her friend's glass first.

"May I?"

"Oh, thanks."

"I'm Stephen, by the way."

"I'm Amy, and this is Lucy."

"Hi Amy and Lucy." (I believe I mentioned my lack of fluency in chatupese.)

I'd asked Emma for the two-minute briefing on the party's hosts, so was able to ask them how they knew Sarah and Joe. They turned out to be work colleagues, at a facilities management company. I wasn't entirely sure what a facilities management company did (other than manage facilities, one presumes), and rather suspected the conversation might be more interesting if I failed to enquire.

It's always quite delicate approaching a woman when she is with a friend. On the one hand, you have to be sufficiently solicitous to her friend to avoid causing offence, but not so attentive that you cause confusion over the object of your interest.

Women seem to have a much better handle on this. I've never fully established whether close women friends are actually telepathic or merely have some secret signal agreed in advance, but it's been my experience that if you're chatting with one of her friends present, you can tell within five minutes whether you're getting anywhere. If her friend is still firmly by her side after five minutes, you failed the interview. Amy, to my delight, excused herself.

I still hadn't quite figured out whether or not I was having a night off from the Dating With Intent business, and to be honest didn't at that moment much care.

"You haven't told me how you know Sarah and Joe," she observed.

"Ah. I don't, actually."

She raised an eyebrow in a way that suggested she'd practiced the move: "A gatecrasher?"

"Not entirely." I explained, pointing out Emma, who was the happy-looking subject of the attentions of a tall guy about her age. "And anyway, I'm a gatecrasher who brings decent wine."

"That does make it forgivable, yes."

We chatted about a range of things before I ventured a casual "No boyfriend?".

"Not as of yesterday, no."

"Oh. Sounds like that might be a subject best avoided?"

"He cheated on me. I ended it."

"Ouch."

"No girlfriend?"

"No, divorced a while back."

"Badly?"

"No, fortunately very amicably."

We finished the bottle. "Shall I go in search of another?" I asked.

"No," she replied, giving me a very direct look.

Did that mean what I thought it meant? Apparently it did: "Do you ever just feel like a night of meaningless sex?" she asked.

My dilemma about my operating mode for the evening had been neatly resolved.

I wasn't under any illusions that this was anything but a belated revenge-fuck on her part, but I never claimed to be proud …

"Is this when I do the 'My place or yours?' line?"

"I somehow think meaningless sex is best suited to a hotel," she replied.

I tried not to groan aloud. I spend so much time in the damned things when working that they have zero appeal as a liaison location, but one must sometimes think of the bigger picture, namely a night of meaningless sex with an extremely attractive brunette.

"Let me make a call."

Another type of shoot done strictly to pay the mortgage is conference platforms. You spend two or three days in an Identikit business hotel in some godforsaken place like Birmingham or Milton Keynes taking a series of tedious photos of tedious businessmen making tedious presentations. But one such conference had been at the Excel Centre in the Docklands, and as I was shooting the dinner speeches too, they'd put me up at the conference hotel – which turned out to be a cruise-liner permanently moored at the dockside. I'd got chatting to the Concierge there, and he'd told me they were usually extremely quiet at the weekend, so if I ever wanted a romantic room at a bargain rate … At the time, I had no interest at all, but it was a halfway-fun option for present circumstances, so I made a call. Three minutes later, I had a balcony room for what was indeed a bargain price. I managed to catch Emma's eye and waved goodbye; she also looked to be having a good evening.

The taxi ride there was like a return visit to my teenage years. We spent the entire journey necking. (Is it still called necking? No wonder this return to the single life feels so complicated when I'm not even sure of the terminology any more.)

I was grateful to the hotel receptionist for avoiding the pointed 'No luggage, Sir?' question, and a few minutes later we were in our cabin.

You know that fabulous thing they do in the movies, where the couple move from doorway to bed, removing clothes en-route and all without ever breaking their clinch? A brief experiment led to the conclusion that the necessary set of manoeuvres must require a great deal of training, planning, practice and probably a formal Risk Assessment; I resorted to the less glamorous but more achievable single-tasking approach.

I have found certain bedroom skills to be both appreciated and reciprocated. The activity was indeed reciprocated on this occasion, only .. well, there really isn't any kind way to say this .. not very well. In fact, really quite badly. If there had been any doubt before about which mode we were in, this fact settled it decisively.

Now, some people may consider it shallow to place such great emphasis on a single characteristic of an otherwise delightful woman. But I guarantee you that not a single one of those people is male. Sex is a crucial element of a relationship, and blowjobs are, let's be clear, a crucial component of sex.

It would not, of course, be fair to reject a woman out of hand after a single poor performance. More than one woman has, I'm sure, had to provide a hapless male with a map, compass, illustrated diagram, operating instructions and guided tour of her clitoris. It behoves one to find a gentle means of tuition, and then to provide an opportunity for redemption. But when the result of this second foray into the field the following morning proves equally incompetent, it is time to move swiftly on.

Thank god this wasn't one of Helen's friends: there would be no possible way of explaining this one.

Chapter 5

We can become so adept at filling our lives with activity that we even manage to seal the tiny gaps we might otherwise use for reflection. Plane journeys are spent working, watching movies and sleeping. Train journeys spent reading a book. Car journeys listening to Radio 4. Laptops, iPods, Blackberries ... all that time we once spent in idle thought is now spent in equally idle doing.

It can become habitual, but every once in a while I catch myself in time. Coming straight from a shoot to a restaurant for dinner with a friend, and finding myself with 40 minutes spare, I settled into the restaurant bar with a drink and was just reaching into my bag to pull out a newspaper when I stopped myself, and instead used the time to mull over the less than stellar start to my Dating With Intent phase. DWI. Hmmm – sounds disturbingly similar to DUI, which I vaguely recalled was Americanese for drink-driving: Driving Under the Influence.

I reflected on my track-record so far. One embarrassing dinner that should have been a drink. One very enjoyable afternoon tea with a somewhat abrupt ending. One date that never was. And a one-night stand with lousy sex. Not exactly Romeo & Juliet. Though, given the way things turned out for them, I'm not really sure why we hold them up as the romantic ideal.

Was I going about things the wrong way? Was I too quick to write people off? I revisited each date.

Alli. Well, that one was simple: you can't have a relationship with someone you don't fancy, and that's before we even get into the religion thing. I knew from conversations with female friends that it's not necessarily quite the same for women: they can sometimes grow to find someone attractive over time. Men are simpler creatures – it doesn't really work like that for us. We can be oblivious to someone, but once we have noticed them, if we don't fancy them immediately, that's exceedingly unlikely to change.

Kathy. A tricky one. The baby issue is not an area of life on which compromise is an option. If a woman wants babies, or thinks she may, that does, realistically, rule her out. But was she right about me being so dismissive about it that I was giving a false impression of myself as some kind of 'my way or the highway' type? And was it a false impression anyway? I was that way about babies, was I the same way about other things? I filed that one away to mull on another time.

Sumi. How to make sense of that one? Was Helen right, or did my own stubbornness over a point of principle rob me – rob us both – of what might have been an amazing relationship? No way to know, so no sense fretting over it.

Lucy. Sexual mechanics aside, I don't think she was in the relationship space. And even if the sex had been great, I'd been living that life a bit too long. Much as it made me feel old to admit it to myself, I needed something more fulfilling than that.

I smiled a little at the 'grass is greener' syndrome that always operates in this area. My male friends in relationships envy my freedom. The ability to do what I'd done that night would have made them jealous. Yet the truth was, I envied them their lives. It had been too long since I'd enjoyed the simple pleasures of sharing my life with someone I loved.

Close friends are great, of course. You can do 50% of it with them. The dinners, the movies, theatre, parties ... If they're 'affectionate friends', you can do snuggles and holidays too. My married friends were right that the life had much to commend it.

But it's only 50%. The 'affectionate friends' routine only lasts as long as you're both single. And you don't have all the little stuff. Waking up next to each other every morning, not just random weekends. Shopping together, even if it is being told that buying five identical shirts is not permitted. A walk together after work. Even the tedious stuff – washing-up, changing the bedding, DIY – becomes something fun, shared, when you do it together. The little stuff, but life is, in the end, mostly made up of the little stuff.

Ok, you don't marry the first person you meet. The wrong person is far, far worse than no-one at all. But was I setting impossible requirements? Did I have too many pre-conceived criteria? Did I have too many rules? Too many check-boxes? Should I have a more open-minded approach? At what point do relationship criteria stop being reasonable and start becoming barriers to love?

But then, what I seek in another is surely a reflection of who I am. Aren't, in truth, our relationship criteria one of the most fundamental ways in which we define our identity? If I start sacrificing those, then who am I?

But (how many levels of 'but' could there be to this?) what if one's criteria rule out most women? Didn't my attitude to babies in fact rule out most of the female population between the ages of 18 and 40?

But (at least one more, it seemed) isn't that always going to be the case? We don't, after all, need there to be a million compatible partners, only one.

But (I decided to stop counting at this point) isn't some of it a numbers game? How many women do I meet in a month? In a year? In a lifetime? If there was really only one, the odds against happening to meet her would be pretty astronomical. And anyway, nobody over the age of 14 believes in the concept of 'the one.'

Perhaps, I thought, this whole reflection business was over-rated. My musings weren't exactly clarifying matters in my mind.

I was waiting for an old friend, Laura. Young, quirky, energetic, quick sense of humour, slight hippyish tendencies, and a habit of doing a job for a year before getting bored with it and switching to something completely different. Her most recent move, which had so far lasted for two years and three months (exactly two years and two months longer than my estimate) had been to a post in the Foreign & Commonwealth Office.

Stereotypes are often grossly unfair, failing to do justice to the rich diversity one finds when one looks beneath the surface. The stereotypical FCO is a deeply out-dated, sexist and ageist Old Boys club filled with old duffers who spend their dwindling days practising the great British art of Muddling Through.

The real FCO is, of course, exactly the same. Laura did not entirely fit in.

The reason Laura was still there was because she'd developed a love affair with China. That this passion had been developed exclusively on the basis of travelogues and an interesting programme on Radio 4 was, to Laura, of little consequence. After a year in London, combining induction with an introduction to Mandarin, she had succeeded in getting a two-year posting to Beijing.

It's a pretty cushy number by any standards. For the entire first year, you are officially a student, spending 20 hours a week in language lessons. In the remaining time, your job is to soak up the culture and generally get to know the place. Who would guess? All those backpackers staying in dollar-a-night dives and getting by on a couple of bowls of boiled rice a day could be having exactly the same gap year but with decent food, an ok apartment and a government salary.

FCO staff on overseas postings get a travel budget intended to allow them to return to the UK twice a year, business class. In reality, of course, almost everyone used most of their budget on cheap weekend trips to Hong Kong, Shanghai and Xi'an and made their trips to the UK in cattle-class.

Since we only got to see each other twice a year, we'd decided to splash out a little with dinner at Club Gascon, a French restaurant that had received excellent reviews. We justified the cost on the grounds that we were having dinner only twice a year instead of the 10 or 12 times we used to when Laura was in the UK. I've always felt that being able to come up with convincing-sounding rationalisations for things we want to do is one of life's handier skills.

The popularity of the restaurant was the reason I was here straight from work: we'd only been able to get an early table, at 6.30pm. I realised I'd barely taken in the surroundings in my reverie, and since we were going to be paying for the décor as well as the food, I decided I should take some time to look around.

The surroundings were indeed appealing: about 5'6", looked about my age, average build, very simple black silk dress, a very simple gold necklace that I suspected was much more expensive than it looked, fabulous cheekbones, a nose that should have looked too long but somehow didn't, and something of a Latin look.

She was the only other customer in the bar at this early hour. She noticed my surveying of the scenery, and gave me a slightly amused look. I gave her what I hoped was a slightly apologetic smile, and raised my glass to her. I think it was the nose that gave me the confidence, otherwise she'd just have been too perfect.

I'd decided not to worry about my lack of pickup vocabulary, and to treat any failed approaches as training.

"Have you eaten here before?" It seemed I desperately needed the training, as I realised I'd pretty much just used the 'Do you come here often?' line.

"No, but my companion has."

'Companion' is one of the most ambiguous words in the English language, meaning anything from 'ageing aunt' to a lover you've slept with but haven't entirely made up your mind about. But the practice was useful, so it didn't matter which definition applied.

"Were they as impressed as the critics seemed to be? One review spent several columns extolling the delights of the tasting menu with matching wines."

"That's what my friend had last time: she raved about it."

'Friend' can also be rather ambiguous these days, but 'she' was at least statistically promising.

Of course, it was entirely possible that there was a six-foot-something boyfriend at home, but I think I may have mentioned that I'm an optimist.

"Sorry, I haven't introduced myself. I'm Stephen."

"Nice to meet you, Stephen; I'm Eva."

The misuse of the word 'nice' is a small bugbear of mine, but I wisely decided to let it pass.

She presented a hand in that slightly high, angled pose common to some Latin women that always makes me wonder whether I'm being invited to shake it or kiss it. I decided that I would need to be ten years older and wear a cravat in order to go for the kissing option, so went for the safer bet.

We made small-talk for a few minutes, during which time I learned that Eva managed a small art gallery in Kensington, lived in Fulham, enjoyed skiing and was owned by two cats.

I realised that the latter piece of information was revealing, and made a mental note to make it a standard question. Not just because she was a cat person, though that is always an excellent sign, but because answering a question about pets elicited a pronoun: "I have two cats" rather than "We have two cats." I made a second mental note to arrive in restaurants early more often.

I also learned that she was waiting for Phoebe, a friend with whom she had dinner on the first Thursday of the month, something they'd done for the past couple of years. I felt a slight twinge of envy at being able to have a life that organised; messed-up social arrangements were a fact of life with me.

"And you?" she asked. "Who are you waiting for?"

That, I decided, was a distinctly encouraging question.

"A friend who lives in China and comes over twice a year." The additional information was intended to make it clear there were no inverted commas involved.

Eva smiled.

I was feeling brave. "Shall I give you my number before our friends arrive?"

"That's a little presumptuous, don't you think?" For a moment, I thought she might be serious, but she held the stern expression for only a few seconds before grinning. "And besides, it is always up to the man to call." She passed me a card. Just her name, the gallery name and a phone number; clearly people were supposed to know where it was.

She got up to greet a 40-something woman carrying the world's largest handbag.

"Enjoy your meal," I smiled.

"And you," she replied with a casual wave.

I'd settled on the view that life was too short to play courtship games, so called her the next day. The phone was answered by an overly-cheerful American woman who, when I asked for Eva, announced that she was "Bethany, Eva's assistant." Eva was apparently with a client "but said text her a few dates and she'll confirm one of them." Bethany gave me Eva's mobile number.

That was two firsts: arranging a date via an assistant and by text. I felt distinctly behind the times. I texted her a choice of three dates.

Half an hour later, she texted back: Next Friday. Dinner. Where? And I thought I had a business-like approach to dating ...

I know a little French place, just below Covent Garden. Meet outside Charing Cross tube at 7.45?

Almost immediately: I've eaten French quite a few times recently – I feel like Italian.

It struck me as a little odd to initially leave the choice in my hands and then come back with a very specific preference, but Italian was good too, so: Italian is fine. Did you have somewhere particular in mind?

Let's just meet in Soho and wander

I knew a good bar in the area, so: Ok, let's meet in the bar in The Hampshire, bottom of Leicester Square at 7.45pm

She again replied immediately: Actually, I know a lovely pub in the area, the 12 Bar Club on Denmark Street. Let's meet there, ok?

It seemed she liked to call the shots.

I considered this for a moment. It has been my observation that most successful relationships, however egalitarian they may be in essence, have one partner who tends to take the lead, and one partner who tends to go along with them. They may sit down together and discuss the big stuff, but on a day-to-day level, usually one of them will be the default decision-maker.

This had been one of the challenges in my marriage: we were both default decision-makers. It wasn't that either one of us considered that this was our role by right, it was simply habitual. We had some clashes ...

Of course, being a boy, I thought it was a simple matter of figuring out a system. Let's divide things up into logical categories, I proposed, and for each domain of our lives, one of us will take the lead. For example, I had no interest in the garden, so whatever we did there could be her decision; she had no interest in hifi, so whatever we did there could be my decision. Not that we wouldn't consult each other, just that there would be a default leader for each area. I reckoned that in 90% of cases, it would be immediately clear which of us should take the lead, and for the other 10% we could flip a coin. It seemed simple and obvious to me.

Of course, being a girl, and a redhead to boot, she didn't see it the same way. Life, she informed me, didn't work like that. I responded that just because it hadn't so far didn't mean it couldn't in future. She replied that you can't systemise a relationship. I argued that I wasn't attempting to do so, just trying to make our lives easier by-

Well, let's skip the next 20 minutes of that conversation and simply say that an accord was not reached and the following day I had to replace two wine-glasses and make a call to a carpet-cleaning service. Despite twelve years of marriage to one, I never did quite manage to get the hang of redheads.

Why do I never meet the quiet demure ones who simply want an easy life?

"Stephen, you'd be bored within 24 hours and the relationship would be over within a fortnight," was Helen's answer to the question.

We were drinking tea in her Extremely White Kitchen. It had become a bit of an in-joke: the kitchen had been fairly white when they moved in. White walls, floor and worktops. Their fridge and cooker were white, and they'd joked that no colour should be permitted in it. A few of us bought them white kitchen items as housewarming presents, and it had sort of taken off from there.

"You're probably right," I replied, "Maybe I just need to get out of the habit of being the leader and let someone else do it."

Helen merely looked at me. She didn't even bother to raise an eyebrow. Was it too much to ask that she could humour me that much?

"Besides," she continued, from her unspoken argument, "there's also the Singleton Effect to consider."

"The Singleton Effect?"

"What was the best thing about getting divorced?"

"Apart from cheaper glassware bills, you mean?"

"Yes. What did you most enjoy when you first set up home on your own afterwards?"

"Well, being free to fuck any woman I could talk into bed was quite agreeable for a time."

I knew that look. I moved swiftly on.

"The freedom. The fact that, for the first time in a decade, I had no-one else to answer to but myself. I could choose my décor without reference to anyone else's taste, play whatever music I wanted at whatever volume I wanted, stay up to 3am – all that kind of stuff."

"Exactly. The Singleton Effect. You've had two years of that. Being able to make all the decisions – where you go, what you do – you are master of all you survey."

"Or at least of the remote control and the central heating thermostat."

I was doing it again.

"But yes," I continued, quickly. "I do see what you mean. Habit, plus self-employment, plus a couple of years being free to please myself .. going from that to going along with someone else's lead in a relationship wouldn't be entirely straightforward, I agree. But I can't keep writing-off lovely women after one date. Well, not even one date, in this case."

I filled Helen in on my restaurant musings.

Good friends tend to offer us a mixture of predictability and surprise. Much of who they are, we know: that's why we love them. But every now and then, they surprise us, and that's the other half of the equation. Helen's cynicism and matter-of-fact manner occasionally peeled away to reveal the romantic within.

"No. It's not about finding the perfect woman, I agree – it's about finding a woman who is essentially right and then finding the perfect way to love her."

It was my turn to look at her.

"And perhaps she wants to step back," I hazarded. "After all, she was initially offering the baton to me, so to speak. Perhaps it was just habit that she kept taking it back."

That got me a slightly less sceptical look than I expected.

The pub was crowded. Really crowded. It took several minutes just to find Eva.

"Sorry," she said, "it's not usually like this."

"No problem," I lied. I hate crowded pubs. "What would you like to drink?"

"V&T, please."

The bar was about three layers deep. Judging from the number of people waving tenners in the general direction of the harassed-looking bar staff, this was going to take a while. It was hard not to be slightly irritated by the fact that, had we gone to the place I'd suggested, we would be sitting in comfy leather seats being waited on by smartly-dressed, attentive staff. I felt this was a thought I should keep to myself.

Five minutes later, there were still two layers in front of me. I have long held the view that patience may be a virtue for patient people, but it's a pain in the arse for the rest of us: executive action was required. I returned to Eva.

"This is hopeless – shall we just go find somewhere to eat and settle for wine?"

"Sure. I'll take you to one of my favourite places."

A friend in the wine trade had once given me an excellent tip about choosing wine in a restaurant. "If it's a decent restaurant," he'd told me, "the house wine will be good for the money. They are associating the name of the restaurant with the wine: it will be carefully chosen, and often better than wines costing significantly more. The mistakes, the wines that aren't selling, they make those the second or third cheapest on the list. Those are the ones chosen by the punters who know nothing about wine, don't want to spend too much but are afraid they'll look cheap if they go for the house wine."

It had been a tip that had stood me in good stead over the years. It also fitted well with my philosophy that first dates have enough variables already without risking experiments of a gastronomic or oenological nature. I braced myself for the Actually …

"Fine."

That was a surprise. I crossed my fingers that the wine would meet with her approval when it arrived.

"Tell me about your gallery."

"Well, I have the luxury of owning it," she began. That would explain the lack of title on the business card. "So I can pander to my own tastes. So far it seems that there are enough people out there who share those tastes to keep us ticking along."

"And how would you describe your tastes?"

"Whimsical would probably be the best description."

"Whimsy is good. I enjoy whimsy." It wasn't a line: I've always been amused by the faintly absurd, a taste I was able to indulge on some advertising shoots. "I did a backstreet shoot for a brand of sunglasses a few weeks ago, and we discovered an old upright piano abandoned at the roadside. We tugged it into a cobbled sidestreet, sent an assistant back to the studio to grab something that would pass for a piano stool and made it the central theme of the shoot. The client loved it."

"I suppose you don't always have the opportunity to follow your muse like that. A lot of commercial shooting must be quite constrained by the brief?"

"Some is. Few are fortunate enough to earn a living without having to do tedious shoots, but you can inject your own style into a lot of it. The biggest constraint is generally time rather than any requirement to work to a formula. But I don't imagine that any business is 100% fun. I'd hazard that even running an art gallery has its duller moments."

Somehow we seemed to have entered a very mild sparring match. It wasn't quite what I had in mind for a date. Was it just me, I wondered, or did a huge proportion of communication just somehow happen, rather than being actively chosen by either party? I resolved to do my bit to inject a more amiable tone.

Eva smiled. "Yes, that's true." Perhaps she had made the same decision.

"Do you include photography, or is that not considered art?" I grinned. Hmmm. Given that I'd made my resolution less than three seconds ago, I wasn't doing too well, despite my playful tone and grin. The second half of that sentence just sort of tacked itself on without consulting me.

"I think some of our artists would have opinions on the subject," she replied with a curious sort of half-smile, half-frown expression that should have been topologically impossible. "For my own part, I view art as a broad church, but feel a gallery should have some kind of focus. We don't include photography just as we don't include sculpture."

"Do you paint, yourself?" I asked. "That is, paint comma yourself, not paint yourself."

"Is that a polite way of asking whether gallery owners are frustrated artists?"

It was my turn to smile. "The theory has been voiced."

"I paint a little, when I have time, but I bring art to far more people by running a gallery than I would by devoting myself to painting."

Why was it that every conversational turn with this woman seemed to have an edge of challenge to it? I couldn't quite get to grips with how or why it was happening.

The wine arrived. The waiter poured a little for me to taste.

"I'd like to taste it too, if you don't mind." This was addressed to the waiter, who looked momentarily startled but quickly covered it with a smooth: "Of course, madam." He poured a little for Eva too.

Most people think they are being offered the opportunity to see whether they like it. I suspected Eva knew that, in fact, the tasting is only to check that it is not corked: if you order a wine you turn out not to like, that's not the restaurant's problem.

We both declared it fine. The waiter, having been implicitly accused of sexism by offering it only to me, hesitated slightly before topping-up Eva's glass first.

"It's a little project of mine," Eva explained. "Even when the woman orders the wine, most restaurants offer it to the guy to taste. I'm trying to train them to either ask, or offer it to both parties."

I immediately liked that. Both the goal itself, and the idea of taking it on in the way she had. It required some determination, to be willing to consistently risk being seen as aggressive or rude, by waiting staff and possibly by her dining companions. I felt it said good things about her.

"Ok," I replied, "I'll join you in that one, and rope in some friends. We should set ourselves a deadline, that every decent restaurant in London will do it as a matter of course within a year. What do you think?"

"Sold. I know the directors of some of the top hotel chains, so I can push it from the top too." This information didn't surprise me.

I was glad we'd found some cooperative territory.

I wondered how teetotallers managed first dates. The disinhibiting effects of alcohol aside, the pouring of the wine always seems to have an important psychological effect too. It signals the crossing of a line, somehow: a move into territory that is more intimate, more open. There's a tangible shift in the conversation, in the way we interact, that I can't imagine would be quite the same with a bottle of Badoit. Or perhaps it was the effects of the wine that were leading to my theories on the effects of wine ...

"Besides art, what are your passions in life?" I asked. It was a sort of compromise question: it opened the door to more meaningful conversation but still allowed someone to keep things on a more superficial, activity-based level if they wanted to. I was pleased to find Eva didn't want to.

"I'm quite involved in the prison reform movement," she said. "What we do at the moment plainly doesn't work. We imprison people for relatively minor offences, then put them in an environment which tends to both brutalise them and provide an apprenticeship in more serious offences."

"Good thing I'm not a Daily Mail reader."

"I don't think we'd be here if you were a Daily Mail reader."

"You didn't check."

"They tend to identify themselves."

"You're probably right. What do you see as the solutions?"

"Honestly?"

"Of course."

"Probably the single biggest difference we could make is to legalise all drugs. The majority of burglaries and street robberies are committed by addicts looking for the cash for their next fix. A huge proportion of prison inmates wouldn't be there were it not for the fact that they committed crimes to fund their drug habit. Legalise drugs, institute some sensible controls in the way we do alcohol and tobacco, and have enough programmes to help those who want to kick the habit."

She gave me a slight wary look that suggested she was used to being challenged on this view. Ironically, given the fact that we'd earlier seemed to be challenging each other over the most innocuous of things, her most provocative statement drew no argument from me.

"I agree completely. It's all arbitrary. We ban marijuana yet permit tobacco. We ban cocaine yet allow alcohol. Given the natural teenage desire to rebel, making something illegal virtually guarantees they'll try it. I suppose heroin is another matter, but you're probably right that legalising and controlling it would be an improvement on the mess we have now."

"You definitely don't read the Daily Mail."

"True. So what else do we do, besides legalising drugs? There will still be criminals, and we will presumably still imprison some of them?"

"For starters, imprison far fewer of them. We need to distinguish between people who make mistakes and those who are committed to a life of crime, and respond differently to each. Then for those we do imprison, we need to decide whether we want to punish them or rehabilitate them; the two aims demand completely different strategies."

I have to admit I was slightly surprised. I was beginning to pigeon-hole her as someone with a privileged background and a semi-socialite life, used to getting her own way. What she was revealing instead was a thoughtful, caring woman who was not afraid to get her hands dirty in a cause which would be unpopular with many of her peers.

Most people, when we give them the chance to show it, are deeper than we would have guessed.

The rest of the evening passed quickly, and we talked easily. Despite the slightly awkward start, I was finding myself quite taken with her.

The bill arrived, and we each placed our cards on the tray. We, or at least I, live in somewhat ambivalent times: does the guy pay or is it 50/50? The question didn't arise with Eva. We paid the bill, and I was putting my card back into my wallet when-

"Are you coming home with me?" she asked, in much the same tone as one might enquire as to whether I'd listened to the weather forecast.

When I'd ended my casual sex phase, I'd formed the view that Dating With Intent presented something of a dilemma. You can't just hop into bed on the first date, because then there would be nothing to distinguish it from the previous phase of Just For Fun dating. But you can't leave it until the eighth date because by then you may have invested two months in someone with whom the sex turns out to be distinctly lacking in the fireworks department.

My target compromise was date three. Enough to show sincerity without compromising efficiency. I did know enough about women to feel I ought to keep the 'efficiency' part to myself.

My 'third date' tactic was, of course, based on the fond and rather sexist belief that I would be the propositioner rather than the propositionee. So far, I noted, I was zero for two.

Sometimes you just have to go with the flow: "I am."

Given Eva's apparent desire for control outside the bedroom, I was a little wary about what to expect within it. While I wasn't exactly expecting thigh-high boots and a riding-crop, I did briefly wonder whether I might be hearing the phrase "Actually, I know a better position".

My concerns, it turned out, were entirely groundless. As soon as we set foot inside her stylish but surprisingly messy apartment just off the Kings Road, her manner made her expectations clear: matters carnal were one area in which Eva apparently preferred to cede control.

Though, thinking about that one for a moment, I wasn't entirely sure which of us was in fact taking the lead ...

We had fun. A great deal of fun. Twice.

Chapter 6

"The sex was good," I told Helen over lunch in Upper Street, "I've arranged a second date with the same woman for the first time in my brief DWI career – and you & I can have a relaxed lunch putting the world to rights rather than you acting as my relationship counsellor. These seem like good signs."

"And the battle of wills?" she asked.

"Seems to be becoming a little less fierce." I didn't go into specifics on the bedroom side; there are some things that even close friends don't need to know.

"So when are you seeing her again?"

"Thursday. There's apparently an excellent restaurant near her that specialises in exotic steaks – ostrich, kangaroo and the like – so we're meeting at hers then wandering round there."

"Well, if you're not going to need relationship counselling, you'd better at least have some salacious details next time.

"I promise much salating."

The conversation with Tom was shorter. I led with the 'first date to bedroom' part, and he was suitably approving.

"See what you get when you walk away from the bunny-boilers and find the right kind of woman?"

When I arrived, Eva had a glass of wine in one hand and a phone in the other. She gave me a quick kiss and pointed me at a bottle of Syrah on the kitchen table and a glass cupboard with Bordeaux glasses.

I topped up her glass, poured myself a glass and attempted the impossible task of not eavesdropping on a conversation taking place three feet from my right ear. She was apparently trying to impress upon an artist that their exhibition date was fast approaching and usually by this stage the mounting and framing would be well underway, so she wasn't sure that having a good idea for a new pair of paintings was quite the stage they should be at. Well, I did say my attempt was unsuccessful.

I passed the time by admiring the figure-hugging red silk dress Eva was wearing and the figure it was hugging.

Eva finished the phone call with a small "Sorry!" and a large kiss. It was less of a 'Hello, good to see you' kiss and more of a 'You remember where the bedroom is, don't you?' kiss. I did remember where the bedroom was.

"I trust the appetiser was to sir's satisfaction?" she enquired, some time later.

"My compliments to the chef," I answered.

Discounting her initial "Sorry" and my occasional request/instruction of a positional nature, these were the first words we'd exchanged that evening. That was, I discovered, to be the extent of the pillow-talk: she stepped gracefully from the bed and slipped back into her dress in what seemed like one fluid moment. "Time for steak, then." Apparently Eva's non-bedroom persona didn't waste much time in reasserting itself.

Slipping back into my own clothes was less of a single fluid moment as I reached behind a chair to retrieve my boxers and spent a good 30 seconds searching for an errant sock.

By the time I was dressed, Eva had run a brush through her hair and touched-up her lipstick. How do women do that, I wondered? If I let my hair grow much beyond a close crop, it requires a shower to tame it.

The restaurant was only a couple of streets away. I offered her my hand as we walked away from her apartment, but she ignored this, smiled and set off at some pace. Ok, no pillow-talk, no snuggling and no hand-holding. If I'd been the wham-bam type, it would have felt like a rather bizarre role-reversal. As it was, it just felt slightly .. odd. I wasn't sure whether to be offended or amused.

We both opted for the ostrich steak which was, as promised, superb. It had that melt-in-the-mouth texture that only the best steaks manage. The waiter had recommended a wine, and it was an excellent choice.

Great food, fabulous wine and discreet yet attentive service always helps to set the mood, so I made some light-hearted remark about the role-reversal thing.

"I'm not a romantic," said Eva.

"You don't like romance? I thought everyone liked romance."

"It just strikes me as silly."

"Isn't it supposed to be silly? Isn't that part of its charm?"

"I guess I can't see past the silliness of it. I like love. I like relationships. I like two people trying to make each other happy. But romance .. that's like the Hollywood substitute for love."

It was an interesting debate. I could fully understand her perspective on it. The movie myths create all kinds of expectations that aren't particularly helpful in real-life relationships. But romance as a spirit ...

"Well," I began, "if you mean romance as in Valentine's Day and red hearts and all that commercialised nonsense, I'd abolish all that in a heartbeat. But romance, to me, is more a state of mind. It's about taking the time to show someone we care, and if some of the mechanism happens to be a bit clichéd, well, there are worse crimes. I never yet met a woman who didn't appreciate being bought flowers."

"You have now."

"Really?"

"Really."

"I'll cancel my order with Interflora."

"Spend the money on something more imaginative."

"And holding hands? Is that silly too? Or just too early?" We live in interesting times: two people might sleep together on a first date, but holding hands .. that might take five or six dates.

"Perhaps a little of both. But I'm not really into public displays of affection, and I've never really been a great hand-holder in public or private."

I paused to consider the matter for a moment.

"Ok, I think I can understand where you are coming from. Why inherit someone else's idea of how to relate, how to be together, when you can invent your own?"

"Exactly."

"But we are a species which lives by symbolism, and we can't reinvent the wheel for every aspect of our lives, surely? A kiss, a touch, a gesture ... these things all have inherited meanings. We might just as easily make a case for abandoning our inherited language as our non-verbal symbolism, surely?"

"Language is an immensely complex construct. It's not practical to reinvent it – though it's enlightening to learn other languages and appreciate just how many assumptions are encoded within it. But romance .. we don't have to adopt that."

For me, something clicked in that moment. It wasn't just that she was a woman with strong views and the confidence to express them – that was true of most of my friends, it was kind of a pre-requisite. It was more the way she expressed it. She wasn't on a mission to convert anyone. She didn't give any impression of thinking she was right. She simply came across as being who she was, without consideration of any other way of being. That's rare.

From romantic symbolism to views on marriage was but a short step. I was somewhat surprised to learn that a woman who didn't appear to do romance, least of all established symbols of same, had been married.

"It was a mistake," she said.

I'm always interested in the way people describe their previous relationships, feeling it to be quite revealing. It's a bit like the waiter test (you don't judge a person by how they treat you on a date, rather by how they treat the waiter): the way people talk about an ex tells you a lot about their attitude to relationship and their readiness to move on. Someone who is bitter about an ex is a big red-flag to me, so I tend to probe just a little ...

"In what way?"

"I'd rather not talk about it."

"Ok," I smiled. "Sorry, I didn't mean to pry."

She smiled too. "And I didn't mean to snap. It's just .. well, exes are exes for a reason, aren't they?"

"True."

"And you probably wouldn't want to do chapter and verse on yours."

"It's not a sore subject. We just gradually developed different interests and priorities."

"How long were you married?"

"Ten years. Well, twelve if you count the two-year separation bit."

"Ten years longer than me."

"It was good for most of it, and by the end the recognition that it was time to go our separate ways was a mutual one .. well, from a couple of weeks after The Conversation, anyway."

"I can hear the capitals in that!" she grinned.

"Yes, it's never an easy conversation to have, even when you think you're actually both of the same mind."

"Which, in my case, he wasn't."

After her earlier reaction, I wasn't going there.

"Right."

"Anyway, I don't think I'll do it again."

"Nor me. Actually, I never intended to the first time either. My parents are divorced, so it's not like I ever believed there to be any significance to marriage. It's just that Isabel one day decided she wanted to, and I was young enough or naïve enough to believe it was for life, so why not?"

"It's funny the way we sometimes make the most fundamental decisions in the most casual ways, isn't it?"

I gave a wry smile. Since we'd done one of The Big Two, I thought we might as well complete the set:

"And kids?"

"Do I have any secreted about my apartment, you mean?" she grinned.

"Well .. that or any plans for same secreted about your person."

"Maybe someday, but definitely no immediate plans."

'Maybe someday' can mean a lot of different things, I thought, but a second date wasn't the time to press the matter.

"But," Eva continued, "rehearsal is always fun, don't you think?"

"Oh yes, always helps to be prepared."

"So shall we get the bill and head to the dress rehearsal?"

The dress rehearsal went well.

Tom's "Wahey!" didn't shed a huge amount of light on the matter, so I tried Helen.

"You know," I told her, "I think I may know what it feels like to be used for sex."

I ignored her sceptical look.

"I mean, she doesn't do romance; we do, admittedly, have some good conversations, but mostly we have sex."

"Sounds dreadful."

"You're not taking this terribly seriously. I mean, how do you know whether there's any real relationship potential when there's no pillow-talk, no snuggling, no hand-holding, and the conversation just sort of fits into the gaps between the bedroom gymnastics?"

"Sounds like a pretty good relationship to me."

"Seriously, though."

"Seriously, though, you're being mathematical again."

"I am?"

"You are. You're wanting to turn something inherently unpredictable – the evolving relationship-"

"Or not."

"Or not – between two people into something predictable. But if it is the right relationship, you have the rest of your life to allow it to unfold – what's the rush?"

"Hmmm. But if it isn't the right relationship, you don't want to spend months realising that, do you? I could spend a lifetime slowly getting to know a series of women who aren't going to be right."

"You can't rush it; life doesn't work that way."

"It should."

"It doesn't."

"It did before, with Isabel. We knew in a week. Actually, most of our friends knew before that, it just took us a bit longer to catch on."

"You were 20 years old then."

"True."

"Not much in your life is fixed when you're 20. You don't have some great long checklist at that age: you need to fancy them and find them interesting to talk to, that's about it. By the time we get into our thirties, we invent a whole load of other things that we decide matters."

"You think that's the problem? Lots of acquired criteria?"

"Too many, probably. But it's not that I see it as a problem, it's just the reason things work differently when we're 20."

Did I mention that Helen can be annoying? Insightful, but annoying.

"Anyway," she continued, "things come together, if they do, in different orders with different people. This time, the sex is good from the start, the romance needs some work. Another time the romance could be good, but the sex need time to work itself out."

"Um, if the sex isn't good at the start, there isn't going to be anything else to work out."

"What, you expect it to be perfect from the first time? Before you've had a chance to get to know each other's tastes and bodies and those little things that really do it for you?"

"No, not perfect," I replied, "but, you know ..."

"No," answered Helen. "Enlighten me."

"Maybe it's different for guys," I said, "but if the sex just totally doesn't work, then it's a lost cause from the start."

I shared the story of Lucy, expecting Helen to laugh with me and agree. She did neither, but fixed me with a hard look. "I love you dearly, Stephen, but you can be a real arsehole sometimes, you know."

I looked at her, bemused. "What?"

Helen just looked back.

"What?" I repeated.

"You think guys get things right first time. You think you get it right first time?"

"Listen," I protested, "like I say, I don't mean perfect. I don't mean we-"

"You. Talk about you. That's another thing you do, you know: talk about how it is for men, like you're speaking for all three billion of them. You're not: you're talking about you."

I sat there wondering what the hell just happened. One minute we were having a perfectly friendly conversation, the next I seem to have stumbled onto the set of a new reality TV show: Friends Tell Friends Some Home Truths. Helen had always been straight with me, but now she seemed actually pissed off. I didn't know what to say.

"Ok," I said. As a means of stalling for time, it had tradition on its side, but the amount of time it bought was not very much longer than the time taken to voice the two syllables.

"Look," said Helen, "I don't mean to have a go at you, but have you any freaking idea how sexist you are at times?"

"How is it sexist?" I asked. "It would have been just the same if I'd been a woman and she'd been a guy demonstrating equal incompetence in the oral skills department."

"Stephen, do you honestly think men have a clue without coaching?"

"Not the first time. Ok, first few times. No. Sure. But ..."

"But after that you know how to get off any woman?"

"Well ... no, not any woman, obviously, and anyway, as you say, we always have to learn each person's own preferences."

"Stephen, have you ever had a woman, on say, the second or third time you've gone to bed with her, look at you with a naughty expression and say something like Hey, you know what might be fun to try?"

"Um, yes. Sure."

"Well, hello, I have news for you. That wasn't because they just had this sudden, spontaneous thought about something new they wanted to try. That's a woman's gentle way of instructing a guy in how to get her off. Because women, if they like a guy, will give him more than one or two chances to catch on."

"Oh."

"Yes: oh. Meantime, you think that because she didn't do things the way you like them, she's a lost cause. Maybe the stuff she did drove her last guy wild. Maybe there's nothing lacking in her skills, maybe you, like many men, just haven't learned successful ways to communicate to a partner what it is you like, you just expect women to be mindreaders Either that, or you communicate so badly about it that they lose all interest in trying to please you."

"Hmmm."

"You're 36 and you're like a fucking teenager in some ways. Or like a teenager fucking."

"Ok. Point taken. I think."

"Give it some thought."

"I will."

Straight-talking friends can be rather like tax demands, I decided: you know the world would be screwed without them, but you don't always greet them with a smile on your lips and a song in your heart.

Chapter 7

I texted Eva: 'Friday or Sat night?'

She replied a couple of minutes later: 'Shall we make it the whole weekend?'

That was a slight surprise. 'Sure, got anywhere in particular in mind?'

'I have access to a cottage near Oxford. Bring wine.'

'Pick you up 8pm Fri?'

'Perfect.'

It seemed I was getting the hang of this arranging dates by text business.

I will confess to some sexism here: I assume when I arrange to pick up a woman at 8pm that this means arriving at eight, chatting while she finishes packing and then leaving at around nine. Eva was ready, bag packed and in the hall, at 8pm precisely. The bag was small and singular. The only addition was a couple of carrier-bags of food: we'd arranged that Eva would take care of the food and I'd take care of the wine.

I looked around suspiciously: "Is that it?"

"That's it. I travel light."

"Me too, but when a woman tells you she travels light, that generally means three bags rather than four." Um, nice one, Adams. Just STFU, will you?

"This one means what she says."

"So tell me about the cottage you 'have access to'," I asked as I carried her bag to the car."

"It's a weekend cottage belonging to an old school-friend. She lets me use it whenever I like."

"Ah, the scene of one or two trysts, then," I grinned.

She stopped and looked at me. Was I organising a one-man national Put Your Foot In It Day or something, I wondered? But what she said took me rather by surprise: "No, I don't take casual lovers there."

Oh.

What I needed to do at that point was smile and kiss her. What I did not need to do at that point was make a mocking remark like 'I am suitably honoured.'

"I am suitably honoured."

One across, three-letter word, usually followed by an exclamation-mark, made famous by Homer Simpson.

"Sorry, I didn't mean to make fun. I was actually pleased but embarrassed. It's a boy thing."

"You should be pleased, actually." This was spoken with that kind of neutral tone that could mean she was really pissed-off or could mean nothing at all. I hate neutral tones.

My car was a Saab convertible. Practical photographers buy estates, but if I'm going to spend time stuck in traffic, I'd rather do it with the roof down, and convertible estates are an as-yet untapped market. (Think how practical it would be for loading! There's a definite gap in the market.) I also rather like the fact that nobody forms any opinions about you based on the fact you drive a Saab: they are BMWs without the image problem.

I opened the door for her, put her bag in the boot and pulled away into the traffic. The Kings Road on a Friday night makes for a slow start to the journey, but we had the roof down and the stereo on, Eva had a relaxed smile on her face, and I was still enjoying her surprising comment, so the traffic couldn't dent my mood.

By the time we got onto the A40, it was late enough that the traffic soon thinned-out and we were able to make reasonable progress. An open-top car at speed isn't entirely conducive to conversation, but it provides an opportunity for another couple of little compatibility tests: the ability to enjoy companionable silence, and an absence of complaints about the effects of slipstream on hair. Eva seemed to be passing both tests in a pleasing fashion.

The cottage was amazing. Tucked away in the middle of nowhere, thatched roof, a river at the bottom of the garden ... it was like something out of the 1940s.

The evening was turning chilly, so Eva started cooking dinner while I fetched some wood from the shed and built a fire in the huge fireplace in the living-room. 1940s roles, even.

Fire-making is one of those skills men are supposed to have, but not one we tend to be taught these days. Not us city types, anyway. I relied on a combination of vague memories of physics and poking at it in a random fashion until it caught.

I washed my hands and nuzzled Eva from behind as she stirred what smelled like an amazing sauce. She turned her head to kiss me.

"This is fantastic," I said.

"It's my little hidey-hole," said Eva. "I quite often come here on my own when I want some time away from it all."

"It's made for the job." Given her earlier comment, I felt it safe to add: "It makes a pretty wonderful location for a romantic weekend too" before remembering that she didn't do romance.

"It does," she said, simply.

Dinner too was perfect, simple but delicious. Some kind of bouillabaisse style dish with French beans and a garlic mash that set it off to perfection. I'd bought an Oz Clarke-recommended St Emillion that lived up to expectations, and we chatted easily about anything and nothing.

"The more time I spend here, the more I'm thinking it might be time to buy a house," said Eva. "Oh, nothing quite like this – it still needs to be in reasonably central London – but somehow a house feels much more like a home that an apartment."

"Yes, I know what you mean. I love my apartment, but there is something about a house. And more rooms would be a real luxury. Two completely different living-rooms, for example, to suit different moods."

"Yes, having some space to play with. A dressing-room in the old-fashioned sense: wall-to-wall wardrobes and an entire cupboard for shoes, Carrie-style. A little study stroke office stroke nursery tucked off to the side somewhere. A really big kitchen and a dining table big enough to have a dinner-party with 10 or 12 guests."

There are no prizes for guessing which of those words grabbed my attention with the kind of intensity of concentration one might afford a glint of steel spotted in the hand of a lurking stranger in a dark alley whilst on the way home at 2am.

I tried to reassure myself that the mention had been a vague one, in the style of an abstract list rather than a specific intent. A kind of 'here are the sort of things houses tend to have that apartments don't' rather than a 'here's what I plan to have'. Wasn't it?

I took a sip of wine. Well, possibly more a gulp, than a sip.

Eva didn't seem to have noticed my sudden stiffening (no, not that type .. definitely not that type at that particular moment), and was continuing to develop the theme.

"Plants. Lots of plants. The garden should just be laid to lawn, for ease of upkeep, but having the space inside for big plant pots. Yucca plants, that sort of thing."

"Bare wooden floors?"

"Yes. Real ones. Maybe oak."

"Other décor?"

"I guess I want something a little more homely. Nothing chintzy, but perhaps less open space and more soft furnishings. Burnt reds. Browns. Cosy colours. A big solid old dining-room table."

"Sounds like putting down some roots."

"Yes, I think it is. I think I'd want it to be the last place I buy."

I smiled. "There's something very appealing about that idea. I mean, it's very different from my place, but I can see it."

"What's your place like?"

"Archetypal bachelor pad, I'm afraid! Minimalist. Light wooden floors. Black leather sofa. A bit of stainless steel. Not much else."

"I shall have to see it sometime soon."

"You will."

I had to admit, she was painting an appealing picture. Not all of it was to my taste, but the overall feel was pretty close to what I might have envisaged for a few years down the line.

We cleared away the dinner things and took our wine glasses and the rest of the bottle into the living-room. The fire had died down to an orange glow, so I added some wood to the fire, did more random poking and then we snuggled on the sofa by the fire.

For a woman who didn't do romance, this was pretty impressive.

We had the usual dessert.

I am not a morning person. Actually, to say I'm not a morning person is akin to observing that Pol Pot was not really a people

65

person. I need at least three cups of tea in order to come to terms with the mere concept of a morning having arrived, let alone actually taking any active role in its unfolding. So when Eva kissed me good morning, my response was more of a 'Mmmb Mmmmming'.

"I'll make tea," she said brightly.

"Mm, mmmm mmmmm it," I replied, slightly less brightly.

"It's ok, you can make breakfast later," she answered, springing out of bed in a worryingly energetic fashion. People who can understand my morning speak do get bonus points, though.

While Eva made tea, I struggled through the task of opening my eyes and focusing on my watch. Twenty-five to twelve? I focused a bit more and succeeded in distinguishing the big hand from the little hand. Good grief.

By the time Eva arrived with the tea, I'd accomplished an entire series of tasks: fully opening my eyes, propping up our pillows and sitting up in bed. I'd even managed to look out of the window to see that it was raining lightly.

Eva sat next to me in bed. One advantage of not being a morning person is that even if all you have done is sat up and sipped tea, you get an enormous sense of accomplishment from having done so before 7.15am. There are also few better feelings in the world than sipping hot tea in bed while listening to the rain outside. I turned to kiss Eva. She smiled and placed her hand in mine.

The aforementioned lack of morningness may explain why it took me a couple of minutes to notice that this non-handholding woman was in fact holding my hand. Or, at least, allowing me to hold hers.

"Do you like walking in the rain," she asked.

"I love walking in the rain," I answered. "Well, at least, summer rain."

"Good – it looks like it's set in for the day. So you cook breakfast, then we'll go for a walk. Sound like a plan?"

It did.

Eva had bought bacon, eggs, sausages – the works. She made fresh tea while I grilled the sausages & bacon and cooked scrambled eggs. A German friend had once expressed surprise at the English habit of eating cooked food for breakfast, and I'd had to explain that we didn't exactly do it every day, but I think it's more-or-less compulsory in a thatched cottage on a rainy weekend.

A few minutes later, we were sat at the kitchen table tucking in.

"Wow," said Eva, tasting the scrambled eggs.

"Good?" I asked.

"Amazing."

"You should taste it when I have access to both my secret ingredients instead of only one of them."

"Do tell."

"What kind of secret would it be if I told everyone?"

"I'm not everyone."

"True. Ok. My main secret ingredient, which we don't have here, is a generous splash of cream. The second, which we do, is to cook the eggs in an equally extravagant amount of butter."

"Aha. So there are about a million calories in the twin-secret version."

"Give or take a hundred thousand, yes. But hey, it's a fry-up. Might as well do the cholesterol bit properly."

"I think that walk will have to be a long one."

"That's a reasonable deal, I think."

The walk was indeed a long one. Awake at seven, cooking before eight, embarking on a lengthy walk before nine – what was the woman doing to me? But there's something fantastic about summer rain on your face, even if it is the hitherto unfamiliar slightly chilly pre-9am variety.

There were even some public displays of affection! Admittedly, the public in question comprised a few ducks and a rapidly-disappearing blur that we think was a fox but may have been a cat.

I think I even succeeded in turning off the mathematics, just enjoying the weekend for whatever it was: great company, a delightful location and the kind of mix of lazing and activity that always has you feel like you've had a week off when you return to the fray on Monday morning.

"Could you live in the country?" Eva asked.

"No," I replied. "I love it for a weekend away, but I'm a city boy. If I can't buy milk at midnight, I start to feel slightly panicky."

"Plus there's all those theatre productions we like to know we can go to, though never do."

"Quite. But it's vital that we could if we wanted to."

"And the choice of hundreds of restaurants even though we mostly frequent half a dozen of them."

"Ah, but we wouldn't be able to select our half dozen favourites were there not hundreds to choose from, so that one's legitimate."

"True."

"Why, are you having second thoughts about your house-in-London idea?"

"No," she replied slowly. "Not really. I mean, it wouldn't be practical. Well, not unless I sold the gallery and bought something out in the sticks, and I can't see that. No, it's just the whole real-fire-rustic-kitchen thing."

"Buy an old enough place, and you could have the real fire in London."

"Smokeless fuel just isn't the same. I want the crackling of logs and the smoky aroma."

"Yes, I'm with you there. If I could have that in a penthouse apartment somewhere overlooking Tower Bridge, I reckon I'd be set for life. And mortgaged for about a dozen lives, of course."

"I wonder if they police the smokeless fuel thing? There can't be too many real fires in use in London, so maybe you can get away with it nowadays."

"They seem to police just about everything these days," I frowned. "I don't know how we ended up living in such a restrictive society; England used to be about common sense and muddling-through, and somehow we have become a land with a rule and a regulation for every occasion. Whenever anything goes wrong, we seem to think the appropriate response is yet another law, as if every misadventure could be prevented by declaring it illegal. Even where laws might be the answer, we invent new ones instead of enforcing the perfectly sensible laws that already exist. I'm half-expecting a new law making it a specific offence to break the law. It's the great political disease of Being Seen To Be Doing Something." I paused, and smiled apologetically. "Sorry, that's a little soapbox topic of mine: I shall stop ranting now."

"You're preaching to the choir here."

We'd reached a makeshift bench someone had created from a fallen tree trunk beneath the shelter of some overhanging branches. It was a little damp, but not really wet. We sat and looked out over the river.

More bonus points for Eva: a girl who isn't afraid to get her clothes a bit damp and dirty.

"What?" asked Eva.

"What what?" I asked.

"That smile."

"Oh." I hadn't been aware I was smiling. "Just .. this. The view, the walk, the rain, the company – it's just .. right."

She considered this for a moment.

"Yes, it's nice, isn't it?"

"Anyway," I said, "my rant interrupted your musings about your house."

"So it did."

"Any more thoughts on it?"

"I think, realistically, I have to buy in London. But maybe somewhere greener. Richmond is a bit far out, but maybe Hampstead, Highgate, somewhere like that. Leafy. Places for kids to play. A bit of fresh air and peace."

It's amazing how quickly a mood can dissipate.

It was a real bugger, to be frank. Being with her just felt so comfortable, so .. right, somehow. And yet there was that issue of The Kid. Or, it appeared, Kids Plural. God, I haven't even got as far as thinking that she might want more than one of the little sods.

But c'est la vie. Back to Plan A: enjoy the liaison for what it is, and stop trying to turn it into something else. And while I might be looking for A Relationship, there's no law to say that a man can't entertain himself in the meantime.

But I needed to be upfront about it with Eva. Much as I hated to break the mood of the weekend, and could see the sense in Helen's counsel to be less head-on about these things, I didn't want to run the risk of misleading Eva.

"Uh ..."

"Mmm?"

I suddenly felt a little silly. I mean, this was only a third date, and it felt terribly presumptuous to assume that Eva viewed the whole thing as anything more than an enjoyable temporary dalliance. I wasn't sure how to address the issue without sounding arrogant, pompous even, making some Big Announcement. Maybe it was best just to let things take their course.

But she had made that remark about not bringing casual lovers here. And- Oh sod it. Rightly or wrongly, tackling these things head-on is just who I am, and frankly I'd rather make a fool of myself than lead someone on.

John Harvey Jones was once asked how he could make decisions affecting thousands of jobs and hundreds of millions of pounds, and he'd replied that sometimes you'll get it right and sometimes you'll get it wrong but what you have to do is make a decision. You just do what you think is right.

"Sorry," I said, "I was just having a little debate with myself. It's just that .. I mean, I really like you .. and I don't know quite how you're viewing .. this ..."

"You're not about to get down on one knee, are you? It's a little muddy down there."

I laughed, grateful to her for easing the tension.

"No, no cause for panic there – I rarely propose before the 4th date."

"Glad to hear you have standards with these things."

I smiled.

"Oh god, this is silly, but- Well, I like to be upfront, and ..."

"You're gay?"

I laughed again. Damn, Eva. This was so unfair. Stop making me like you so much, I thought, when I'm trying to tell you this isn't going to go anywhere.

"Only in the old-fashioned sense right now."

"So are you going to tell me, or are we playing 20 Questions?"

"Ok. I like you. I like you a lot, actually. And you said that thing about not bringing casual lovers here. To the cottage, I mean."

"That sentence sounds like it has a 'but' on the end of it."

"Um, yes. The kids thing. I mean, that's a stupid conversation to have on a third date, I know, but I just like to be clear about things. Too clear, according to a female friend. But anyway, there are definitely no kids in my future, and I just wanted to be clear about that." I paused. "Ok, I feel officially silly now, for that rather presumptuous speech, but still better for having said it."

Eva smiled. I was trying to work out whether it was an appreciative smile or a 'What the hell is this guy on, I'd better just smile and nod' type of smile.

"Well, I'm a direct kind of girl, so no need for apologise for being a direct kind of boy."

"Ok. Good."

"And yes, it is the first time anyone has ever raised the issue of kids on a third date."

"Er, yes, I imagine it is." How stupid did I feel?

"And I don't even know that I want any." Pretty damn stupid, now that you ask. But ...

"Well, no. But if I were to guess .. well, I think there are a few clues in the way you talk about your house."

"Like I said, I want this to be the last place I buy. And since I might one day want kids, it makes sense to buy somewhere that would be suitable for that."

"Makes sense. Ok, can we talk about something else now? The weather, or something?"

"It's still raining."

"Yes, it is."

"Ok, now that the subject is safely changed, shall we head back for some tea and then see if we can figure out a way to pass the time indoors?"

We figured something out.

"Do you like cakes?" asked Eva, some time later.

"Mmm," I replied.

"Ever made one?"

"Never. My cheffing repertoire is fairly limited."

"Want to learn?"

"Sure."

Eva had brought ingredients for a ginger and marmalade cake. She introduced me to the intricacies of textures and peaks and the difference between mixing and folding (a concept I'd encountered before but never really quite grasped) and then we poured the mixture into a cake tin and put it into the oven.

"So," I asked, "how long before we get to sample our wares?"

"About 40 minutes. Have you ever cooked a soufflé?"

"I have, actually. It was a bit ambitious for someone with my somewhat limited kitchen skills, but I adore them and fancied a challenge. Amazingly, it did work."

"Ok, so you know about never opening the oven before it's ready."

"Yes."

"Think of cakes in the same way. They're not quite as sensitive, but they can still collapse. So mostly you have to judge it visually, by how much it has risen. You then do the skewer test, and provided it's almost there, you can put it back for a few more minutes if needed."

This whole thing, I decided, was unfair. I mean, if two people can enjoy bedroom gymnastics, putting the world to rights over a decent bottle of red, walking in the rain and now domestic intimacies .. for all that to be right and yet still be fundamentally incompatible. Well, it just isn't fair.

"What are you thinking?" she asked.

"Oh, nothing really," I lied. "Just random thoughts drifting by." Much as I like to be straight with people, I felt that after my earlier speech, more of the same would be too much.

The cake was excellent, as was working off some of the calories afterwards.

The cottage had a few concessions to the 21st Century, one of which was a stereo with Bluetooth connectivity. We got out our phones and spent some time comparing music collections and introducing each other to some of our lesser-known favourites.

I do not dance. Over the years, I've taken lessons in everything from jive to salsa, and in all cases have concluded that continuing was going to result in a broken leg, the only uncertainty being whether the leg in question would belong to me, my partner or some innocent bystander.

Yet the two of us managed to dance around the living-room with that kind of uninhibited silliness usually reserved for couples who are way past the stage of feeling they need to impress each other.

We declared that under the 1986 Weekend In The Country Act, it was legal to open a bottle of wine at 3pm. We sprawled on the sofa with our glasses.

"You seem very definite on the kids thing," observed Eva.

"There are few topics on which I am quite so definite."

"What are you afraid of?"

I seemed doomed to have this conversation over and over. I tried to short-cut it, but felt she deserved more than the cocktail-party response.

"It's just not for me. The life I lead, the priorities I have, the things I enjoy – they're just not compatible with having a screaming brat in tow."

"That's a naïve way of looking at it."

"Naïve?"

"Yes: thinking that you take your existing lifestyle and add a kid to it. That isn't how it works."

"How does it work?"

"You have to invent a new lifestyle. Not one in which you give up things, but one that you design to incorporate a child."

"I just can't imagine living a life that includes a child."

"No, but you've never tried. You've just thought about your existing life and all the ways a child would spoil that. You've never tried imagining a life that is designed with a child as one of its components."

I had to admit she was right. I mean, I really, really cannot envisage any way of doing it that would work, but it was true that I'd never completed the exercise.

"Hmmm! Well, I don't think the outcome would be in much doubt, but it might be an interesting thought experiment," I replied, cautiously. "Tell me about your designed life with a kid."

"Actually, now I'm doing your thing. It's a bit of a serious conversation for a third date."

"It is, but I'm at least intellectually interested in the concept, so let's pretend we're on whatever date it is where such subjects become permissible. I haven't checked the rule-book so I'm not sure offhand which one that is."

"Maybe eight or nine."

"Ok, we'll pretend we're on date 10, just to be safe. So: tell me."

"Well, the first element is support. Two people bringing up a child on their own is a recipe for no life. So: the grandparents play a key role. My parents would absolutely love to have a kid around the place again, so they'd be good for at least one evening a week.

"Ok."

"That would also be part of the rationale of moving to a child-friendly location. I'd want a street with lots of other mums, where we could set up rotas where each family has say two other kids round one night a week, in return for which they get to unload theirs for two nights. So that's already three child-free evenings a week. Add a babysitter to that once a week and you've got more evenings without the kid than with it."

She'd clearly thought this through.

"I have to say I'm impressed! But – and you understand I'm merely playing devil's advocate here – isn't the point of having a kid to, er, have a kid? Wouldn't you be better off borrowing one from time to time if you want more time without it than with it?"

"No, they would still be my kid. I'd still be responsible for them. I'd be the one choosing the people he or she spends time with."

"But – again, I speak here as legal representative of the satanic one – wouldn't the kid end up screwed-up, being passed around from pillar to post, not really sure where its home was?"

"Quite the reverse: I think it would be healthier for the child. They'd have more people who love them, and more places that feel like home."

I had to admit, she made a bloody good case. I told her so.

"Actually," I continued, "I can relate to that a bit. My parents divorced when I was five, and for a few years I lived with my mum. But I think there comes an age when girls want to be with their mum and boys want to be with their dad, so when I was nine, I sent my dad a postcard saying I'd like to come and live with him now."

Eva laughed. "A postcard?"

"Well, life is pretty simple when you're nine, isn't it?"

"Had you mentioned this to your mum at all?"

"Er, no, it seems I forgot that bit."

"Must have been some interesting conversations going on there!"

"I imagine so, yes."

"So did the postcard do the trick?"

"It did, but there was a complication. My dad was building his own house at the time, and currently living in a tiny caravan on a building-site. Since there wasn't really anywhere for me to stay, and I think they wanted me to see that things were happening, they arranged for me to live with my gran for a year while he finished the house."

"So you've had a bit of the multi-home experience. It doesn't seem to have damaged you too badly," she smiled.

I laughed. "No, the irony is I learned from my dad years later that he'd felt terribly guilty about the fact that it was a year before I could join him, and had expressed the concern that I must have felt like I was being passed around like a parcel. In fact, nothing could have been further from the truth! My gran absolutely doted on me, so I had a year of no bedtimes, lots of cakes and basically being free to do as I pleased. And since I'd spent most of my summer holidays there anyway, I had lots of friends there already. I didn't quite know how to break it to my dad without him taking it the wrong way, but it was probably the best year of my childhood," I grinned. "My gran would even set off in her little Daf chasing fire-engines for me so I could watch them put out fires."

"So, the devil may need to be persuaded of the virtues of the multi-home childhood, but no need to convince you."

"I guess not."

"So ... he or she is home three or four nights a week. You're away on business some of the time. There'll be holidays with grandparents. I think you can see that having a child doesn't have to be the 24/7

"If there was ever a sane way to have a kid, I think you have the corner on it."

Eva looked thoughtful.

"What are you thinking?" I asked.

"Didn't anyone ever tell you it's girls who ask boys that?"

"They did, but I ignored them."

"This is date ten, right?"

"It is. Officially. All signed, stamped and certified."

"Ok. So, we like each other. We've had ten dates. We've discussed kids."

"All true."

"So it wouldn't be unreasonable to invest a week in a thought experiment?"

"It wouldn't."

"Alright, here's the deal. You spend a week designing a life that works, that incorporates a kid. I'll spend a week designing a life that works that would give me the things I'd seek from motherhood without having a child of my own. At the end of the week, we have dinner and compare notes. Deal?"

The woman was more mathematical than me!

"Deal."

Chapter 8

"Help!" It was Sunday night, and I'd just got home after dropping Eva back. Wine in hand, I'd called Helen.

"What have you done?" asked Helen.

"Look, it wasn't my fault."

"Uh-huh."

"Well, ok, it was partly my fault."

"She's pregnant?"

"No! Jesus, Helen, don't even say things like that!"

"So what have you done."

"Agreed to spend a week thinking about what a life with a child could be like."

"So I was close, then."

"It's just a thought experiment."

"So what's the big deal?"

"Did you not hear the word 'child' in that sentence?"

"You'd better start from the beginning."

"Yes, I better had. Dinner tomorrow?"

"There had better be salaciousness as well as angst."

"There is indeed both."

"7pm, my local Italian, then."

Helen was already sat at a table with a carafe of wine, two glasses and a plate of garlic bread; I like my friends.

"What's new in Helensworld?"

"I might have a chance to get some Microsoft work."

"Really? Wow."

"They have a big UK agency, of course, but one of my clients is working with them on a new product, and there's talk of handling that through a separate entity that could do its own thing. Since I do their PR, I should get a chance to pitch if that happens."

"Very cool! Any idea what it would be worth?"

"Not sure yet, but they should have a decent budget, and it would definitely look good on the client list."

"For sure."

"But anyway, you owe me tales of sexual adventure."

"What, that's it for Helensworld? One admittedly rather exciting news snippit about your business and we're done? What about your sexual adventures?"

"You know we married women – such things are behind us."

"Yeah, right." Helen and I had known each other for a long time, and I knew some of her stories from before she met David; she was not lacking in adventurous spirit.

"You know the rules."

"Hmph."

While she'd often shared her dating stories over the years, including some of the more .. ah .. specific elements, when things got serious with David and I'd met him a couple of times, the rules of course changed; it's one thing to share tales of anonymous encounters, and something else to reveal bedroom secrets about someone they know.

"So, tell all."

"But what if the rules are changing with Eva?"

"Stephen, she wants a child."

"May someday want a child," I corrected, with more emphasis than conviction.

"Yeah, sounds like it. So, this, er, thought experiment ..."

I told Helen about Eva's perspective that I'd never properly considered the matter, and her saner-than-average approach to parenting.

"Hmm. She's a smart cookie."

"Yes. Also cute, interesting and an amazing cook. Hence me wanting to conduct The Experiment, despite its rather far-fetched nature."

"I think I'll join you in the experiment, actually."

"You will?"

I was surprised. While Helen was also theoretically in the 'someday maybe' camp, my money would have been very firmly on that someday never arriving.

"Well, you know David is keen."

I did know that, but I also knew who wore the trousers in that relationship.

Helen continued: "So I owe it to him to at least think about how we might make it work, and your Eva seems to have a good handle on it."

"Ok, then you first: I think I need a good example to follow."

Helen thought for a moment.

"I guess, in a sense, mine is pretty simple. In principle, at least. I've always been a career girl, and my business comes first. I've never been able to see a way to run a business while also being a mum, and I think that's exactly it. I can't be a businesswoman who's also a mum, I can only be a mum who also runs a business."

"And could you do that?"

"That's the big question, of course. But it does at least become a question, considered that way round."

"I suppose for both of us," I mused, "part of it is a question of identity. You're not someone who does PR for a living, you're a PR person. It's a big part of who you are. And I'm not a guy who takes photographs, I'm a photographer. Or, at least, that's how I've always thought of myself."

"Yes. Being a mum would be a big shift in my identity." She paused. "Hmmm – interesting ..."

"What's that?"

"I'm not sure whether this is just an old-fashioned sexist attitude, or the reality – but I would say being a dad is less of a shift in identity."

"Hmmm."

'Hmmm' was going to make up a high proportion of this conversation, I thought, before continuing: "I don't know. I mean, yes, just from a practical perspective: you carry the baby inside you, breast-feed, etc. That's an undeniable qualitative difference. But otherwise, I think the shift in identity is just as huge."

"I suppose the crux of it is who stays at home. I mean, there has to be a period in which one of you does, and generally that's the mum."

I was momentarily filled with terror at the thought of being a stay-at-home dad. Me and a baby in the house for 24 hours a day.

"Oh my god. Call me a sexist bastard, but the idea of me being the one who stays home to look after the screaming vomit-generator hadn't even crossed my mind!"

"That's what I mean," said Helen. "We haven't moved on from those old role ideas as much we might like to imagine."

"I suppose for me, it's always been the case that, if I did ever have a baby, it would be because my partner wanted it, so I would see it as primarily her thing."

Helen shook her head firmly: "No way. That is definitely something you would have to factor into your redesigned life. It has to be an absolutely joint project. If you can't view it in that way, you can't have a kid: it's that simple."

She was right, of course, and it was obvious as soon as she said it; I'd just never thought about it seriously enough to get that far.

"You're right, and in that case – whoever stays at home – I would say being a dad is as big a shift as being a mum."

Helen gave me a sudden quizzical look.

"You don't agree?" I asked.

"No, it's not that," she replied. "I just had a thought. Er, you may want to cross your legs for this question ..."

It was obvious what she was going to ask.

"You haven't had a vasectomy, or we wouldn't be having this conversation. Given your claimed absolute certainty that you never want kids: why not?"

"I guess two things. One, it's supposed to be bloody painful, and two, you need some time off, so it would take a degree of planning that I've never got around to."

"I'm not sure I buy that. In fact, I'm fairly certain I don't. I mean, you plan a thousand other things, including finding the one day in a million when you can fly-"

She was referring to the fact that I'd recently started flying lessons. As a student pilot, you need three things to allow you to fly: wind speed below 10 knots, cloud-base above 2000 feet, visibility of at least 10 miles. You can imagine how often the three coincide in the UK. I spent a lot of time sitting in a portacabin on an airfield staring forlornly at the sky.

"- so no sale on the organisational excuse. And forget the pain –
you are, in case you have forgotten – the man who can break his
arm without realising it."

That was an incident I hadn't been allowed to live down. I
stupidly tripped up at an airport in Germany, arriving for a 5-day
shoot. I hit my elbow on the ground, and it hurt a lot, but a brief test
seemed to show that I had movement in all directions, and I was on
a tight schedule, so I shrugged it off as a ligament injury and
carried on with the work. It was only 10 days later when I still
couldn't straighten the arm fully that I had it x-rayed and learned it
was broken.

"So you think I have some Freudian desire for kids?"

"I think the evidence suggests you are not quite as decided as
you like to pretend."

"I have to say I'm not convinced, but I guess I'll know for sure at
the end of this experiment."

"I'll be convinced when you have the snip."

"It's a deal."

"So, my primary issue in designing a life with a kid would be not
defining myself by my work. What would be yours?"

"Well, let's make the question more manageable by assuming,
for now, that I don't become a stay-at-home dad. I think my brain
would explode if I tried to cram that concept into it, and you
wouldn't want brains spattered all over your pizza."

"Thank you for that image."

"My pleasure. So. What would be my primary issue ... ?"

Time to insert another 'Hmmm' accompanied by a lengthy
pause.

"I think, actually, it would be about going from a controlled life
to an uncontrolled one. I mean, yes, there's lots of my life that I
don't control now, but, overall, I at least harbour the fond illusion of
being in control of large swathes of it. With a kid, so much of your
life is chaos. From simple things like temper tantrums when you
want quiet to major things like a teenager getting arrested for
taking drugs. Realistically, you just have to accept that huge
chunks of your life are in the lap of the gods."

"Well ... yes, but, actually that's true now. Mr Kopp again. It's
just a question of degree."

"Actually, I don't think it is. The shift is so radical that I think it
has to be considered a whole new game."

"Ok, so your issue is giving up control. Going from the studio to a
location."

I smiled. It was an apt analogy for a photographer. In the studio,
you control the light: intensity, direction, quality, colour, position ...
everything. There is no excuse for failing to pull off a shot because
you are in complete control of the environment. On a location shoot,
you have varying degrees of control, but to a much larger extent
you have to work with what's there. Even the things you can
control, you have to do in ways sympathetic to the surroundings.
You can enhance, but not replace.

As a photographer, I enjoy both. The studio is great because you can do whatever you like (at least, given enough time and budget). Location shoots are very satisfying because you often have to overcome significant obstacles to pull off the shot. Could I view parenting in the same way?

"Smartarse," I said.

"That's why you love me."

"Ok, there's one big- no, make that huge, enormous, massive, gigantic and assorted other adjectives describing largeness of scale- difference."

"Namely?"

"The 18-year commitment." I almost said 'sentence', but was making a concerted effort not to be flippant. "Well, lifetime commitment, really, but I have enough trouble contemplating the 18-year bit. With a kid, that's it. No end, no relief, no escape clause."

"If that were true, there wouldn't be single mums. Plenty of men do walk away."

"Well, yes, but you know me: if I make a commitment, I see it through."

"Ok, so you'd need to design a life in which dealing elegantly with uncertainty and chaos became a source of satisfaction and fulfilment."

Like I said, she's a smartarse.

"I think you just summed it up in a sentence. Only, before I could design it, I'd have to believe it were possible."

"There are a lot of parents out there; at least some of them must pull it off."

"I've always thought of parents as a different species to me." You're trying not to be flippant, Adams, remember? "Ok, that's flippant phrasing, but I really do think their mindset is so different to mine, their outlook so alien to me, that it's utterly impossible for each to understand the thinking of the other."

"Well, as you always say, defining the problem is 90% of the way towards solving it."

"I do say that, don't I?"

"I think we've defined the problem."

"I think you're right. Ok, so, problem defined, now we need a plan of attack."

"Well, since the issue is thriving on chaos, I reckon you need to spend the week actively seeking it out. Give up your plans, your preparation, your mathematics, and spend the week winging it. You need to deliberately place yourself in situations where you don't have your usual levels of control."

"Ok, that sounds reasonable. My only problem is that Thursday is the only day I have free – I have an ad shoot tomorrow and Wednesday, then a property shoot on Friday."

"And that is a problem because ... ?"

"I can't wing it on shoots. Half of my reputation is based on the fact that I always have a Plan B, and – if that fails – a Plan C."

"I don't think you've quite grasped the idea here."

"I get the idea," I argued. "I think it's great. I just can't do it with work."

"That is what is known as missing the point in its entirety," said Helen. "You want to control when & where you give up control! The whole exercise is about living chaotically for a week."

"But what if something goes horribly wrong on a shoot? I can't say to the client 'Sorry I don't have a backup plan – I'm thriving on chaos this week'."

"You seem to have missed the 'thriving' part of the equation. The point is you go with the flow and figure things out as they happen. If something goes wrong, you don't deploy a pre-planned alternative, you think on your feet and figure it out on the spot."

"Fuck."

"I think you're finally getting it."

This was heady stuff. Until this conversation, I hadn't fully appreciated just how much I prided myself on always having everything under control. Attending to every detail. Having contingency plans. To deliberately give all that up, and tempt fate, was almost unthinkable.

"Shit."

"Yes, I would say you're definitely getting it."

I was appalled. But somewhere very far away was a very quiet voice acknowledging that she was right: it had to be done. It was the only way I could get any real sense of whether I could live such a life. I was also strongly motivated to complete the task: not only did it hold the key to a potential relationship with a woman with whom I was growing increasingly smitten, but I'm also a sucker for a challenge.

There was worse to come.

"Ok, so that's part 1 of the gameplan," said Helen.

"You mean there's more?"

"Of course! Living with chaos generally is only part of it – you also need to have a real experience of what it's like to be around kids." Helen paused. "What's the longest time you've spent with young kids in one stretch?"

I thought about it for a moment. "Oh, you know, evenings with friends with kids. Four or five hours."

"How long were the kids around before they were put to bed?"

"Er ... Well, maybe two or three hours."

Helen raised her eyebrows.

"You probably meet for dinner at, what, 8pm?"

"Are you sure you shouldn't be a cop?"

Helen ignored me.

"And the kids probably go to bed no later than 9pm, so probably an hour tops."

"Now who's being mathematical?"

"So, you've probably experienced kids for an hour at a time. What we need is for you to spend an entire day with some. It's the school holidays – do you have any friends who have kids and work from home?"

I didn't like the way this was heading.

"Um, yes. Alice. She has two kids."

"How old?"

I made vague, oscillating height-related gestures suggesting something in the 1-12 years old range.

Helen sighed. "When did they have them?"

That was an easier way to think of it. "Er, the first must have been about four years ago. Yes, four years ago. And the other one, uh, since."

"And you have Thursday free."

"Well ..."

"Sorted, then. Give her a call, arrange to go over Wednesday night so you have the full-day experience, from getting the kids up in the morning to putting them to bed in the evening."

The worst of it was that Alice would find the whole idea hilarious. Even if she had plans, I was sure she'd rearrange them for this. It was a bloody conspiracy between two friends who'd never even met.

A sudden thought struck me, and Helen saw the dismayed look on my face.

"What?" she asked.

"I never did this for Isabel."

"The experiment?"

"Yes. I was married to her for twelve years. Eva and I have had two dates and a weekend together. I should have done this for Isabel."

"You didn't think of it then."

"I should have done."

"Shoulda, woulda, coulda. Do you think it would have made any difference if you had? That wasn't the only reason you guys split."

I sighed. "No. No, I don't. But I do still feel guilty. I should have done that much."

"The nature of relationships that end: there's generally stuff we should have done and didn't."

We'll draw a veil over Tuesday and Wednesday's shoot; it's an experience I want to erase from my memory as quickly as possible. I reckon a decade or two ought to do it.

It's not that anything disastrous actually occurred. I'm fairly sure that the client wasn't even aware of any difference. When unforeseen things happened, I was able to solve them and maintain an appearance of composure. It was the way it felt inside. I absolutely hated it. I mean, really, really hated it.

With two issues, I'd had to completely abandon my original plan and instead work out a completely different tack, then shift things around in such a way that it appeared to the client that I'd had the second plan in mind all along. It was stressful, unpleasant and just felt so .. not me. It wasn't how I worked. More than that, it wasn't who I am.

I didn't ever want to work like that again. I was already firmly decided that, whatever the stakes of The Experiment, I was absolutely not going to be repeating it on Friday's shoot. I would probably introduce an extra layer of contingency just to compensate for the terror of the previous shoot.

But, I rationalised, I wouldn't need to live that way at work, I just had to be able to live that way outside it. Work could remain an island of calm and control in an ocean of- The metaphor just sort of trailed off there. I didn't know what the hell the ocean would be, but I would shortly be acquiring the necessary education.

Sometimes ad clients choose the final shot on the day, other times they reduce it to a shortlist, and I need to do the initial stage of processing on a series of shots. In this case, it was the latter, so it was 9pm by the time I'd finished, and just after ten by the time I arrived.

Alice and Paul lived in a leafy street in Crouch End. I'd never thought of it as anything other than a pleasant area, but now I was looking at it in terms of Eva's child-friendly criteria and realised it probably fitted the bill rather well. Perhaps a whole segment of parents had figured out the same approach?

The extent of my former lack of interest in micro-persons is revealed by the fact that I couldn't actually remember the names of the two kids. I figured they'd be mentioned at some point, so no need to confess the omission.

Paul was one of those guys whose dress-sense I envied: he had that knack of looking fashionable without looking like he was making any effort to do so. On me, a polo-neck jumper with a suit jacket would look contrived; on him, somehow, it didn't.

Alice was five years older than her husband and ran more to a Bohemian look: Big Hair, chunky jewellery and clothing that looked slightly rumpled in a way that made her look relaxed rather than untidy.

Paul was still rather stunned at my sudden interest in parenting; Alice still hadn't made up her mind how seriously to take it. To be fair, neither had I.

They'd eaten while I hadn't, so we sat around their kitchen table eating cheese & biscuits and drinking wine. I looked around at all the cupboards with kid-locks: beautiful furniture with nasty-looking cream-coloured plastic things stuck on them. Ugh.

"So who is this lady who has achieved this miracle?" asked Alice.

"Steady on the miracle bit," I protested. "This is merely a thought experiment."

"You spending an entire day with kids is more than a thought experiment."

"Well, you know me: I don't do things by halves."

"True. So is it serious?"

"I honestly don't know. I mean, it's ridiculously early, and there's a tonne of things we don't know about each other yet. But there are a lot of things that are right, and she has an approach to the kid issue that had never even occurred to me before, so I want to take a fresh look at it, however unlikely it seems."

"Well, 24 hours in this household will certainly give you a taste!"

"One thing I was chatting with a friend about .. Paul, is becoming a dad as big a shift as becoming a mum, would you say?"

"Absolutely," he said, without hesitation. "It changes everything. Being a dad is a completely new life."

"Do you agree?" I asked Alice.

She waggled her hand in a 'yes and no' gesture. "I don't think a man can ever experience it in quite the same way. When you carry the child inside you, it is literally part of you before it's even born. However involved the father is – and Paul was and is absolutely fantastic – it's still different."

I turned to Paul again: "Did you ever have any doubts? About being a father at all, or about the whole 18 year thing?"

Paul smiled. "God yes. And that '18-year thing', as you put it, goes out the window the moment you hold the minutes-old baby in your arms. You know at that moment that it's a lifetime bond, and all the doubts you had before just melt away."

"That easily?" I asked, doubtfully.

"Oh, I don't mean there won't be times when you want to murder the bloody thing. There are good days and bad days like anything else. But beneath that, there's always a core feeling of connection, of wanting to do everything you can for this new person. The feeling of .. feeling of this being what life is all about, that overwhelms everything else."

"Wow," I said. "I don't know that I'd ever feel that."

"You would," he said.

"You're very quiet," I said to Alice.

"I'm thinking," she said. "I've known you a long time. In all of that time, you've been adamant about this. Nobody ever goes into it without doubts, and I've known plenty of men go from ambivalence to doting dad .. but I've never known anyone be as consistently certain about it as you. I don't know that Paul is right. I don't know whether it would be that way with you. You might never make that leap. It could be a truly horrible mistake for you."

That comment hit me hard. I'd always experienced parents as advocates for the joys of parenthood. Not, as Paul said, that it was all sweetness and light, but that, ultimately, everyone would find it worthwhile. Their utter conviction that to experience it was to be converted to it was something I'd considered endemic to the breed. In fact, that patronising 'if only you knew' attitude was one of the things I found annoying about parents. To have one now saying 'Maybe not for you' was a real wake-up call.

"I guess tomorrow may give me a better idea," I said.

"It won't be the same," she replied. "They're not yours, and it's just a day, but yes, I think if you're still wondering about it by this time tomorrow, then that would be a positive sign."

Somewhere in my apartment, there was a horrible noise. The kind of noise you want to silence with the aid of a baseball bat. What the hell could it be?

It was not stopping. It was somewhere very close and to the right, which was odd because that put it directly outside my 3rd-floor window.

I may have mentioned in passing that I have limited familiarity with low-digit hours of the ante meridian variety. Well, actually I'm extremely familiar with those tacked onto the end of the night, just not those which some people inexplicably choose to lever into the beginning of the day. It thus took me a couple of minutes to remember that I was not, in fact, in my apartment, and that terrible noise was a crying baby. Or child. Or whatever the hell you called them at that age.

Please god make it stop. Why didn't they make it stop? You surely can't get used to something like that? They have to make it stop!

I looked at my watch. It was the middle of summer and it was still almost dark, for chrissakes! I waited for the face to come into focus. Three minutes to six! No, wait, that was the polite way to put it: it was actually 05:57. I was being woken up by the most insanely irritating racket imaginable at a time with a five in front of it! A five!

They must hear it! Nobody could sleep through that. It seemed to be getting louder with every moment. The next-door neighbours must be able to hear it. The guy down the street had to be able to hear it. When will they make it stop?

It had been going on now for 10 or 15 minutes. I looked at my watch. It had stopped: it was still reading 05:57.

Finally, eventually, after several aeons of dreadful, painful noise, I heard signs of movement.

Alice was speaking to it in soothing tones. This had converted the noise from a high-pitched wailing into a lower-pitched moaning.

I was seriously tempted to call an end to The Experiment there and then. More than one day of that and I would be clinically insane.

The moaning got louder and there was a knocking at my door. I did some moaning of my own. Alice appeared with the source of the noise in her arms. It was the younger of the two. Female. I realised that the names hadn't been mentioned. Had I heard it in Alice's attempted pacifying? If so, I hadn't been able to make it out. Oh well, plenty of time later for formal introductions.

"Good morning, and welcome to parenthood," Alice said, with a degree of chirpiness that must surely be illegal under international non-proliferation treaties.

"Gmmb mmmbing," I replied.

"Sophie, meet Stephen; Stephen, meet Sophie. I know you've met before, but knowing you, you'll have forgotten her name." It was too early in the morning for me to muster the energy required for a denial.

With great effort, I levered myself up onto one elbow.

"Does this happen often," I asked.

"What?" asked Alice.

"Sophie waking up in the middle of the night."

"Ah," said Alice. "Time for lesson one of parenthood. This is not the middle of the night. This is the time that kids wake up."

"Every day?" I asked, incredulously.

"Every day."

"Dear god! How do you cope?"

"You go to bed early."

I let this revelation sink in. Come to think of it, I realised, we had gone to bed at about eleven last night.

"Um. So what's first on the agenda?"

"The kids have to be washed and dressed, then we get them breakfast. Do you want to wash one of them, or just watch?"

"Either one means getting out of bed, right?"

"Right."

"Do I have time for a shower?"

"After the kids are washed and dressed. That's lesson two. You always have to attend to the kids first, then fit in your own stuff around them. I'll get one of Paul's dressing-gowns for you."

What the hell kind of life was this, I asked myself?

Alice returned with a dressing gown. "See you in a minute," she said.

"I think I'll ease into this gently," I told her, as I wandered sleepily into the bathroom in the dressing-gown. "You wash them, I'll just sit here." I sat on the toilet lid.

"Michael, you remember Stephen. Stephen, you remember Michael, though probably not his name." Michael looked at me suspiciously. Quite rightly, I thought. I tried to smile and wave. His look of suspicion didn't change.

Sophie (I'd repeated the name to myself several times in an effort to achieve the complex task of remembering something at such an ungodly hour) started crying again as soon as Alice started wiping her with a wet flannel. Oh god.

"Don't be silly, Sophie, you know you like being washed." I'd noticed that parents often lied to their kids in the hope that they might be taken in by it. I wondered if it ever worked.

A minute later, Sophie was done and it was Michael's turn. At least he didn't cry.

Dressing them was remarkably quick.

"Ok," said Alice, "you grab a quick shower and get dressed. All I'll be doing is preparing some breakfast, and I think even you know how to do that."

I showered, shaved and dressed, and felt marginally more human by the time I wandered downstairs. Paul was already dressed and making coffee.

"Sleep well?" he asked.

"Until about ten minutes ago."

"You get used to it," he smiled.

I didn't know which was the more terrifying thought: my belief that you never would, or the idea that you actually might.

"Did you bring any other clothes?" asked Paul. I looked down at my shirt and chinos, bemused. What was wrong with my clothes?

"Um, no, should I have?"

"Well, those look a bit expensive, and you being new to kids, and all, you might not duck in time when they throw stuff."

"Oh. Right. Thanks for the warning. I'll allocate some dry-cleaning costs to the budget for The Experiment."

I was introduced to the feeding rituals. Even a two-year-old can feed herself, I learned, but has to be supervised quite closely, and will typically end up with as much food on the floor as she does in her belly. Four-year-olds are relatively automated in the feeding department. My clothes were, so far, food-free.

I gratefully accepted the proffered mug of coffee from Paul.

"So, what's the plan for the day?" I asked.

"Paul leaves for work at seven, so feeding the grown-ups is next on the agenda. After that, I generally try to keep the kids occupied for a couple of hours while I do some work, then we need to do a quick supermarket run."

"Don't you have stuff delivered?" The idea of actually setting foot in a supermarket was foreign to me; I always used the home delivery service.

"We do, but you always need odd bits & pieces." She looked amused at my expression. "Call it lesson three of parenthood."

"I can't say that any of the lessons so far fill me with joy," I complained.

"You get used to it," said Paul.

"Or not," added Alice, cheerfully.

Breakfast passed reasonably uneventfully, the only noteworthy events being Sophie announcing that she'd had enough by pushing the plate off the high-chair, spilling banana and yoghurt all over the kitchen floor. I noted that mum and dad had the forethought to make sure it was a plastic plate. Well, forethought or experience, anyway. Neither of them made any immediate move to pick it up, so I did. Perhaps, I speculated, you just got used to having a kitchen floor coated with various foodstuffs?

Paul left for work with a cheery "Enjoy your day!", and Alice cleared the breakfast things into the dishwasher while handing me some wet-wipes: "You wipe off their faces."

Um. Hmmm. I tentatively brushed Sophie's lips with one of the wipes.

"She's not made of porcelain!" Alice exclaimed. "Here ..." She wiped Sophie's face with the kind of force you might use on a stubborn worktop stain. Sophie didn't appear to notice.

"Your turn."

I compromised with Michael, using enough pressure to remove a good 80% of the jam (how do kids manage to get jam on their eyebrows?) without removing skin in the process.

Alice was a freelance magazine journalist specialising in financial articles. How we can all save £1500 a year by organising our finances in clever ways, why we should start a pension at age 20 even if we're only paying in a tenner a month, how to pay off our mortgage five years early, that kind of stuff. In short, the kind of worthy things it really would make a massive amount of sense to do but which few of us ever get around to.

Alice worked in what was once the dining-room and was now a study, because what used to be the study was now a kid's playroom.

I didn't have any project work to do, but one of the banes of a photographer's life is the need to constantly update your website, so I'd brought along my laptop to do some tinkering with that while Alice was working. I looked around for a power socket, and noticed they all had covers. Just how much conversion did one do to a house, I wondered, to make it compatible with kids?

"No," said Alice.

"No what?" I asked.

"No you don't get to bury yourself in your laptop. I need a couple of hours to work, so you can look after the kids while I do."

"But I don't know how to look after kids," I protested.

"I know," said Alice. "You'll figure it out. Or not." She led Sophie and Michael (I had remembered their names for a good hour now – I reckoned I was doing well) into the playroom. "Right, all yours, see you in a couple of hours. Try not to kill them." On which cheery note she waved and virtually danced out of the room.

I looked at Michael. Michael looked at me. I looked at Sophie. Sophie looked at me.

"Listen, guys, you know the drill here, don't look at me for ideas."

Both kids continued to look at me.

"Ok, ok," I said. "Um ... stuff to do. Kid's stuff. How hard can that be? We're in a room full of kid's stuff." I looked around at the astonishing number of plastic boxes full of brightly-coloured ... um ... stuff. Oh, Sticklebacks, I thought, spotting some plastic bricks with lots of pins sticking out on all sides. I remember those. At least, I think that's what they were called. But I can at least do building things. Yes, let's start with those.

I tipped them onto the floor, picked up a yellow one and a blue one, stuck them together and then handed them to Michael. Who promptly threw them to the far side of the room.

"No, Michael, let's make something. Look ..." I went and fetched the bricks, added a third to make a kind of arch and then handed them to him. He threw them across the room again.

"Ok, not Sticklebacks. Or whatever they are really called." I was beginning to doubt my vague childhood construction memories; it seemed like an unlikely name. "No problem, we'll do ..." I looked around some more. "Ok, crayoning. All kids like crayoning." I picked up a set of crayons and a roll of ... wallpaper lining paper? I guess it's cheap. I looked at the box of crayons. Non-toxic. Suitable for children of all ages. There: right there in black-and-white. Suitable for children of all ages, which is what I have here. Right. A few crayons each – I handed several to Michael and one per hand to Sophie – and some paper, instant toddlerific entertainment. Sorted.

Michael threw the crayons across the room. Sophie started eating hers.

Hmmm.

Ok. Don't panic. I know only, like, thirty seconds has passed, and Alice has threatened to leave me in here with them for two hours (or 120 minutes, or 7200 seconds, but who's counting?), and all I seem to have achieved so far is to teach Michael a sort of reverse game of Fetch, but I can do this. I'm a bright, resourceful, creative chap. If I can't outwit a 2-year-old and a 4-year-old, I'm in trouble.

Right. Deep breath. I looked around again. A teddy bear. A cute, furry teddy bear. Ok, that has to be a safe bet for a 2-year-old. She has to like teddy bears, right? I picked it up and handed it to her.

She tried to throw it across the room, only being less coordinated than Michael she mostly just sort of smashed its face into the floor. Mental note: do not hand her any live animals.

I needed to get them off this whole throwing thing. I needed something they couldn't throw. I looked around again. A baby rocking-horse. Ok, it was admittedly the smallest rocking-horse I'd ever seen, more of a rocking Shetland Pony, but it seemed large enough that neither of them could throw it anywhere and small enough that they were unlikely to hurt themselves much if they fell off it. Perfect. Rocking horse time.

I dragged it into the centre of the room. "Who'd like to be first?" I asked. Both were looking quite interested; I congratulated myself on a smart move. Michael was closest, so I picked him up and lifted him onto the 'saddle' of the horse. I wasn't sure whether he could hold on on his own, but didn't want to have to return a toddler to its owner with a broken nose within my first two minutes of caretakership, so decided to hold him under his arms and kind of rock the horse by rocking him. He started crying.

Ok, no rocking-horse. I put him back on the floor and asked him "What do you want?" He continued crying. "It's ok," I said. What was it parents said when kids cried? Oh yes: "There, there." I had no idea what it meant, but they always seem to say it, and they wouldn't say it unless it had some kind of success rate at shutting up crying kids. "There, there," I repeated. He continued crying, and then Sophie joined in. Two crying toddlers. I'd been left alone with two toddlers in a room full of things specifically intended to make toddlers happy and I'd reduced both of them to tears within about the first three minutes.

"There, there" wasn't cutting any ice with Michael; I decided to try it on Sophie. I picked her up. "There, there." What else did parents do? If it was a grazed knee, they rubbed it, but there were no grazed knees. Did you pat them on the head, or was that only a metaphorical thing? I suspected the latter, but having no other ideas decided to try it anyway. Sophie's decibel rating increased by about 50%. Yes, that must be a metaphorical thing.

Ok, what else? There-thereing hadn't worked, head-patting had made things worse, there must be other things I can think of. I mean, I was a kid once, I thought, what worked with me? Ah! Sweets! Yes, those work. I looked around. No sweets. Maybe in the kitchen, I thought. But can you leave kids alone while you go to the kitchen? They're in a playroom, so you'd think it was designed for kids to be ok on their own for a little while at least, but what if that's the one thing you never do with toddlers and I end up having to explain to a distraught Alice & Paul and an incredulous coroner and a baying pack of Daily Mail reporters how I thought it would be ok, just for a minute or two? Best not.

Why wasn't Alice coming, anyway? These were her beloved kids, and they were clearly upset, and she was seemingly still in her office tapping away at her keyboard.

"Um, Alice!" I called. Nothing. I went to the door and opened it, standing half in, half out of the doorway so I could call again without taking my eyes off either kid. "Alice! They're crying."

"I can hear that." She didn't seem terribly concerned. Ok, calm down, kids probably cry all the time, it's nothing to worry about.

"Um ... how do I make them stop?" I considered that for a moment and decided the phrasing could have been better. "Make them happy again, I mean."

"Just distract them with something. Now shoo back in there – you won't learn anything if you keep running to me every five minutes" That sounded distinctly like something one might say to a child, not a grown man who was trying, with a remarkable lack of success, to be a temporary guardian to a pair of them.

"Uh, ok."

Right. Come on. How difficult can this be? Millions of parents deal with this every day. You have a roomful of stuff to distract them with. Ok. I looked around, trying to spot the box with a large, colourful 'Guaranteed to stop kids crying' label on it. There must be one. I mean, it's an obvious need, Mothercare must surely have the matter in hand?

There were some soft balls. Well, balls and cubes and pyramids. Soft shapes. I didn't know what one did with them, but maybe the kids did.

The kids. Wait a minute. They're not crying any more. Neither of them. How did that happen? Fuck, I've inadvertantly hit on the solution and have no idea what it was!

Ok, now what? Proceed with the soft shape plan, or go back to the crayons or the horse or-

"Painting."

"Sorry?"

It was Michael. He was tugging at a box. A box underneath a whole pile of stuff that was about to fall on top of him. I lunged across the room, slid on the pile of Sticklebacks and launched myself head-first into the pile of toys I was trying to prevent falling. I extracted a piece of Lego from my left ear.

It wasn't a 100% successful attempt at stopping the toys from collapsing, admittedly, but I don't think that any of them landed on Michael's head.

I gingerly extracted the box Michael was reaching for. Face-painting Kit. Non-toxic. Suitable for kids of all ages. I was beginning to spot a theme here.

Right, face-painting. Except, um, I'm rubbish at painting. Listen, Adams, I thought, they are not art critics, they're toddlers! They're hardly going to know the difference between a recreation of the Sistine Chapel and something Pollock would have created when he was in nappies. Slap several colours on their face, show them the result in a mirror and they'll be happy.

I opened the box. A small warning light flashed dimly somewhere in the back of my brain. Paints. Kids faces. Probably ought to run that one past a parent.

"Ok, one minute," I told my canvases, "I just need to check this with your mum."

I nipped next door and presented my plan. "Sure, they wash right off."

Right. Good. This was good. I had a plan, nobody was crying, it was something they wanted. This was Good.

I went back into the playroom. The room I hadn't left more than 90 seconds ago, tops. Not time enough for the kids to have got into any kind of trouble. Definitely, absolutely and categorically not enough time for them to have taken the face-paints and daubed at least three colours all over the walls. And the carpet. Oh fuck.

"Um, Alice?"

"Yes, In Loco Parentis?"

"Those paints that wash right off … do they wash right off walls? And, er, carpets?"

Alice looked at me: "You left them alone in there with an open box of paints?!"

"No! Well, yes. But only for a minute."

"Washing-up liquid and warm water, in the kitchen. Bowl under the sink. But put the paints away before you leave them again."

"Right."

I put the paints back into their box and took the box with me to the kitchen. My mobile rang as I did so. My hands were covered in paint, and my phone was in my pocket. I dashed over to the sink, ran my hands under the tap and reached around to grab a towel. In my haste, I knocked a large pasta jar onto the kitchen floor. It shattered, depositing glass and pasta shells everywere.

"Fuck!" I exclaimed. Alice came rushing over to see what the hell was going on. As she did so, there was another crash from the playroom. "Oh Christ!" I ran to the playroom, slipped on pasta shells and slide across the floor, cutting my arm on the glass and leaving a trail of blood across the floor before finally catching a potted plant with my foot and depositing it and its earth on the floor.

Alice stared at the floor. Glass. Pasta shells. Earth. Yukka plant. And blood.

"Are you ok?" she asked.

"I'm fine. Go check on the kids."

I picked myself up and grabbed some kitchen towel to dab on my arm. I examined the damage. There were lots of small, shallow cuts, but nothing to worry about. My shirt, however, was ruined: both torn and bloodied. Having made sure I wasn't still dripping blood, I walked back to the playroom, trying not to tread more glass into the floor.

The playroom looked almost as bad as the kitchen: a large box of Lego was now distributed across the floor, adding to the crayons and Stickleback bricks I'd left there earlier. Sophie and Michael, having been deprived of their paints, had seemingly found crayons a suitable alternative for drawing on the walls, and it appeared Michael had been climbing one of the piles of toy boxes in order to reach high enough to put the finishing touches to one of his masterpieces.

I looked at the devastation. Alice looked at it too, then looked at me. She alternated between the two a few times. Finally she spoke.

"Unbelievable. How long had it been? Five minutes? Ten tops?"

There didn't seem to be any reasonable response.

"How is that even possible?" continued Alice? "I mean, how can that all have happened in ten minutes?"

I didn't have an answer to that one either.

I finally ventured: "Um, shall we declare this a failed experiment, and I'll slink off as soon as I've reconstructed your home?"

Alice paused. "No. No, it's fine. I think we'll just ensure you have a grown-up supervising your efforts from now on."

I focused my efforts on clearing up the chaos while Alice did most of the childcare duties. Michael seemed to be in a questioning mood. Why does daddy eat mouldy cheese? What are rocks made of? Why does glass break?

"How the hell do you do it?" I asked Alice.

"What?"

"This! The questions. The multiple suicide attempts. The destruction of property. The demands to be fed, watered, accompanied to the loo. And please don't tell me you get used to it."

"Well, you do or you don't. I have. Paul has. Most parents do." She gave me a sharp look. "But I'm really not sure about you."

"Makes two of us," I said.

Next on the agenda was a visit to Sainsbury's. This was a three-minute walk. So: three minutes to walk there, five minutes to whiz round grabbing the bits & pieces, a couple of minutes queuing at the checkout, three minutes back, cup of tea, sorted.

Er, no. First, the kids had to be dressed. I'd thought, not unreasonably in my view, that they were already dressed, but no: they had indoor clothes and outdoor clothes. That took ten minutes. Not including shoes and coats: that, somehow, inexplicably, took about another five minutes.

Michael wanted to walk, and that, apparently, meant Sophie wanted to walk too. A three-minute walk with two small kids in tow is about a 20-minute walk. Partly because they have small legs, and partly because they stop every five feet to look at something.

"That's one of the great things about kids," claimed Alice. "They make you notice things. To them, it's all new, all exciting, even the most mundane things, and you start looking at the world through their eyes."

I was sympathetic to the argument – the same applied to a camera viewfinder – but I did not personally start to view dog turds, weeds, wheelie-bin wheels, slugs, yesterday's Metro, gravel, bus-stops, old women, fat men, empty Coke cans, potted plants or cigarette butts with renewed enthusiasm.

Sainsbury's was the same only more so. I had fondly imagined that both kids would go in those pairs of kiddy seats they have in the trolleys. I was wrong: 2-year-olds go in the seat, 4-year-olds run amok in the aisles. Michael's role in the proceedings appeared to be to disappear out of sight and return clutching something we didn't need to buy, whereupon Alice would take him back to where it came from so he could put it back on the shelf. En-route, he would stop to look at something or to ask a question ("Why are those biscuits made of cake?").

"You're just doing this on purpose, aren't you?" I accused Alice.

"Doing what?"

"Stopping at everything they want to see. Usually you'd just tell them to shut up, hold on tight and you'd scoot round and be out in five minutes."

"Sometimes," she admitted, "if I'm in a hurry, but then you risk temper tantrums. More importantly, you want them to be stimulated by the world, to be interested in everything they see."

Alice looked at me for a moment, then laughed.

"What?"

"I've just realised: you think it's all neat compartments. You think that now we're shopping, and later we'll sit down with them and teach them stuff, and then after that they'll play ... It's not like that. Most of the learning kids do takes place in everyday life. A trip to the supermarket is an educational visit. So is catching a bus or walking down the street."

"So it's relentless."

Alice looked amused. "A parent would tend to say continuous. I think your instincts are correct: you are so not parent material."

Eva was due at 7.30pm, and I was preparing dinner. I have a rather limited range of dishes, but do well at those. Tonight it was Stilton and celery spread (to be served with toast) followed by honey and mustard glazed steak with fine beans with egg (you sort of scramble the egg in a frying-pan then add the beans).

I'd decanted a bottle of Grenache and made a start on it. I had REM playing on the hifi, and the windows open with a pleasant breeze blowing through.

It would be a lovely evening were it not for the fact that it would probably be our last. At least, there didn't seem much point in continuing given the outcome of my experiment.

Bugger.

I'd debated whether to advise Eva of the outcome of The Experiment prior to dinner, but decided it would be better done in person. There was always the lurking hope, of course, that she may have had more success with her experiment, but I was not optimistic on that count.

We were all cheery hellos and kisses when she arrived. I poured a glass of wine for her when we disentangled ourselves.

The obvious thing to do now was to ask about her week, but that would lead inevitably to discussion of The Experiment, and I needed more wine before that conversation.

It was Eva who broached the subject. She gestured at my batcheloresque apartment: "Ok, I can see you're not going to fit a kid into this. Put a single cuddly toy in the middle of the floor and it would make the place look untidy. I feel I should stand in pre-defined places in the room, selected for their Feng Shui properties."

I smiled. It was a bittersweet feeling. One of her real talents was defusing tense situations; I was going to miss that. I was going to miss a lot of things.

"Yes, your child-friendly home would definitely need to be part of any redefined life."

I was trying to arrive there obliquely; my theoretical phrasing gave its own clue as to the outcome.

It was usually me who tackled things head-on, but this time it was Eva.

"The experiment didn't work for you, did it?"

"No," I said, simply. "And yours didn't either." I realised as I said it that it was a statement, not a question.

"No."

We both gave sad little smiles, and stood there silently for a while.

"Let's have dinner," she said.

So we did.

"I tried," I said. "I really did." I told her about my day as a deputy parent. I realised I'd already turned it into an after-dinner anecdote; it was that firmly in the past.

"So did I," she said. "It was a real surprise, actually. I honestly did think it was an undecided issue for me. It was only when I contemplated a life without a child that I realised it wasn't; I really do want one. Maybe not soon, but I do want one."

"I know. And knew."

"Yes, you knew before I did."

"So."

"So."

"It's not going to work, is it." It wasn't a question.

"No."

We finished our food and drank more wine, then I cleared the plates. When I came back in, Eva was sat back on the sofa with both wine glasses. I sat next to her, leaned back and kissed her on the forehead. She turned and lay her head against my chest, snuggling up next to me.

"Thank you," I said.

"For what?"

"Everything. The time we had. And this. Making it easy. Easier," I corrected.

"We could carry on as we are, for a while at least."

"No." I wasn't sure where she was at, but I couldn't do it. I was falling for her. Had fallen for her, actually. I couldn't keep seeing her, knowing it wouldn't last.

"Ok."

We snuggled for a long time.

"Do you want me to go?" she asked, finally.

"No," I said. "Stay."

"Let's go to bed."

We slept together, but only slept.

Chapter 9

"Shame," said Tom, "but if you want different lives, better to know it now."

"Right," I said.

"Onwards and upwards."

I was still hurting, and wasn't in the mood for cheerfulness. Helen would be more understanding, I felt.

"Life can be bloody unfair sometimes," I told her. "I miss Eva."

"Are you really sure she wouldn't make kids worth it?"

"Totally sure. I wish I weren't, but I am."

"Ok."

Helen was uncharacteristically quiet.

"Anyway," I said, with forced cheeriness, "what about your own kid experiment? What was the outcome?"

"It was rather confronting."

"I bet. And the verdict ... ?"

"The verdict, to my surprise, is yes."

"Wow."

"Yes, wow. Not yet, not for a couple of years, I think, but yes – there will come a point where I'm willing to switch roles."

"Wow."

"I think you mentioned that."

"I guess I did. But: wow."

"Ok, you can stop wowing now."

"I'll try."

"You're still thinking 'wow', I can tell."

"I can't be responsible for what the voices in my head get up to without my permission."

"Hmph."

I resisted the temptation to add a further wow.

"Anyway," said Helen, "changing the subject back to your love-life, what now?"

"I don't know. I don't much feel like thinking about it at the moment. I'm considering becoming a hermit. Or maybe a recluse. I'm not quite sure what the difference is between the two."

"I think a hermit has to live in a cave while a recluse can live in a mansion."

"I'm veering towards the recluse option, then."

"No."

"No?"

"No."

"What do you mean, 'no'?"

"I mean we can't have you moping about. You need to get back in the game."

"That's what Tom said, but I'm really not in the mood for playing it just at the moment."

"I know, but you have to anyway."

Helen's tough-love approach was generally something I appreciated about her, but just at that moment it wasn't what I was looking for. I wanted to go lick my wounds for a while.

"I'm going to sit on the sidelines for a while. Maybe go have some meaningless sex."

"That's ok. You just shouldn't hide in the dark. And anyway, I have a plan."

"A plan?"

"Speed-dating."

"Speed-dating?"

"There's a terrible echo in here."

I had heard of speed-dating, of course, but I had no idea how it worked and wasn't keen on finding out.

"It sounds dreadful."

"It's tailor-made for a man with a mathematical approach to dating. Anyway, a friend went – she thought it was great fun."

"This is not another fix-up, is it?" I asked, warily. I didn't think I could cope with another of Helen's fix-ups just now.

"No, you're not to be trusted with any of my friends at the moment."

"So you want to palm me off on strangers instead."

"Quite."

"Hiding in the dark sounds preferable."

"You can hide in the dark after the speed-dating. Which is on Thursday, by the way."

"Um ... I'm sure those hideous things happen all the time. What's special about the one on Thursday?"

"Well, Joanne is going again, and apparently they are short of men."

"There's probably a reason for that."

"7.30pm in a bar in Notting Hill. I've emailed you the link."

"Do I get any say at all in this?"

"Not so's you'd notice, no."

"Remind me why I'm friends with you?"

"I keep telling you, I'm very loveable."

"Hmm."

The bar looked crowded and loud. I was relieved to find we were in a private bit of it.

"Here's your badge," smiled the woman greeting us as we arrived. It was one of those fixed smiles that didn't get as far as her eyes. "And here's your sheet and pen. I'll explain how everything works once everyone is here."

She handed me a cheap plastic biro with the web address of the dating company in tacky gold lettering, and sheet with the numbers

1 to 30. Alongside each number were two tickboxes, labelled 'Date' and 'Friends' respectively. My badge read 'Stephen' and under it in a smaller typeface the number 24. The only thing they could have done to make it any more clinical was to stamp a bar-code on our foreheads.

I put on my badge and looked around to see if I could spot Joanne. Helen had reminded me that we'd met a couple of times, and I vaguely recalled her as a frighteningly sociable redhead in her late 20s. I had no idea what that sort of woman would be doing at a speed-dating event. For that matter, I had no idea what I was doing at a speed-dating event.

I spotted Joanne, who was chatting to two other women. One was a short and somewhat nerdy-looking brunette, the other was a goth-looking woman with purple hair. Both looked in their mid-20s. I wandered over.

"Hello again. I gather this is your fault."

"Stephen!"

She leaned over for a cheek kiss. Cheek kisses are incredibly confusing things these days. Among the many unknowns are: who do you do them with? Is it an air-kiss or an actual peck? Do you do one, two, three or even – I discovered one time in the Champagne region of France – four? What's wrong with a good old-fashioned handshake?

"Ah, yes. Karen, Susan: Stephen – we have a mutual friend."

That's the other weird thing about cheek-kissing: once two of you have done it, everyone has to, even if they're complete strangers.

Once the ritual was complete, I peered at their name badges.

"Uh, just out of idle curiosity, why does Karen's name badge say Felicity, and Susan's say Liz?"

"We're just here for moral support," said Susan/Liz. "I'm actually married, and Karen lives with her boyfriend."

I processed this information.

"Um .. is that common, do you think? Non-single women coming to singles events to provide moral support to their friends?"

"Of course," said Susan/Liz, in a slightly pitying tone that implied any fool knew that.

She looked at me. "You look shocked."

"Well, I hadn't known quite what to expect from the sort of women who would go to a singles event, but I had imagined that they might at least be, you know-"

"Single?"

"It didn't seem too unreasonable an expectation, under the circumstances."

"Consider yourself educated."

"So, based on our sample of you three, out of the thirty women here, perhaps ten of them are even single?"

"Well, yes," said Joanne. "But then two-thirds of the men here are desperate losers who still live with their mums, so it balances out."

I wondered how soon it would all be over.

Our host with the non-smiling eyes explained the system. In a few minutes time, the women would be asked to take their places at tables and would stay where they were. The men would rotate. Each meeting would be for three minutes. After each encounter, we would tick the 'Date' box next to their name if we were interested in meeting them for a date, 'Friends' if we didn't want to date them but thought we could be friends, or nothing at all if we never wanted to see them again. Afterwards, we would hand in our sheets and they would match up the choices. Only if both parties ticked a box would contact details be passed on, and we would then be told whether that person had ticked 'Date' or 'Friend'. This had all the romance of a hospital waiting room.

Joanne gave me her tips.

"Most of the men spend the entire three minutes talking about themselves. No-one ever ticks them. Don't say exactly the same things to each woman because we all compare notes in the Ladies, and there's nothing worse than a prepared speech."

I had a feeling the men might also be comparing notes, only I wasn't convinced the basis for comparison would be conversational skills. How many times in one evening could I wonder what I was doing there?

"Obviously don't say anything tacky-"

"I'm not five."

"No, but at the same time, you do have to flirt with the ones who interest you. Women will only tick men they're sure will tick them, so you have to make it clear when you're interested. Though some men will tick 'Date' for all of them, but they're the desperate losers I mentioned, and no-one will tick them."

"But why would the women only tick the ones who they feel sure will tick them? If I understand the system correctly, and it rather depresses me that I think I do, the guys who don't tick them will never know whether or not they were ticked."

Even discussing the system was making me cringe.

"Yes, but the speed-dating people will know, and anyway, it's the principle of the thing."

That sounded about as comprehensible to me as ticking yes to everyone, but I was saved by the bell – or, in this case, by Non-Smiling Eyes instructing the women to take their places.

There were numbers on the table, and we started with matching numbers, so I needed to go to table 24. Which was Joanne. Great.

"Ok," I asked, "can we please just agree now that this is too weird and spend three minutes discussing the weather?"

"Or I could give you more speed-dating tips."

"Please don't. I assure you that this is my first and last speed-dating event. How the hell are you supposed to have any even halfway informative conversation in three minutes. That's 90-seconds each. All you can do is see whether you fancy them, flirt a bit if you do or have a pointless and probably excruciating conversation if you don't."

"That's the whole point. Three minutes is enough to decide you fancy someone and make sure they have enough brain-cells to be allowed out in public, and with the ones you don't fancy, you have the delicious comfort of knowing you can stop talking to them after 180 seconds."

Remembering my dinner with Alli, I had to admit she had a point there.

"Well, ok. On the subject of which, exactly what do Karen and Susan do for these little encounters? I assume the pseudonyms mean they don't admit their real status?"

"It depends. With the guys who seem genuine, they confess. With the guys with their heads up their arses, they play them along."

"I see."

"With the most full-of-themselves guys, Karen tells them she and her girlfriend want to break into the porn business, and do they have a camera?"

"Whose phone number does she give them?"

"Last time it was Lambeth Police Station. I think it's Buckingham Palace tonight."

"I hope some Lady In Waiting answers the phone. Does Her Maj still have Ladies in Waiting?"

"I don't know, but I guess they'll find out. Oh, and Helen asked me to remind you of something."

"Oh yes?"

"You are not to ask them about their child-bearing plans. That is not the sort of conversation one has within a three-minute date, even if the only reason you're asking is for elimination purposes."

A gong was sounded.

Joanne winked at me: "Go have fun."

"Hmm."

I had to admit that Number 25, aka Michelle, aka who knows what if she was one of the fake singles, was rather aesthetically pleasing. Maybe 30, West Indian, impeccably-dressed, a silk scarf over her blouse, beautiful eyes.

"Hello," I said.

"Hi."

I concentrated very hard on not asking her whether she'd been speed-dating before as I was determined to get through at least one 'date' without some variation on 'Do you come here often?'.

Prepared speeches might be naff, I thought, but some kind of bullet-point plan might have been an idea. Oh well, I was only here to make up the numbers, so what the hell.

"Do you feel as at ease with this process as you look?" I asked.

"No," she smiled.

"Oh good."

Have you ever tried to have a three-minute conversation, whose sole purpose is to find out a bit about someone, without resorting to any clichés? It's almost impossible. What are the two things you want to know about someone to begin getting some sense of who they are? 'What do you do?' and 'What do you enjoy when not working?', right? Otherwise known as cliché questions A and B. But if you don't ask those, what the hell do you ask?

"Sod it," I began. Ok, perhaps that wasn't the ideal beginning. I explained the cliché dilemma and added "at least I won't be the 30th person in 90 minutes to ask you what you do for a living and what your hobbies are."

"No," she said, "only the second so far."

Ah yes, I'd escaped the first round; she hadn't.

"Perhaps we should all be issued with laminated cards with the answers to the first three questions on, and we can just hold them up."

"So what's your third question here?"

"Actually, my third question should probably be the first: are you really single, or are you here as moral support for one of your mates?"

"Ah, you've done this before, then."

I explained, and Michelle laughed.

"No, I really am single."

"So let's get questions two and three out of the way."

"I'm a barrister."

"I'm impressed."

"Don't be. It's not all Kavanagh QC and murder cases at the Old Bailey. Most of it is traffic offences in Barking Magistrates Court."

"Do you think any career is as glamorous as the image?"

"Self-made billionaire, maybe."

"I don't think I'll be giving that one a try."

"Ok, then, cliché question one: your turn."

"I'm a photographer."

"That's not all gorgeous models on Caribbean beaches, right?"

"Right."

A gong sounded. Was that it? Three minutes already?

"Oh," I said. "We didn't get very far, did we?"

"CV-wise, no, but it was good to meet you."

"Likewise."

Guy number 23 was hovering impatiently beside the table. This wasn't just a meat-market, it was a conveyer-belt at a supermarket checkout, and I was apparently the product that was caught in the mechanism and failing to move smoothly down the belt.

"Bye, Michelle."

"Bye, Stephen."

Number 26 was Sonia. Her face was ... well, there was no other word for it: orange. Fake tan is never a good look, and too much of it says all the wrong things about someone. I began to see the virtues of the three-minute time-limit.

We had nothing in common. Not a single thing. Admittedly, three minutes is not long to decide such a thing – I had, after all, spent longer than that waiting for a tube train, but in this particular case, it was long enough. The gong came as a relief.

Number 27 was Erin. The view, at least, had improved. Short, red hair, small ear-rings, one of those sort of triangular faces that just kind of work. I decided to make question three question one. If they couldn't cope with an upfront approach, well, it wouldn't work, right?

"Hi."

"Hi Stephen."

"I am reliably informed that about two-thirds of the women here are ringers, dragged in to lend moral support to their friends. How do you plead?"

"You don't waste any of the three minutes, do you?"

I grinned. "I don't know whether that means I'm getting the hang of this speed-dating lark or not."

"It makes a change from the answering the same questions over and over, anyway."

"Oh, I'm not promising you'll escape those – but you haven't answered the first one yet."

"I was considering my options. But yes, I'll confess – I am a ringer, as you put it."

"So a husband and fifteen kids just around the corner somewhere."

"Actually, not. An ex a few weeks around the corner. All ended a bit messily, and I'm absolutely not interested in another relationship for a while."

"You must be a very good friend to come to a speed-dating event in those circumstances, then."

Erin smiled appreciatively. "Yes, I guess I am, at that."

"So who are you here to support?"

"I think that's classified information."

"So I can't get the low-down on her from you, then. The things that make her go weak at the knees, that sort of thing."

"Ah, no."

"Fair enough. So have you confessed to any of the others yet?"

"None of them have asked."

"Serious question: what do you do in these three minute sessions? How do you play-act an interested single woman, tell them they're not your type, or what?"

"Most of them talk about themselves non-stop so I barely have to say anything at all. Mostly they brag about the careers and cars."

"That must make it easier."

"Yes. So how did you find out about the whole ringer thing anyway?"

I explained.

"Ah, inside information."

"Something like that."

"So have you met anyone interesting?"

Gong! Saved by the bell, almost literally.

"Enjoy your subterfuging."

"Enjoy your hunting."

Number 28 was Rita. Not physically my taste, which simplified matters. I was beginning to feel that three-minute dates were even less use for deciding whether or not you were interested in becoming friends with someone than they were for deciding whether or not you want to date them, so I concluded that it didn't matter what the hell we talked about. Which was just as well, as I didn't get any say in the topic of conversation: it was immediately defined as 'the life and works of Rita'.

Rita was a small-scale property developer. Her current project was an old house she'd bought in Brixton and was converting to six studio flats. The secret, apparently, was all in making them look as stylish as possible for the lowest possible expenditure. Fake wood laminate flooring, fridges with stainless-steel-look finishes made of plastic, rugs that looked expensive but were bought from Ikea for seven pounds fifty each, saving money on things people wouldn't notice on viewing but would only curse later, like only three power sockets ...

I couldn't help feeling that property developers finding themselves in a dating situation would be well advised to invent some more appealing career for themselves, like street robbery or drug-dealing, with perhaps a spot of child pornography thrown in at the weekend.

I tried to glance surreptitiously at my watch, then realised that as I didn't know what time this ordeal had begun, it wasn't going to help. Surely the three minutes must have been up by now? Was the gong broken? Had Miss Non-Smiling-Eyes fallen asleep, a state I expected to enter at any moment?

'The life & works of Rita, Chapter two' concerned her mother. Long-running discussions she was having with her mother, things her mother didn't appreciate about Rita's life, why despite the aforementioned issues she still went on holiday with her mother every year ...

I used the time to mentally plot a route to the fire-exit.

Gong!

My entire contribution to the conversation had been, in sequence: 'Hi Rita', 'Oh yes?', 'Right' and 'Bye, then'. I now understood how the ringers were able to pull it off, and was beginning to get a handle on the origins of theism and prayer. Speed-dating, it appeared, could be surprisingly educational.

On the plus side, I thought, if Rita was typical of the behaviour of most of the men in the room, it was a buyer's market ...

Number twenty-nine. Elana. Mid-20s, slim, blonde, and quite exquisitely beautiful. This woman had to be a ringer: even allowing for the intimidation factor, she must get asked out about fifty times a day.

"Hi Elana."

"Hello."

An East European accent. Polish? Czech? I'd often wondered what the secret was to Eastern Europe that it produced such a high proportion of incredibly beautiful women.

This woman could have gotten away with being a property developer and being obsessed with her mother. She could have talked for three minutes solid and I'd simply have enjoyed looking at her. Hell, she could have just counted down from 180 to zero and I'd have been entertained.

Elana was looking at me with a slightly amused expression, and I realised that perhaps I ought to say something, rather than just drinking in her beauty.

"Hello."

Er, you did that bit, Adams: try something else.

Yes, but what?

Anything. Well, ok, anything except a third greeting. Just open your mouth and say something.

Elana saved me.

"You don't make a habit of these events, I think?"

Russian? No. Latvian? Lithuanian?

Um, Adams ... Oh yes: speak.

"How can you tell?" I managed.

"You haven't prepared a speech, and you look uncomfortable."

"Er, thanks. I think."

Beautiful and direct.

I explained how I'd ended up there, a story that was rapidly turning into a prepared speech. I included the bit about the moral supporters to see whether she'd confess.

"Ah, then I should perhaps tell you that I am one of those supporters. I have a husband and a child."

"I didn't doubt it."

"You men are funny. You meet a beautiful woman and you make all these assumptions. We are married. We are stupid. Every married woman has been single, you know."

I laughed: "Am I to defend the entire male species?"

She laughed too. A beautiful laugh, naturally. "I would like to watch you try."

"Perhaps another time. So, who is your single friend?"

I did, to my surprise, resist adding '... and is she as beautiful as you?'. Perhaps all men are equally clueless in the presence of a stunning woman, just that some of us manage, on occasion, to refrain from actually broadcasting the fact. Are women as hopeless when faced with a muscular guy with Clooneyesque looks and Patrick Stewart's voice, I wondered?

Elana laughed again. Actually, I thought, it would be worth saying clueless things just to hear that laugh.

"No, I think you will have to work that out for yourself. So are there any ticks on your sheet yet?"

Oh yes, the sheet. "Um, any plans for divorce?"

"Sorry, no."

"Well, then, one."

I didn't feel I'd spoken with Michelle long enough to gain much of an impression of her, and Eva was too painful a memory to be ready to date again, but Michelle was single, cute and had an IQ above room temperature, which seemed to be pretty much the jackpot in such an environment, and Helen was right that I had to move on at some point; maybe Michelle would understand a deferred date. I ticked both 'Date' and 'Friend' boxes.

I will skip the rest of the evening; suffice it to say that I had no further use for the cheap biro.

"Please assure me you didn't ask any of them about their child-bearing plans?"

"No, I was good."

"Glad to hear it. So ... any candidates?"

"One. Maybe. Which is to say, one who didn't manage to eliminate herself from the running within the first 180 seconds. You may be picking up on the fact that I don't necessarily consider this the most ringing of endorsements."

"It's pretty good going, actually."

"Oh?"

"Yeah, Jo was a zero this time."

"How many the first time?"

"Two."

"Neither of which turned into the love of her life, one presumes."

"No, but she's still fucking one of them."

"There are less painful ways of finding FWPs, believe me." (Perhaps I have genteel tastes, but I prefer the term Friends With Privileges to 'fuck-buddies'. An even more genteel FWP of mine uses the phrase 'affectionate friends'.)

"I think Jo may be coming round to your point of view on that. Still, it got you out of the apartment and back into civilised society."

"There was nothing civilised about it."

"So what's her name?"

"Michelle."

"And what did you learn in your three-minute interview?"

"90-second interview – it's three minutes between the pair of us."

Helen waited silently. She does a pretty loud silence at times.

"She's a barrister."

"Good start: you need someone capable of matching your capacity for argument."

I reviewed what else I knew about her.

"Um, that's kind of it, really."

"I know three minutes isn't long, but you must have learnt something else about her!"

I double-checked.

"Oh, and she's cute."

"That's it. That's three minutes' worth."

"Apparently, yes. We talked a bit about speed-dating."

"Only you could spend an entire speed-date talking about speed-dating."

"Well, in fairness, Michelle can too, it seems."

"You must be made for each other. So have you called her yet?"

"I only got the email with her phone number half an hour ago, as I presume she did mine. Anyway, like I said, she only survived the three-minute elimination test; I don't want to see her yet. I don't want to see anyone yet."

"You know the rules: no moping around."

"I think I missed the bit where I promoted you from confidant to manager of my love-life."

"It's a seniority thing: I've been confidant long enough to have been promoted to at least supervisor."

"I'll consider it."

"What's to lose?"

"The will to live?"

"You have neither the temperament, wardrobe nor hairstyle to make a drama queen."

"I think the 'neither/nor' thing limits you to two objects, actually."

"Pairing you off may take some time."

Tom asked only how many of the women I'd fancied. I explained the supporter thing.

"Do those count?" I asked.

"Only if they're open to a fling," he said. "Did you ask?"

I reckoned speed-dating was better suited to him than me.

Chapter 10

Helen might have been right that moping around wasn't going to do me any good moping around, but it was about all I could manage just at that moment. Meeting thirty women in an evening had only served to underline the fact that none of them were Eva.

I'd received an annoyingly enthusiastic email from the speed-dating company congratulating me on 'finding a match'. I resisted the temptation to reply telling them I'd done no such thing, I'd merely met one woman out of thirty who hadn't managed to deter me (or reveal herself to be a fraud) within the first three minutes of our acquaintanceship.

But I at least owed Michelle an explanation of why I'd ticked her when I wasn't ready to meet anyone. I opted for discretion in my initial approach: I sent Michelle a text. 'Hi Michelle, Stephen here, from That Ordeal, as it shall henceforth be known. Free for a chat?'.

'Hi. Need to explain. Can I call you this evening?'.

That sounded intriguing. Had there been two Stephens and she'd mixed us up, I wondered? Well, I guessed I'd find out later.

'Sure, talk to you then.'

"Hi Michelle."

"Oh. You programmed me into your phone already."

"Yeah, but don't worry, it doesn't mean I'm planning our wedding, I'm just efficient like that." My natural tidiness extends into the virtual world: why have a phone number stored in an email when it logically belongs in a phone?

"Ok."

"So were there two Stephens?"

"Sorry?"

"Your need to explain, and your less than lively conversational manner suggests that we are not about to embark upon the path of romantic adventure."

"Oh. Yes. Sorry. Er, I mean, no, there weren't two Stephens, and I did purposefully tick you, but you're right about the second bit."

"Well, not a problem, but indulge my curiosity anyway."

"Um .. it's a bit embarrassing, actually."

"Which naturally increases my curiosity."

"Well, I don't know why I'm sharing this with a complete stranger. Oh dear, that sounds rude."

"No, I know what you mean. Ninety seconds each doesn't exactly qualify us for bosom buddy status."

"It's just that, after you, I met this other guy. At the end of the evening, after we'd handed in our sheets, he suggested heading off for a drink, and-"

"Enough said."

"We just got on so well. I mean, I don't usually do .. that .. but I did, and .. well .. I think this could be it, actually. Oh god, this is too cringeworthy! Sorry. It's just that I liked you and felt you deserved an explanation. Can I stop talking now?"

I laughed. "Probably best. And thank you: I appreciate it. Hope it works out for you."

"You too. Sorry. Nice to meet you, anyway."

Speed-dating indeed.

"Soulmates?" I asked Helen. "I'm not convinced I'm trying online dating at all, but if I do it most definitely isn't going to be on a site called Soulmates!"

"Guardian Soulmates," replied Helen, calmly. "Guaranteed intelligence, liberal, interesting."

"Guaranteed the sort of person who signs up to a site called Soulmates," I countered.

"Am I your relationship consultant or not?"

"Not."

"I've been sacked? I'm sure you have to give me a month's notice."

"Suggesting that I join a site called 'Soulmates' is grounds for instant dismissal. Any employment tribunal in the land would accept that as Gross Professional Misconduct."

I couldn't believe Helen was seriously suggesting it. It was bad enough that she was suggesting dating at all, when I'd made it clear I needed time to lick my wounds. It was worse that she was suggesting Internet dating. Worst still that the reason she was suggesting it was because Joanne had moved on from speed-dating to a personals site. And utterly beyond the pale that the site in question, apparently owned by the Guardian, who one might reasonably expect to be above such things, was called 'Soulmates'.

"I'll forward you the link from Jo."

"What part of 'Under no circumstances' was unclear?"

"You know you won't be able to resist the experiment."

"I won't?"

"No. It's your natural curiosity. Now it's been mentioned, you'll want to take a peek, then you'll have a look around the site, then you'll wonder what you'd say about yourself, and finally what sort of women would respond, and there you are."

Ok, so she was right about the first bit: I couldn't resist clicking on the link, just out of idle curiosity.

Helen had reminded me about her own little dabble in the world of personal ads. It hadn't lasted long. She'd placed a one-line ad in Private Eye: 'Nymphomaniac, own brewery, seeks compatible partner.' She'd had one reply: 'Please send photo of brewery.' Unfortunately, his sense of humour was the only thing he'd had going for him. Much as we'd enjoyed the moment, it didn't strike me as a ringing endorsement of personals as a means of meeting someone.

I enjoy taking photos a lot more than I enjoy processing them. Admittedly Photoshop in a nice bright home-office beats the smell of chemicals in the darkroom, but there's still only so much I can do at a time before seeking distraction.

The net is, of course, a convenient form of distraction, and after visiting the BBC news site and reading enough stories to enable me to sidle over to the Soulmates site in a suitably casual fashion, I clicked on the link in Helen's mail.

Ok, the homepage at least didn't look tacky. Quite professional, in fact – one might almost have mistaken it for a site that normal people visit.

My first thought was to check Joanne's ad to see what she'd written about herself, but I didn't know her surname and it wouldn't have helped if I had: all the names were exceedingly silly ones like BlondeinBalham4U. Ok, I was right, this was completely beyond the pale.

Unfortunately, Helen was right too: my curiosity about anything and everything has been responsible for many a misadventure. Solemnly summoning my most bored expression, I clicked on Search. Habitually, actually, I clicked on Advanced Search (blame my geekish tendencies for that). So, what was I searching for?

[X] Woman

Well, that narrowed it down to 50% of the population. A good start, I felt.

Age range? Hmmm. I had to say one thing for this Internet dating lark: it's an interesting exercise. It makes conscious what is usually instinctive. I mean, clearly we all do have an age-range we look for, but the filtering process is normally unconscious. We don't meet someone, learn they are single, consider them as a possible date and then suddenly realise they are ten years too young or too old: if they are outside our instinctive age-range, we don't notice them as a potential date in the first place.

For the first time, I was being forced to examine my own criteria for a potential partner. Well, I don't mean I've never done that at all, of course. We all give the matter some degree of thought, but not like this. Not as .. baldly as this.

It helped that this was an entirely academic exercise. Helen might be right about having to move on at some point, but I missed Eva too much for that point to be now.

Ok. Focus, Adams, focus. Age. Much as I might enjoy the classic 30-something male fantasy of an 18-year-old, at some point you do actually have to talk to her, and however bright and mature she might be, we're not exactly going to have much life-experience in common. So, we need a lower limit.

But how low? I'm 36. Sexist or not, you often get older men and younger women as couples, but how much younger? I vaguely recalled Tom quoting some rule about it. Half your age plus something, I think – but I couldn't remember what the something was, nor did I have any idea whose rule it was.

Ten years was silly, so had to be over 26. In fact, twenties seems wrong. Let's say 30.

Christ, I thought, if typing one number into a search-box is going to take me this long, it'll be next week by the time I've even hit the Search button.

Ok, upper limit? Interesting the way this brings one face-to-face with one's own sexism. I was ok with someone six years younger than me, but six years older – 42 – felt too old. Well, I could challenge my outmoded assumptions about the nature of the mating process in a modern society some other time, I decided. Let's just take the simple approach and say 30s. I typed 39.

Ok, what's next?

Did I want to see only those profiles with photos? An examination of the roots of the obsession with superficial appearance over deeper qualities was another issue that could wait for another day, I felt; yes.

Height. Another one of those unconscious filtering things we do. And more sexism, I realised – although my wife had actually been an inch taller than me. Which was, I thought, the fatal flaw in this process: we enter all our believed requirements and thus filter out all the thousands of women who would have been so deliciously enchanting we wouldn't give a flying fig that she was an inch too tall, or two years too old, or had a strange fascination with cross-stitch.

I was, I decided, taking this far too seriously. It was, after all, just an exercise in idle curiosity and an excuse to delay colour-correcting 140 frames of interiors shot under an ungodly mix of daylight, tungsten lighting and strobes.

Ok. So let's say 5'2" to 5'9". The Guardian did at least speak Imperial.

Body type. Well, while body-shape might be an odd basis to choose a friend or an employee, one could hardly be considered politically-incorrect for having physical preferences in a sexual partner. Slim to average.

Appearance. This was a series of tick-boxes ranging from Very attractive to Below average. Since everyone thinks they are at least one notch up, and people with self-esteem issues struck me as too much like hard work, I ticked those from Above average up.

Hair colour. Do people really select on that? I mean, anyone can have a preference, but specifying hair colour as a requirement? I ticked Any.

Eye colour. Ok, this was getting silly now! Any.

Star sign. Oh, FFS! This is the Guardian not the Sun! That one didn't require an Any box, it needed a Can we please get on with it? box. Could I exclude anyone who ticked anything other than Any, I wondered?

Ethnicity. This was growing more surreal by the minute. 'I'll have a very attractive East Timorean 31-year-old 5'8" size 12 brunette with grey eyes born in March, please.' The Any boxes were getting a lot of use.

Religion. That, I supposed, was a reasonable one. But on the other hand, how many people carelessly tick the religion of their upbringing when filling in forms, however token a nod their parents may have made towards it and regardless of the fact that they themselves had never engaged in a single religious ritual in their entire adult lives? On the other other hand (you may have noticed that I frequently find myself running out of hands when having these little debates with myself), did I want to select someone who ticked a religion box thoughtlessly? I was over-thinking this again. Agnostic. Atheist. Spiritual but not religious.

Education. Regardless of actual educational attainment, anyone with any nous is going to tick the box that reflects their intelligence, so I could safely tick everything from Graduate upwards.

Occupation. We were through the looking-glass again. Ok, I could understand a preference for someone in a creative profession, but did people really specify that they wanted to date someone working in the food industry? Seriously, that was one of the tick-boxes. I did a quick scan to see if there were any occupations I wanted to exclude, but neither Drug dealer nor Property developer were in the list. Any.

Income. Hmmm. Another surprisingly thought-provoking one. In turning this into a dinner party story later, should I ever admit to this little foray, I'd claim to have searched in vain for a Billionairess box. In fact, I had to confront my sexism again: how would I feel dating a woman who earned substantially more than me? Perhaps, I thought, the entire website is a clever ruse on the part of the Guardian to raise the sexual-political consciousness of its readership.

I again decided to defer navel-gazing and be pragmatic. Earning more than me might be ok, but 'Wealthy', assuming it meant no need to work, could be tricky, with potentially an entirely different perspective on life. At the other end of the scale, 'Struggling' might be the stuff of romantic novels but in practice was either likely to limit the things we could enjoy together or lead to guilt issues about me paying for everything. I excluded those two and ticked the rest.

Smoking habits. Now there, I thought, is another tricky one. I hate cigarette smoke. Can't stand it. Nobody was happier than me when smoking was banned in pubs because it meant I could happily visit them again, safe in the knowledge that I wouldn't end up with clothes stinking of tobacco smoke. And as for kissing a smoker ...

But, when I was younger, I dated a smoker for a year, and we had a great time. I didn't like the smoking even then, but she was considerate about where & when she smoked, and mints were a reasonable solution to the kissing issue. What if I was excluding the perfect partner who was in any case considering quitting and her undying love for me would be the final push to do it?

I looked at the clock in the taskbar of my screen. So far, I'd spent five minutes filling in two numbers and ticking & unticking a handful of checkboxes. This was absurd! Never.

Right, what else was left, I asked myself, apart from shoe-size and mother's maiden name?

Relationship status. The Guardian being a respectable paper, there wasn't any 'Married but looking for no-strings sex because my spouse doesn't understand me' option, so that one was easy. Single. Divorced. My finger hovered over the Separated box for a moment, but then moved on: separated was too recent and/or too ambiguous.

Have children. Hurrah! Another simple one. No.

Want children. And again! No.

And that, finally, was that. Now all I had to do was click the Search now button.

105 matches. Blimey. That was a bit worrying. How many thousands of women are there on this site? And only 105 of them match my requirements. Were my criteria that unreasonable? Were compatible women really that rare? Surely I wasn't asking for anything too outrageous?

Oh well, I thought, I'd better check out these rare creatures.

Each match had a thumbnail and a few details. Scanning the matches, I realised I needn't have worried so much about the age-range selection, since it appeared to operate on much the same basis as a price-range given to an estate-agent. Actually, that wasn't quite fair: an estate-agent starts at your price-ceiling and works upwards; the Soulmates site apparently started at your age-ceiling and called it good. Or perhaps there was no-one under 40 on the site.

I looked at the first thumbnail. It may be harsh to reject someone on the basis of a postage-stamp-sized photograph, but the first one was, ah, not my type. The perils of modern dating: one now not only has to look good in a dimly-lit bar, but also in the cold light of a colour-calibrated computer monitor.

The second one had an okay-looking thumbnail and wasn't called BlondeinBalham4U, so I clicked on her. In an idle, just-out-of-academic-interest fashion, you understand.

I scanned quickly through. I clicked on another. Then another. Then two more.

The ads were surprisingly witty. Clearly the site was not entirely the preserve of the socially inept and the desperate. In fact, the more I clicked, the more the women here looked like a reasonably broad cross-section of- I was about to say 'population' then realised I actually meant 'Guardian-reading population': there was an unsurprising but nonetheless slightly disturbing tendency towards worthy occupations. The average woman here was, from the evidence so far presented, a social worker who spent her spare time recycling carrier-bags to raise money for a disabled rights organisation.

But, worthiness aside, and the fact that the dating-pool comprised 105 women, I had to admit to being pleasantly surprised.

Describing oneself in a few words struck me as an interesting exercise. Damn! Helen would be so smug when she discovered this. But there was worse news to come: reviewing further profiles, I realised that a good third of them began with some variation on the same words: 'I wasn't sure how to describe myself so I asked my best friend, and she said ...'. It struck me as a good cop-out, but then I'd be forced to 'fess-up to Helen before I could go any further. Double-damn!

"I want it clearly understood that this is purely an intellectual exercise."

"Of course." She was attempting to disguise her smugness with a studiedly neutral tone, with, it must be said, a notable lack of success.

I told her about the cop-out tactic and asked her how she would describe me.

"Hmmm ... let me think." She paused for a few seconds. "Arrogant, eccentric, mathematical, dubious dating skills, grammatically pedantic and prone to over-analysis."

"How come everyone else on there gets glowing reviews from their best mate and I get this?"

"Ok: Arrogant, eccentric, mathematical, dubious dating skills, grammatically pedantic, prone to over-analysis and yet inexplicably loveable anyway."

"That's it? That's my glowing review?"

"Oh, and demanding. We should add 'demanding'."

"Thanks."

"My pleasure. Am I reinstated as your relationship consultant now?"

"That depends."

"On?"

"Whether I am inundated with emails from adorable (and adoring) women."

"So, seriously: tell me your impressions. Feed my vicarious need for new experiences."

"It was unexpectedly thought-provoking," I admitted, explaining all the things you have to think about just to do a search. "And that's before I've written a single word about me and what I'm looking for. Perhaps attempting to write the latter bit will help me figure out the answer."

"Tell me the stuff you know, the stuff you don't even have to think about because it's obvious."

"You know all that stuff. In fact, you tell me, I'll take notes and make any corrections and additions as required."

"I think we need to add 'terminally lazy' to your description."

"I prefer to think of it as having good delegation skills."

"Ok. You're shallow, so you want cute."

"That's not shallow, that's being an aesthete. But you talk and I'll translate."

"Hmph. You're an impatient sod with a short attention-span, so need someone bright, articulate, interested in anything & everything."

"I don't think we need bother people with the preamble there."

"You need a chameleon – a woman who can fit in anywhere, be equally happy in a cocktail dress or jeans and walking boots."

"Good phrase – consider it stolen."

"We'll discuss the licensing terms later. Oh: definitely not the jealous type. Having close female friends, and spending half your working life travelling abroad with 19-year-old size 8 models for

111

company, is not a good recipe for a relationship with a jealous woman."

"This is true. Insecurity isn't an attractive trait anyway."

"You should probably mention the business travel too – not everyone is going to want a partner who's away a lot."

"Hey, this is supposed to be an ad, not a warning notice! The dating pool is already down to 105; by the time you're done listing my drawbacks, they'll be nobody left."

"Well, ok, perhaps you don't need to mention all this stuff in the ad, but you should probably slip it in at an early stage in the dating process."

"More good points, please."

"Well, this is the Guardian, so you should probably mention your charity stuff."

I did fairly regular pro-bono work for a couple of charities, partly because I wanted to support their work, partly because it refreshes me when I'm feeling a bit stale in my work and partly because it provided the opportunity for some creative work that made good portfolio fodder. Perhaps I wouldn't mention that latter bit.

"Ok."

"I think you can get away with mentioning your eccentric political perspective: eccentricity will probably go down well in the Graun."

Helen was referring to my complete refusal to recognise the concept of party politics. The original concept of representational democracy was exactly that: we voted for the individual person we felt best able to represent our views. We voted not for parties, but for people. The low quality of today's politicians was, I felt, almost entirely due to the fact that too many people would elect a donkey provided it was wearing the correct-coloured rosette. I did my best to maintain the original concept by meeting each of the candidates, quizzing them on the issues that mattered most to me and then voting for the candidate in whom I had most confidence. Accordingly, I had variously voted for Labour, LibDem and Tory candidates in different elections. This did, at least, make for interesting conversations, especially with those who had strong party affinities.

Ten minutes later, we had the first draft of an ad.

"Joanne did let me know about one little quirk of the site."

"Oh?"

"When you tick the things you are seeking in a partner, those things are visible to people reading your profile."

"Why is that a quirk? Sounds perfectly sensible to me. Well, in so far as any of this is sensible, anyway."

"You'll see."

I did see.

When you create your profile, you tick the same boxes as in the advanced search. These preferences are then stored as part of your profile, and the system uses them to direct you to profiles it considers good matches.

There is, however, one additional layer: for each category, you not only tick the boxes you are after, but also state the relative importance of that category. So, for example, if you've stated that you want a woman who is 5'3" to 5'9" tall, you can say that is slightly important, decidedly important or crucial. The importance you assign to it, as well as the tickboxes you have selected, will be visible to everyone reading your profile.

This creates a small dilemma. If I am honest, things like body type and age are, once you have figured out your acceptable ranges, crucial. No matter how great someone may be as a person, and however much I might be attracted to them as a friend, a 50-year-old woman who is 4'7" and 20-stone is not going to be potential partner material.

But if you select 'Crucial' for physical attributes you can't help but appear shallow. I thus compromised on 'Moderately important' for each.

The system duly informed me that I had over 1000 matches. Well that, I thought, was a considerable improvement on 105. I started browsing them. And saw the flaw in my plan. The first match was 48. The second was rather rotund. The third was-

Well, let's say that being politically correct with my physical criteria did not appear to be a viable approach.

I modified my profile, changing each of my physical criteria from 'Moderately important' to 'Decidedly important'. Ok, it would make me appear a little more shallow than I felt was ideal in a Guardian-reading populace, but at least it should make my matches a little more realistic.

No.

Whatever algorithm the site employed for calculating its matches, the difference between 'Moderately important' and 'Decidedly important' was, it seemed, a subtle one. The matches were not noticeably improved.

I was forced to go back and change both age ranges and body type to 'Crucial'. There went my image as a caring, sharing, open-minded, Guardian-approved kind of a guy. It was just as well I wasn't ready to date.

Since I'd already revealed myself to be a shallow character, I figured I might as well complete the offence by ticking 'Crucial' to 'Has photo'; I didn't want another Alli experience ...

Ah well. It was time to tackle the 'About me' section ...

Noting that most of you adopted the approach of asking your best friend to describe you, I thought I'd be equally lazy and do the same. She said I was: arrogant, eccentric, mathematical, grammatically pedantic, had dubious dating skills, and was prone to over-analysis. Anyone interested in trading best friends? She did, on prompting, add that I was inexplicably loveable.

I should probably be advertising with the Independent rather than the Guardian as I don't have any party politics. I'm firmly convinced that we get the politicians we deserve precisely because we've effectively abandoned the original concept of representational democracy in favour of party machinery. But perhaps that's a conversation best had over dinner.

I'm a photographer, working mostly in the commercial field. I also do a little pro-bono work for a couple of charities I support.

My interests sound rather worryingly generic when I list them out: books (usually a non-fiction one for daytime reading and light fiction to fall asleep to), theatre (more Noel Coward than Pinter), music (tastes best described as eclectic), cycling (40-mile rides liberally sprinkled with pub and tea-shop stops), tea, red wine, good conversation, quiet companionship, Radio 4, occasional bouts of playing dodgy music far too loudly.

You are intelligent, curious about anything & everything, good at what you do, irreverent and are equally at ease in jeans & t-shirt and heels & cocktail dress. You probably love your work but recognise that life is to be enjoyed. You enjoy the simple things – windswept beaches, kite-flying, sitting in a pavement cafe chatting & watching the world go by – but are also able to indulge in guilt-free enjoyment of some of life's material pleasures. You love conversation. You love ideas, opinions, discussion, debate, exploration.

If this sounds like you, perhaps we should talk?

I refrained from adding And, truthfully, still besotted with another woman, so merely doing this as a distraction.

It wasn't perfect, but it gave a flavour at least, and I wasn't going to spend any longer on it. I wasn't optimistic. But that was ok: I wasn't looking.

Chapter 11

Having planted my online seed, so to speak, I headed back to the real world with some sense of relief.

Cycling was my rather token nod towards exercise. I have too low a boredom threshold to contemplate gyms, or indeed anything else comprising exercise for exercise's sake, and my unpredictable travel schedules make group sports difficult. I used my bike as a convenient way to get around London when I didn't have gear to carry, and belonged to a cycle club that held regular weekend runs. The latter were also useful when I felt the need to clear my head and think things through. The truth, which revealed itself in those quiet times when there were no distractions, was that no matter how much I tried to follow Helen's advice to throw myself back in the dating foray, I still missed Eva dreadfully. Maybe a ride out in the country would help me regain some space.

It always amazes me the way human beings manage to divide themselves into factions, even when ostensibly brought together by a common interest. Cycle clubs were a good example.

First there were the 'roadies' versus the tourers. The roadies did 80-100 mile days at an unstinting pace; I did precisely one of those. It seemed to me to be the outdoor equivalent of the exercise bike: head-down, fixed speed, and the only bit of the scenery you got to see was your own front wheel and the posterior of the rider ahead of you (possibly worthwhile if the backside in question belongs to a cute female, rather less interesting if it's the property of a testosterone-fuelled bloke).

The tourers did civilised days out where we hopped on a train or took a short drive to get out of London, then meandered along enjoying the views, stopping for mid-morning tea, a leisurely pub lunch and an afternoon tea. About 30 or 40 miles in total at an average speed that would doubtless have led the roadies to sniff in a disdainful fashion

The tourers had then effectively further divided themselves into what I'd come to label the leisure cyclists and the lifestyle cyclists.

I was a leisure cyclist. I cycled because it was enjoyable, and by happy coincidence also enabled me to burn off some of the calories I'd indulged in during the week. We were there to have a relaxing day out in the country (well, the Home Counties, which was as close as most of us got to rural England). We arrived by train or by car, whichever was more convenient. We might use our bikes for some utility journeys also, but doing so was a pragmatic rather than political decision.

The lifestyle cyclists appeared to cycle because it was good for the planet, and, if anything, appeared slightly embarrassed by the fact that they also enjoyed it. They tended to be vegetarian, take pride in living just above the poverty-line and consider it a moral imperative to ride a bicycle rescued from a skip – even if they'd spent more on adding exotic components to it than most of us had buying a brand-new bike. If they owned a car at all, it had to be a beat-up wreck that put out ten times as much pollution as a modern one, and they would never dream of turning up to a bike club meet in it.

The lifestyle cyclists appeared to view the leisure cyclists with mild but consistent condescension; the leisure cyclists viewed the lifestyle cyclists with varying degrees of bemusement.

While mostly a pragmatist, I do have idealist tinges. One of these tinges is an innate feeling that most human beings have more things that unite us than divide us if we'd only take the trouble to get to know each other a little. So I viewed it as, well, if not a personal mission, then at least a little hobby, to try to get the leisure and lifestyle cyclists to mix. On this particular occasion, I had an additional incentive ...

It's not that we men don't have emotions; we do – much as I wished otherwise at the time. It's simply that sexual attraction can be independent of them. No matter how much my heart might be missing Eva, other parts of my anatomy were more easily distracted.

Her name was Jane, a new member whose colourful clothing and dilapidated-looking bike appeared to put her in the lifestyle category. Early 30s, 5'6"-ish, redhead, no make-up or jewellery, pixie-like features.

"Hi, you're new to the group, I think?" (Look, you know I'm crap at pickup lines, so let's just accept that and move on, ok?)

"Yes, I asked the guys in my bike shop about group rides, and they told me about it."

"I'm Stephen."

"Jane. Do you organise the rides?"

"No, I just come along to them."

"So, do you greet all newcomers, or just the female ones?"

Ouch. Perhaps I needed to rethink my preference for feisty women. I explained my little mission to blend the cyclist factions.

"So before you even knew my name, you could classify me?"

This wasn't going terribly well.

"Hello, I'm Stephen."

She had the grace to smile, but wasn't being deflected: "So which category do I belong to, and on what do you base that assessment?"

"Is it too late to claim that I have absolutely no idea?"

"About two minutes too late, yes."

I felt a slight pang. Her directness and humour reminded me of Eva.

"And which do you belong to, anyway?" she continued.

Hmm. Perhaps I wasn't so obvious, now that she mentioned it. My bike was about ten years old, and while it wasn't a rat-bike and hadn't come from a skip, neither was it still gleaming from the show-room. My fashion sense, in so much as the concept has any meaning while wearing cycling gear, was best described as 'relaxed'. Perhaps I wanted to bring the two factions together because I didn't quite feel that I belonged to either? That did, however, feel like it would make rather a long-winded answer.

"I view cycling as an enjoyable way to meander around, and a pretty practical form of transport in London when I don't have much to carry."

"You could always get a trailer – some of them have about as much luggage capacity as a Smart."

I resisted the temptation to suggest that the comparison would make more sense in reverse.

"Do you have one?"

"Two. A small one for little shopping trips, a larger one for heavy stuff."

A vision of sacks of lentils came unbidden to mind. I kept that to myself, too.

"Well, fortunately nothing more than a waterproof to carry today, eh?"

We chatted for a few minutes more before a few of the regulars I cycled with arrived, and I made the introductions.

I'd become quite good friends with Rachel, a very attractive fellow singleton who was unfortunately a little young for me (that sounds so much better than saying I was too old for her), and we were taking a casual interest in each other's dating exploits. While Jane was busy chatting to one of the other women, Rachel grinned at me: "Hunting?"

She didn't miss much.

I did my best to sound innocent: "I don't even know if she's single."

Another grin: "I'll find out for you."

Large groups can make it difficult to casually end up sitting next to someone during a refreshment stop, but we'd got into the habit of circulating while cycling along so that we all got the chance to chat with a number of different people. Unfortunately, I'd managed to time cycling alongside Jane with the start of a bastard hill, so the first five minutes of the conversation consisted of about 10% chat and 90% heavy breathing. Under other circumstances, that might have been considered encouraging, of course.

The climb complete, I discovered freewheeling down the other side that she was a social worker, working with children with special needs. She had the courtesy to immediately warn me off the phrases "That must be very rewarding" and "You must be very patient." Not that I would have used either, of course; I racked my brains for a third response.

"What's the toughest part?" I asked. Hmmm. Not bad.

"That's not the kids, that's the systems we have to work with," she replied. "We have so many rules and regulations ostensibly designed to protect the kids and provide for their needs, when in reality they often prevent us from doing just that."

"Seems to be endemic to large organisations," I said. "I have friends who work in corporates, and some of the stories they've shared about the obstacles they have to overcome to achieve even the simplest of goals sound to me like something out of Through the Looking Glass. I guess it's even worse in the public sector."

"Why do you think it's worse? Do you believe the propaganda about the efficiency of the private sector and the waste in the public sector?"

How did a supportive comment get thrown back at me like that, I wondered? I deliberately fluffed a gear-change to give me a moment to think.

"From everything I hear, the environments are very similar bureaucracy-wise, but I guess the public sector also has to cope with tighter budget constraints."

"That's true," she said. "It's ridiculous how little money we would need to do some of it, but if nobody thought of that when the budgets were drawn up at the beginning of the year ..."

I decided to quit the work topic while I was ahead, and move onto safe ground.

"What do you enjoy outside of work, besides cycling?"

"I guess you mean apart from the usual books, music and films."

"I guess I do."

"I like photography," she said.

I grinned.

"What's funny?"

"Now it's my turn to warn you off the classic replies," I explained. "I'm a photographer. The phrases to avoid are: 'It must be great, getting paid for something most people do as a hobby' and 'Pressing a button – now there's an easy way to earn a living'."

She grinned back: "What about the naked women?"

"I would have mentioned that one too if you'd been a bloke."

"So do you?"

"Photograph naked women?"

I sensed a trap.

"Not often."

"So sometimes?"

It was definitely a trap, but demurring could only make it worse; I decided to take the rap.

"Sometimes, yes. I had an exhibition of figure work last year."

"Don't you think that objectifies women? Even the term 'figure work' – isn't that a euphemism to lend validity to an activity which is fundamentally exploitative of women?"

It isn't often that a cyclist wishes another uphill stretch would appear in front of them.

It wasn't that I hadn't had the conversation before, of course. There isn't a figure photographer alive who hasn't had the same conversation multiple times. It's simply that it's a conversation far better suited to a quiet bar and a couple of glasses of wine than it is to a semi-shouted conversation between bicycles. I suggested as much.

"So you need time to rehearse your arguments?"

"Not really," I observed dryly, "it's a conversation I've had once or twice before."

"Ok, lunch, then. No later!" With that, she put on a burst of speed and her place was taken by Jason, one of the regulars whose sole topic of conversation was the life and times of Jason, a man whose life was stultifyingly dull. At that moment, his company was almost welcome.

Tuning Jason out (it was ok; he was so self-obsessed he wouldn't notice), I was beginning to reach the conclusion that I couldn't reliably tell when I was being flirted with and when I wasn't. The conversation with Jane had been varyingly pleasant and aggressive, but I did, it appear, have a lunch-date of sorts.

An inability to determine what was and wasn't flirting struck me as a bit of a handicap in the dating stakes. Women should know by now that blokes are spectacularly incompetent at picking up on subtle signals & signs (ok, pretty unsubtle ones too, sometimes) and fit themselves with LED indicators or something.

Where was Rachel? Ah, directly behind me. Not, I suspected, a coincidence. I inclined my head in a 'Come talk to me' invitation. She duly obliged, leaving Jason to find some other audience to continue his tale of what he'd told some other, doubtless equally disinterested, companion the previous day.

"So?"

"It appears we're having lunch."

"Good work!"

"To defend myself against charges of exploiting women."

"Pardon?"

I explained.

"Oh."

"So, your mission, which you choose to accept, is to chat with her before then and find out what's what."

"So, uh, whether she's single, and whether she's baiting you or dating you."

"Step away from the attempted poetry and go do your duty."

"Aye-aye sir."

Lunch was straight out of some English country living magazine: a picturesque pub by a ford. Well, possibly the 25 slightly-sweating lycra-clad cyclists didn't fit the picture, but that was, I realised, one of the benefits of meeting this way: if a potential date had already seen you exerting yourself in lycra shorts and was still interested, there wasn't too much to worry about if & when you made it to the bedroom.

I looked around, aiming to get a quick briefing from Rachel before finding Jane. The good news was that she had made contact; the bad news was that said contact was still in progress, and both were walking towards me, which rather appeared to rule out any advance tip-off.

I had under-estimated Rachel's ingenuity: having delivered Jane to me, she made an excuse of having a call to make and wandered into the pub. About a minute later, I got a text from her. Single – good luck!

There was a further divide between the leisure and lifestyle groups: those of us in the leisure category bought lunch at the pub or café where we stopped; the lifestyle group tended to bring sandwiches and sit outside. Jane had brought sandwiches. I asked her what she wanted to drink, and wandered in to order food and fetch the drinks while she kept an eye on the bikes.

When I came out with the drinks, Jane had commandeered a table. Well, a tree-stump, to be precise. It was to be lunch-a-deux. Whether this was with romantic intent or merely to prevent collateral casualties from the bloodshed that was to follow, I wasn't sure.

"So," she began, "what is the difference between what you refer to as 'figure work' and what appears on Page 3 of The Sun?"

Jane wasn't wasting any time.

"Apart from the originality of the photography, you mean?"

Jane waited.

"The biggest difference is the intent. With Page 3, the aim is to titillate."

"Another word for objectify."

"If you will, yes."

"So how does calling it art change the rules?"

"The aim is different. The aim is not to sexually excite the audience, but rather to create an image whose appeal is aesthetic rather than erotic." Having had the discussion once or twice before at least helped with the phrasing.

"So you can't create an aesthetically pleasing image of a woman with her clothes on?"

"I hope I can, as that's one of the things I get paid to do. But there are different styles of photography, and figure is one with a tradition that goes back centuries."

"So is war, or slavery."

I smiled and tried another tack: "Why do we have photography?"

"I assume that's a rhetorical question and you're about to propose an answer."

This woman really didn't give any ground.

"I'd suggest there are two reasons. The first is to communicate something. To make us think about something, or to make us feel something. To pick up on your war reference, a large part of the reason why the USA had to pull out of Vietnam was the public outrage created by some of the photographs."

"Agreed – that's a worthwhile use of photography."

"The second, and I'd suggest no less worthy aim, is to create beauty. To produce images which give people pleasure."

"I'll accept that, but you still haven't explained why this has to involve women removing their clothes."

"It's a tradition rather than a requirement. Photography inherited most of its styles from painting. Painters gradually developed different categories of painting: landscape, portrait, still-life, and so on – and one of those was life or figure. That particular category involves the removal of clothes. Nobody would seriously accuse Thomas Eakins or John Trumbull of titillating the masses, and the same is true today of figure photography."

"Their work was just as exploitive of women, though, as photography is today. You are presenting women as objects to be looked at, rather than as human beings."

"There's no inherent conflict between being viewed as aesthetically pleasing and being viewed as a person. Kennedy was generally considered to be a good-looking chap, but we still admired him as a President and a person."

"It's different for women, though. Men traditionally have the power."

"Madonna, then. She in very large part created her fame by deliberately presenting herself as a sex-object, or at least playing into that role. She very cleverly took advantage of a particular stereotype to advance her own agenda. I doubt that anyone would view her as lacking in power."

"Madonna is an artist. With figure photography, the photographer is the artist and the model just the raw material – the power is all one way,"

"Actually, that's very rarely true. Most figure photography is a collaborative effort, with the photographer and model working together to create the desired end-result. With a really good model, the photographer's role is half of an idea and the lighting; the model's role is the other half of the idea and the pose. It's the combination of all three elements that creates the work."

"You're not suggesting it's coincidence, though, that it's generally women who take off their clothes and generally men who photograph them?"

"Not for a moment. As a wild generalisation, mon tend to be more visual while women are more verbal, so it's no great surprise that a lot of photographers, and customers for photography, are men – and it's not exactly headline news that men enjoy looking at images of women, whether clothed or otherwise."

"That men enjoy looking at photos of naked women doesn't make it right."

It was clear by this point that this was a debate rather than a date. I figured there was nothing to lose by a more direct approach.

"If you're looking for someone to change biological impulses, you need a genetic engineer rather than a photographer."

"That's a cop-out: the fact that a desire exists doesn't mean you have to feed it."

"True, and I wouldn't feed a desire I felt was wrong. But I find figure photography beautiful, my models find posing an enjoyable way to earn a living, and my customers find buying my photos a pleasant way to spend their money; my perspective is that it's all good. I accept that your perspective is different, of course."

The conversation appeared to me to have run its course, so I diverted my attention to my lunch – which was also lukewarm. I do have a habit of getting caught up in a debate and forgetting to eat.

Jane apparently didn't consider the conversation at an end.

"Ok, let's set aside the purely aesthetic shots. So can you put hand on your heart and say you've never taken a photo whose intent was erotic?"

I debated with myself whether I wanted to go there, but figured by this point there was nothing to lose. I did some boudoir photography. It wasn't something I'd ever marketed, but a portrait client asked me if I would do it, and word-of-mouth did the rest.

"I have taken photos whose intent was erotic, yes."

"So all this talk of art was an irrelevance – avoiding the main issue."

"Let's say it was taking things one step at a time. But, to be honest, if we disagree about figure work, there's really little point debating boudoir photography."

"I'm not saying I'm persuaded to your point of view on the former, but you make a coherent argument. I'm interested in whether you can do the same for erotic photography."

This conversation was going downhill. It had already gone from maybe-could-be date to clearly-not-romantic discussion, and now it seemed I was being tested on my debating skills. I tried to surreptitiously glance at my watch, but it was a skill I never had quite mastered; I was caught in the act.

"Hoping to be saved by the bell?" laughed Jane.

I forced a smile, and decided that I might as well be direct: "It did rather feel like you were viewing me as a performing monkey. Shall we join the others and switch to the usual discussions of hills and the need for diets?"

"Fair enough."

"Another drink?"

"No thanks."

I gave up on the remains of my now-cold meal and took the plate back inside.

The experience underlined my conclusion that I simply wasn't ready to rejoin the fray. Having showered and changed, I checked my inbox to find an email from Kathryn:

Seems you acquitted yourself well at lunch – Jane caught up with me later and asked if you were single. Did you get her phone number? I'm not doing it all for you!

So: we'd had a grilling rather than a tête-à-tête, ended up disagreeing on one subject and deciding there was no point continuing onto the next, and she was sufficiently interested to enquire about my relationship status?

I was forced to conclude that I'd never understand women.

Chapter 12

Soulmates emails you when you receive messages from members. Rather annoyingly, it doesn't email you the text of the messages, it just tells you that you have one, so you have to login to see it.

I had three messages. The first was a passing compliment from a 48-year-old woman in Halifax who said that we obviously weren't a match from an age and geographical perspective, but she really liked my profile. I dropped her a quick reply to thank her for her kind comments, and to pass on my tip about setting 'absolutely crucial' for her age-range unless she really was looking for 36 year olds – in which case, I wished her the best of British.

The second was from Amanda in Upminster and read, in its entirety: Interesting profile – tell me more. I clicked on her profile, which was brief and generic. From her photo, she was clearly quite cute, but neither profile nor approach seemed to bode well for her conversational skills. I hovered over the delete button then remembered the size of that dating pool and decided to keep her in reserve. That seemed like a rather cold concept, but then online dating was a pretty chilly phenomenon.

The third would, had I been seriously looking, have been more promising. Natasha.

My best friend was about as cruel as yours, so perhaps we should try trading to see if they are any kinder to strangers?

Do you find this as excruciating as I do? But my socialising tends to be with the same crowd, and as I run a small business I don't have the usual 'Meeting someone at work' option – at least, not without turning lesbian and risking a sexual harassment suit (my two members of staff being young and female). I can't face the Friday night bar scene, and can't bear opera, so here I am.

I'm not really an online kind of girl, so if my profile seems interesting, shall we speak on the phone and then, if neither of us have made our excuses and left, meet for a drink?

Natasha

I clicked on her profile. I admit that I clicked on her thumbnail to enlarge her photo before I read the text.

The whole thing of 'types' fascinates me. I don't have a 'type' in the sense that some men seem to – a single combination of height, weight and hair-colour that they always seek out; I can be attracted to a range of looks. But there is one particular look that I find particularly appealing, and yet hard to pin down to specifics. It's not the classic ideal of beauty, in fact it's a slightly quirky look, but some combination of face-shape, eyes and- The thought kind of fades out at that point. I really don't know how to describe it in objective terms, but Natasha had just that look.

I read her profile. It was eloquent, witty and – despite her protestations – made meeting this way seem like a perfectly ordinary thing to do. If I was going to take Helen's advice and pull myself together, this would seem a good time to do it.

I realised I didn't know the rules for such interactions. Was there a guide to online dating etiquette, I wondered? How many messages was one supposed to exchange before moving into the real world? I was glad she was suggesting a phone call: that was more familiar territory.

Soulmates may be owned by the Guardian, but it is still a determinedly commercial enterprise: as a free member, you can browse profiles, create your own and receive mail – but you can't send or reply to mail without stumping up for a paid subscription. There were one-month, three-month and six-month options. My faith in online dating was still not overwhelming; I opted for one month.

That done, the site rather condescendingly informed me that I was not allowed to give any contact details until we had each exchanged messages. I wondered whether the site had software scanning emails for text that matched the pattern of a phone number or email address, or whether they had teams of people on minimum wage eavesdropping on the romantic exchanges of electronic optimists – and, if so, what they said when people at parties asked them what they do.

I decided on a brief reply:

Hi Natasha,

Utterly excruciating, but helped enormously by the fact that you seem almost entirely unlike my stereotype of the denizens of online dating sites.

The site advises me that we are not yet deemed sufficiently responsible adults to exchange phone numbers, but I believe when you reply to this, we officially become grown-ups. Here's hoping you don't become a lesbian in the meantime.

Stephen

It seemed a painless start.

The cycling club had an email list. It was used by the organisers to tell us where & when the rides would be, and in theory any member could post any message to the rest of the group, but in practice nobody ever did.

Except this time. Jane posted a message. It was just a brief Enjoyed my first ride with the group yesterday, and look forward to the next one, but it meant that I had her email address.

Hmmm.

Well, if I was going to try to get back on the dating horse, or at least the meaningless distraction horse, a brief email couldn't do any harm. I did take care to be sure that I was sending it to her directly, rather than replying to the group email address. The importance of such checks had been brought home to me when a female friend away on business decided to send a cameraphone picture-message to her boyfriend, Danny. The idea was to give him something to look forward to when she got home, so the photo she sent was best described as not for public consumption.

When two contacts are adjacent, sending it to the contact above or below is an easy mistake to make. The contact immediately above 'Danny' was 'Dad'. She's still cringing, two years later.

My own message was rather more innocuous:

Hi Jane,

Can we chat about the weather next time?

Stephen

I then turned my attention to work. I was doing a shoot for an up-and-coming fashion designer – she didn't have much of a budget, but was very open to creative ideas. She'd emailed me sketches of the designs she was working on and I needed to give some thought to interesting ways to present them. It's the sort of challenge I really enjoy, so a few hours whizzed by as I considered, rejected and refined a succession of ideas.

By the time I felt I had a workable plan, it was nearly 7pm. I emailed my thoughts across and then scanned the incoming mails. There was a reply from Jane:

What makes you think there will be a next time?

Jane

Even I could recognise that as a flirty message. I replied:

Jane,

I think a bottle of wine is in order. Thursday eve?

Stephen

There was also an alert from Soulmates telling me I had a reply from Natasha. I logged in to get it.

Stephen,

No lesbianism as yet. Unkind best friend tells me you may be an axe-murderer and I should get your number rather than give you mine. You're not, are you? I think it's the sort of thing you should mention.

Natasha

I replied, promising her my axe-murdering days were behind me, giving her my number and suggesting she call that evening.

This was another thing I didn't know the rules about, I realised. Clearly two-timing isn't on, but one can hardly be considered to have entered the realms of exclusivity before even the first date. Especially when I'm not even really in a dating mood at all. It would, though, be as well to clarify the deal beforehand, rather than waiting until things got messy.

Tom's view was straightforward.

"That's like a thousand miles down the road if at all," he said.

"So everything's ok unless you're engaged?" I asked.

"Until they tell you they want it to be exclusive, and then you have to make a decision," he said.

"So you can date two women at once and sleep with them both?" I asked.

"Given half a chance."

I felt Helen's view might be more nuanced.

"So, let's say Natasha and I meet, and get on, and I also have dinner with Jane. What are the rules? At what point does it become illegal? I mean, even if I were ready for anything but dating

125

practice, it would take at least a few dates before I knew whether either was going anywhere, so it must be legal to date two women for a while, right?"

"You're being mathematical again."

This was not helpful. I needed answers. Ok, I needed numbers. Numbers of dates, numbers of weeks, something specific. I told Helen as much.

"Girls like to feel special. They don't want to feel like they are just one of your options. If they know you're seeing someone else, they're not going to feel good about it."

"I wasn't exactly planning to issue them with bar-codes, but on the other hand I don't want to feel like I'm deceiving anyone."

"It's not rocket science, Stephen. You know when you're developing feelings for someone, so at that point you stop seeing anyone else. Oh, and if you feel the need to purge your conscience, you can at that point tell her you've stopped seeing other people – even if she hadn't been aware that you had been, that's always a good thing to hear."

"I feel halfway guilty, anyway. I"m not over Eva."

"I know. But the only way you will be is to date other women.

"Hmm. So what do girls do about the multiple-dating issue, anyway? One at a time, even if travel and stuff means there's a few weeks between dates?"

"Usually one at a time, yes. Girls are more selective than boys."

"Hmph. I wish I were less selective: life would be much easier!"

"You're selective about your trademarked Capital R relationships, but women tend to be selective about dating too. Probably because it's usually the girls who get asked, and if you're remotely attractive and not wearing a wedding-ring, you get asked a lot. Annoyingly so."

I'd never quite thought of it in those terms. "Hmm. We tend to think women have the better deal, as you can choose to just sit back and be approached, while guys tend to have to make the running. But being hit on by a succession of people who don't interest you, and to have that continue even when you're in a relationship ..."

"Exactly. When you're the one making the approach, you choose who, how, when, where and how often. You guys don't know how lucky you are. Worse, if a woman does make the first move, many guys will be intimidated – even ones you'd think would be absolutely fine with it."

"Hey, there are no complaints here when that happens!"

"You'd be surprised how many men can't cope with it, even ones you'd think were grown-ups."

"Ok, I shall feel suitably grateful for my lot."

"Sarky bastard."

"So what news from Helensworld? Had any babies yet?"

"I did decide to share the results of the thought experiment with David."

"Oh. I assumed you'd done that at the time?"

"No. I didn't want him thinking it was going to be tomorrow. Or maybe I didn't entirely trust myself, and wanted to let the decision sit for a while in case I changed my mind."

"But you didn't."

"No, in fact, oddly, even though I'm definitely not ready for it yet, I've never been so certain about anything."

I had scarcely formed my lips into a W shape before Helen interrupted:

"Don't even think about starting on that 'wow' business again."

"The thought never crossed my mind."

"So which one of your harem are you seeing first?"

"Can you have a harem of two? Isn't there some quorum requirement or something?"

Helen said nothing.

"I don't know. I don't actually have a date with either yet."

"You don't-" She made a small exasperated sound. "So would you care to let me in on why we're having this conversation?"

"I like to be prepared."

"He likes to be prepared ..."

"You know me."

"Yes. Yes, I do."

Of the many phrases I might have used to describe Jane, 'woman of few words' wouldn't have been one of them, but her reply was best described as brief:

Ok

It seemed I had a date. So, where? I had a horrible feeling she might turn out to be a vegetarian. Not that I have anything against vegetarians, you understand. Some of my best friends, and all that. It's just that I don't personally consider something qualifies as dinner unless there's at least one dead animal involved, and I had no idea which of my haunts catered to those whose tastes ran more to lentils and aubergines.

French clearly wasn't wise. Italian? That ought to be safe. Then there was the question of which one. I suspected attempting to pick up the tab would be viewed as patriarchal oppression, and my assumption about social worker pay-scales suggested it shouldn't be anywhere too expensive. I still cringed when I saw a Bella Pasta logo, so I settled on Pizza Express.

Pizza Express, Dean Street? Oh, and let me know your mobile. I gave her mine.

I can occasionally be brief myself. Not often, but occasionally.

Natasha called at around eight. She had a lovely voice. I don't know why, but voices have always been unreasonably important to me in a partner. I'm honestly not sure whether I could imagine having a relationship with a woman with an ugly accent. It's not that I need an RP accent – some accents are delicious. There can't be a man alive who doesn't go slightly weak at the knees at an Irish accent, for example, and a soft Scottish burr is delightful. But there are some accents which are ... less appealing. Natasha's was, fortunately, pure Home Counties.

"Might we pretend we met at a party, do you think?" she asked. "I don't think I know how to begin this conversation otherwise."

"Please."

"So, we met at the party of a mutual friend, got chatting in the kitchen, you gave me your number as I left and here we are."

"I remember it well. But, as I recall, you hadn't quite got around to telling me what you do – you run a small business, doing ... ?"

"Oh yes, I hadn't gone into details, had I? It's a health food shop."

I have somewhat mixed reactions to anything 'alternative'. On the one hand, I'm a natural sceptic, demanding scientific evidence for unfounded claims and generally finding them wanting. On the other hand, the people involved in alternative things are often lovely. I tried to switch off the former mindset and switch on the latter.

"Aha. How did you get into that?"

"Being a customer of them for years and finding them often rather badly run; I thought I could do better."

"Good reason! Where is it?"

"Notting Hill – fortunately I set up there before it got trendy and property prices went crazy. And you're a commercial photographer? What sort of things do you photograph."

I gave my standard potted summary.

"No, it's no good," said Natasha.

Was she allergic to photographers, I wondered? Was her ex a photographer and he'd given the rest of us a bad rep?

"What's that?" I asked.

"This meeting at a party business – I'm just too curious as to how people end up on a dating site, and what their experiences have been."

I laughed.

"My best friend has appointed herself my relationship consultant, and for some completely inexplicable reason added Soulmates to the agenda. Perhaps she thinks there's no hope for me in the real world. Your email explained your path to sadanddesperate.com – did you get there under your own steam, or were you pushed?"

"Entirely my own doing. I found myself browsing the personal ads in the Guardian one morning, decided to take a look at the website and, well ..."

"Indeed."

"I do have one other confession?"

"Oh?"

"I find phone calls with strangers only marginally less awkward than email exchanges. Do you think we might skip ahead now to the drink?"

"An excellent idea. How does your diary look for this week and next?"

"Well, I'm supposed to be going to some function on Friday, but I'd really rather not, and a date is always a socially-acceptable excuse for ducking out. I don't suppose you're free then?"

I wasn't entirely sure I should admit to having no plans for Friday night, but I figured that, by the age of 36, it's probably ok not to be out clubbing every week.

"As it happens ..."

"Terrific! Could we go somewhere quiet? I'm a little allergic to the typical Friday night bar babble."

"Me too, and I know just the place."

The lounge of the Selfridges Hotel was one of London's best-kept secrets. Not many people even knew of the existence of the hotel, tucked away out of sight behind the store, and the first-floor lounge was generally quiet even on a Friday or Saturday night. I explained where it was, and suggested 7pm.

"Sounds perfect – I look forward to meeting you then."

"Likewise."

In response to Helen's sarky comment, I sent her a text: Being prepared is important. Now I have both dates.

Chapter 13

Men get a much better deal than women when it comes to choosing clothing for a first date. A black suit looks smart but, with an open-neck shirt (also black, of course), doesn't look like you're trying too hard. Not for us the frantic hunt through a dozen or more different outfits in as many different styles.

Except on this occasion. I may have been doing Jane a disservice, but I did currently have her pegged in the 'hippy-ish' category, and a suit didn't really feel appropriate. The problem with my wardrobe, I realised, was that I didn't really do the 'smart casual' thing. Not that I didn't think it was a good idea, I'd just never really learned how it worked.

I can do smart, and I can do casual, but the middle ground is something of a mystery to me.

I settled on the safe option: a black pair of jeans, black shirt and (you guessed it) black leather jacket. While I'd describe the look as more casual than smart-casual, it does seem to be a universally-accepted uniform for anything short of a black-tie ball or afternoon tea at the Ritz.

There's always a certain self-consciousness to a first date. You have the irrational yet persistent feeling that everyone else in the bar or restaurant knows. The Sumi Experience didn't help, with that nagging doubt about being stood up, especially when sat at a restaurant table on my own.

But Jane arrived promptly. It was a good thing I didn't wear a suit: she was wearing something that, well, gave the undeniable impression of having been home-made. It was sort of a summer dress, only longer and in a heavier material. Or materials, perhaps, as it had a sort of patchwork pattern that rather unkindly brought to mind visions of a quilt. I need have had no concerns about my own fashion-sense ...

"How was your day?" I asked, rising to greet her.

"Bleargh."

"Ah. Wine, then."

"Yes, wine and chat about anything other than work."

"Ok, deal. Any wine preference?"

"Something white, light and fruity."

The complete opposite of my tastes; we weren't going to be sharing a bottle.

I caught the eye of a waitress, and we ordered a glass each of house red and house white. When we ordered food, it appeared I was right: she went for one of the vegetarian pizzas. I decided to test my other theories.

"Do you live alone? Flat-share?"

"House-share, yes. Five of us."

"Sounds like you're still living a student lifestyle – does it keep you feeling like you're in your early 20s?" I felt a momentary panic; my age estimates aren't always known for their accuracy. "Uh, you're not, are you?"

Jane laughed: "Not for a while, no: I'm 34. And yes, it does feel rather like I'm cheating time."

"So is it a function of being an impoverished social worker, or a conscious choice?"

"A little of each, but it's a life I love. Most people seem to think that once they're out of their 20s, the options are being in a couple or living alone. I'd far, far rather share a home with friends than come home to an empty house or experience the pressure most people seem to feel to pair up at all costs. Even when I've been in a relationship, we've still lived in a shared house. It puts less pressure on a relationship when you are not relying on the other person to meet all your everyday needs."

The wine arrived, and I took a sip. It wasn't particularly good.

"I have to say it makes a lot of sense. I'm not sure I could cope with it personally, though: it's bad enough having one person's annoying habits to deal with, but a whole houseful ... do you still have arguments about who drank who's milk?"

"Not often, no. Anyway, I drink goat's milk so mine is easy to identify."

Of course she did.

"Do we still need to have the erotic photography debate?" I asked. "It's just, if we do, can we get it out of the way so we can talk about topics on which we might agree?"

"We do."

"Ok, let's start with what you see as inherently wrong with titillation."

Jane shook her head. "This is your case to make."

I managed a small smile. "Ok. Let's say a couple has been married for ten or fifteen years. They still love each other, but things are perhaps not as romantic as they once were, and the sex is perhaps more routine."

"Does that have to happen, in your view?"

"Have to? I don't know. Does often happen? I think so, yes."

"And you think some tawdry photos are the solution?"

"Some fun photos can certainly help to reinvigorate things. The woman sees it as a romantic gift for her partner. The man enjoys seeing her in an unashamedly sexual fashion. And from what I hear, they both tend to have a very pleasant evening when the gift is presented."

"Ok."

"What do you mean, 'ok'?"

"I mean: ok."

"That's it? Interrogation complete."

"Yep."

"You seem to have strong views on the subject – I can't believe a two-minute conversation changed your mind."

"I don't and it hasn't. As I said, this is not about changing minds, this is about the ability to put forward a reasonable case."

I laughed. It was apparently my equivalent of the religion question: the answer isn't especially important, it's the reasoning behind it that matters.

"So you like to test your dates?"

"I haven't decided you are yet."

"What, a date?"

"Yes."

"Um, doesn't the fact that we're here sort of fulfil the technical requirements for a date?"

"Not necessarily. I could be interviewing you as a potential friend. I haven't decided yet."

"Ah, I see. So this evening can become a date or a non-date, depending how it goes."

"Exactly."

"That's a neat way of never having a bad date."

"Yep."

The food arrived. Mine was an American Hot, Jane's looked very ... healthy.

"So are you a full-time vegetarian, or just like vegetarian food?"

"I've been a vegetarian since I was 12."

I decided it was my turn to do the interrogating.

"Why?"

"When I was 12, or now?"

"Both."

"When I was 12, it was probably more to annoy my parents than anything."

I smiled. "And now?"

"In truth, mostly because I haven't eaten meat for 22 years and I don't have any reason to start again. I lost the taste for meat a long time ago, the body actually adjusts to make it difficult to digest meat, and meat makes for more expensive meals."

"So it's habit rather than principles?"

"Principles too, but those are somewhat academic since I have no desire to eat meat."

"What are the principles? That it's wrong to kill animals for food?"

"I don't necessarily think it's wrong to kill animals per se, but I do have a few different objections to the meat trade. The first is the way we've sanitised it. If we went out with a rifle, shot a rabbit, butchered it, cooked it and ate it, that would be one thing. But we don't: we buy neat packages from Sainsburys. We don't take the responsibility for killing what we eat."

"I can understand that. I mean, I get Mr Sainsbury to catch and kill my animals for me because hunting is a little impractical on Borough High Street, but I agree that we should at least be willing to kill animals ourselves if we're prepared to eat them. What's your next objection?"

"The way we farm and slaughter animals. It's simply cruel. You can make the argument that killing animals for food is natural, but there's nothing natural about cooping them up in pens and barns, transporting them packed into lorries and leading them into slaughter houses."

"It's hard to argue with that one. I try to do what I can – buying free-range chickens, etc – but I am uncomfortably aware that it's small beer in the scheme of things."

"Right. The simple fact is that eating meat may be natural, but the amount of meat we eat isn't. With the population size we have, there is no way to satisfy the demand for those volumes of meat without factory farming. Which also links in to my third objection."

"Namely?"

"Hunger. We live on a planet where a sizeable proportion of the population doesn't have enough food to eat. Meat is an extremely inefficient way to feed people. You have to grow 15 kilos of wheat to feed a cow to create 1 kilo of meat."

I felt on somewhat safer ground there. I do a few pro-bono projects a year, and had done a couple of projects with Unicef, so had at least a basic grounding in some of the issues underlying hunger.

"Right, but hunger actually has nothing to do with lack of food. There's plenty of food for all. The issues are much more to do with politics than protein – the politics of both developing countries and the developed world."

"I'm not sure you can compartmentalise things in that way. If you look at what's wrong with the world, it's all interconnected stuff. Hunger, the environment, poverty, the banking crisis – it's all different aspects of the same short-term, selfish approach we take. We need to take a much more long-term, holistic view of the world."

I didn't disagree with the sentiment, but – official date or not – I didn't want to spend the entire time putting the world to rights.

I smiled.

"What?"

"Usually I'm the one who gets carried away with debates and forgets to have normal conversations. You know, about books and music and things that normal people talk about."

"Small-talk, you mean?"

I smiled again: we did have some things in common.

"I must confess I never really learned the art. In fact, the more of this dating-" Jane gave me a sharp look, and I corrected myself: "-potential dating thing I do, the less I think I know about how it's done."

"So don't do it. Just be you."

"You make that sound very simple."

"Isn't it?"

I hesitated. Just how much of one's soul does one bear on a first date? Or potential first-date. Where does genuine communication end and over-sharing begin? I mean, the point of a date is to get to know someone, but Helen's advice to take things one step at a time did make sense.

The truth was: I wasn't quite sure who I was. We're all different in different contexts. With my clients, I'm one kind of person. In fact, I'm different people with different clients. With female friends, I'm another person. With male friends, someone else.

I've always been a chameleon. It's one of my great strengths: I can fit in anywhere. But it's also a weakness: after a while of fitting into so many different environments, you start to wonder which is the real you. Whether any of the roles you play are the real you.

And dating is a whole other arena. One date brings out one side of you, a different date another side. They are all aspects of me. Yet none of them is me. We're all too complex and contradictory to be reduced to a single identity. And right now I was even more confused than usual because I was dating one woman (no, two women) while my thoughts were rarely far from a third.

Jane seemed a very direct person. Maybe even the kind of person with whom you could have this kind of conversation – well, apart from the 'thoughts with another woman' part. But even I had to admit that this was most definitely not first-date territory.

"Perhaps," I replied.

We munched on our pizzas while I tried to find the middle ground between small-talk and levels of intimacy inappropriate for two people who barely knew each other. I want with my 'passion' trick: a question that allows the other person to choose the level at which it is answered. It can be answered superficially, with hobbies or interests, or at a deeper level, as desired.

"What are your passions in life?" I asked.

"Environmentalism is one," Jane answered. "It's just nuts the way we seem to view our planet as disposable." Now it was her turn to smile. "Or is that also too big a topic for dinner?"

I grinned. "Maybe we just give up on the small-talk idea."

"So, where do you stand on the environment?"

"It's an interesting question. I would say I'm an environmentalist in the old-fashioned sense of the word. I care about our surroundings. We do need to plan ahead, and invest in new forms of energy before the old ones run out. But too many of those who call themselves environmentalists today seem to be latter-day Luddites, apparently wanting us to give up all modern conveniences and live some kind of wildly impractical back-to-the-land existence."

"Is it Luddite to look at the kind of consumerist society we live in today and see it as unsustainable?"

"No, some of the things we do aren't sustainable in the long-term – at least, not unless we crack fusion. But neither is it realistic to expect people to simply abandon cars, planes, central heating ..."

"Not abandon them entirely, no, but use them responsibly – take steps to reduce our carbon footprint to a reasonable level. Have you ever calculated yours, by the way?"

I grimaced. I had, once. The amount of business travel I do meant it was something stupid like 70 times the average. I decided tactical vagueness was the order of the day.

"Most of mine comes from business travel, so the exact numbers aren't very meaningful in my case."

"Why? Doesn't it count if you're making money out of it?"

"Some types of work involve travel; that's just the nature of the beast."

"That's a cop-out. Not all photographers travel."

"No, but some of us do, and you can't design your career around your carbon footprint."

"You could."

"Ok, you could, but it's not a very practical approach to life."

"You see, this is the problem. Everyone's willing to consider the environment so long as it doesn't involve actually changing their lives in any way."

"Did you really consider the environment before choosing your career?"

"I considered the kind of world I wanted to help create, yes, and wouldn't have gone for any career I felt was going to make things worse rather than better."

It was a worthy attitude, I thought, no doubt about that. I could respect her for it; I just wasn't sure I could live with it.

Is this how it goes, I wondered? Even if I manage to get Eva out of my head, would I have a succession of dates in which a single failed checkbox on the part of either one of us can bring the whole thing to a juddering halt? If so, what the hell were the chances of finding someone I actually wanted to spend my life with, and who wanted to spend her life with me?

"You seem uncharacteristically quiet," observed Jane, as she replaced her knife and fork on her now-empty plate.

Well, whatever the odds, and however much I might find Jane attractive and interesting, we clearly were not made for each other. But the lesson I learned in date one had remained burned into my mind: if there is one thing you don't ever do on a first date, it is tell them at the time that there isn't going to be a second one. Or, in Jane's terms, a first one.

I did, though, like her. Sometime after the date, I was going to have to figure out a mechanism for saying "I'd like us to be friends" that didn't just sound like a gentle way of telling a date you didn't want to see her again. Though whether that can ever work – telling someone you like them but not enough – I didn't know. I rather suspected not, which would be a shame.

"Pudding?" I asked.

"So how did you leave things?" asked Helen.

"In a non-committal sort of way."

"Then she'll know."

"Probably. And it's not like I'm any better a match for her than she is for me, so it's not going to be devastating news. By the way, is there any way to tell a failed date that you want to be friends and convince her that you mean it?"

"No."

"I figured as much."

"Well, I mean, you might, some way down the road, but certainly not with one breath."

"Right. So. Natasha."

"The one you haven't yet met."

"That one, yes. The simple fact is, I'm not ready to date anyone. I mean, yes, I know you're right, and that sitting at home wishing things were different does me no good, but what's the point of dating when I'm simply not ready?"

"Don't you already have the date arranged?"

"Yes. I'm thinking I should cancel it. She sounds great, but I'm just not in the space for dating."

"Ok, here's the deal ..."

"It is?"

"It is. Go on the date. Pretend you are in the mood for dating. Give Natasha a proper chance. If it doesn't work out, then take a break from dating (though no reclusing!). But on- When are you seeing her?"

"Friday."

"On Friday, you are the very soul of charm and sociability. You accept that she isn't Eva and that Eva is not the only woman on the planet with whom you can be happy. It's one date. If things don't work, having genuinely given her every chance, then you're off the hook for a while."

"How long a while?"

"I'll let you know."

"I see."

"Any more questions?"

"Just one, I guess."

"Which is?"

"Relationships – how the fuck do those work, then?"

"You have done them before, you know."

"Yeah, but I was younger then. Things were simpler. Fewer checkboxes."

Helen made an exasperated-sounding noise. At least, I think that's what it was. It might have been a muffled sneeze, but that's not where I'd be putting my money were I a betting man.

"We've done this. When you meet the right woman, the checkboxes fade away. Or, at least, you can escort them off the premises."

"But you can't always know that on the first date. What if I write them off for Failure to Comply with a Checkbox on date one when they would have revealed themselves to be above such things on date three?"

"You know on date one that you want to see them again. Then you have date two. Do I need to continue, or can you count past two?"

"I think I can manage it. I'm told I'm mathematical."

Chapter 14

I'd discovered the Selfridges Hotel by accident a couple of years earlier. I'd needed something from the food hall, and as the store was crowded I'd walked around the side of the store to get there. As I did so, I'd spotted a further entrance at the far corner of the building. Curious as to whether there was some other part of the store I didn't know about, I'd wandered up to investigate and found the hotel.

The lounge, at the time, was like a 19th Century gentleman's club. All brown leather sofas and chairs, dim table-lamps and only one person in there, who appeared to be sound asleep.

I was disappointed when they modernised the décor slightly, but at least it remained quiet, and it was a great place to meet for a quiet catch-up with friends, especially on a Friday or Saturday night when most places in the West End were packed out.

I had a meeting with a client which finished at 5.30pm. I could just about have dashed home to drop off my laptop, but it made more sense to go straight to the lounge and do some photo-processing. The advent of digital photography meant that photographers no longer have to spend hours inhaling fumes from dodgy chemicals in darkened rooms, but we do instead have to spend hours processing photos on our PCs. This is tedious, so I try to squeeze as much of it as possible into otherwise dead time.

Helen doubtless wouldn't approve of me turning up to a date with a laptop, but she would never know.

I chose a table against the wall, giving me a strategic view of the entrance corridor and allowing me to survey the entire lounge in case I finished my work and wanted to indulge in a spot of people-watching. Not that there were, as yet, many people to watch. A fairly obvious mother and daughter a few tables away to my left, and two thirty-something Arabic-looking guys having an animated conversation with the aid of a large collection of paperwork.

I settled in to do some work.

Natasha arrived a few minutes early. I snapped my laptop closed and slipped it into my bag. Her photo was entirely accurate, and she did have exactly that look. She was wearing a black trouser suit, a thin silver necklace, matching bracelet, heels tall enough to look smart, short enough to look practical. It was a good look.

I realised with a start that sitting and staring at someone is never an ideal greeting, so hastily dragged myself to my feet

"Hi, Natasha – Stephen."

"I'm relieved we didn't have to resort to red carnations and copies of the Guardian."

"One of the virtues of this place – it's not usually heaving with desperate singles, even on a Friday night."

I gestured for her to sit.

"Yes, however did you discover it? It's quite the find."

"Entirely by accident."

"And since then? The scene of many assignations?" Natasha raised an eyebrow. Just one eyebrow. I never mastered that, myself, despite practicing in the mirror for some considerable time during my teen years.

What was a man to do when faced with such a question, I wondered? As it happened, during my .. newly-single phase .. the lounge had indeed played host to a number of meetings. But that would, today, give entirely the wrong impression. Providing the full chapter-and-verse explanation seemed a little long-winded as a response to a teasing comment. I settled on a simple:

"Not recently, no."

"A response worthy of the Diplomatic Corps."

"A former career?" I enquired.

"Not mine, no: my parents."

"Ah. So I'm imagining your childhood was split across a number of countries?"

"Several, yes."

She didn't elaborate, and I was about to ask when a lone woman in her late 50s or early 60s came and sat at the next table. An almost entirely empty lounge, and she has to sit next to us. As if a first date wasn't awkward enough without an audience ...

I turned back to Natasha: "What would you like to drink?"

"A red wine, please. Do you know what they have?"

I wasn't sure I should admit it, given her question about previous assignations, but I did.

"The New Zealand Pinot Noir is pretty good."

"Then the Pinot Noir it shall be."

I gestured to the waiter, who was rather loudly intercepted by the lady next to us, who spoke with a distinct New York accent. The waiter, to his credit, smiled charmingly, explained that he would be with her in just a moment and then turned his attention to us.

"Two glasses of the Pinot Noir, please."

"Certainly, sir. Large or small glasses?"

I turned questioningly to Natasha.

"Shall we be optimistic and get a bottle?" she asked.

It seemed she wasn't expecting to bore of me within the first few minutes. I smiled, and turned back to the waiter: "A bottle, please."

The waiter inclined his head slightly, in that way that would look silly in any other context – at the Tesco checkout, for example – but somehow works in hotels.

"Am I your first foray into Internet dating?" asked Natasha.

I seemed to have a knack for finding direct women.

"You are," I answered, happy to be on more solid territory there than on the hotel lounge history. "And I yours?"

"No," she said, "there was one previous one. It wasn't successful."

"It sounds like there may be a story there?"

"Only a very short one, I'm afraid. He was around ten years older, and two inches shorter, than his profile claimed. Our meeting didn't last long."

"What is the point of someone doing that?" I wondered aloud. "It's not as if you're not going to notice when you meet!"

"My assumption is that they hope to reel you in sufficiently that you'll overlook the matter by the time you meet. The irony is that I wouldn't have had an issue with either his age or his height, it was only the deception to which I took offence."

"Yes, lying to someone isn't exactly the firmest of foundations on which to meet."

We toasted each other when the wine arrived.

"Do you have siblings?" she asked.

"I have a complicated family," I laughed. "Do you want the complete list, or will you settle for the executive summary of divorced parents who both remarried, with various siblings and siblingettes being acquired at each stage?"

"Oh, it sounds to me like we should have the full list."

"Ok, but remember: you asked for this ... So, I have: one sister, two half-brothers on my mother's side, a step-brother on my mother's side, a step-sister on my mother's side, a step-brother on my father's side, and a half-brother on my father's side. Actually, though, since the step-brother was from his second marriage and he's now on his third and, we think, final one, I'm not sure that one counts. Do step-brothers remain so after a divorce?"

"That is complicated," said Natasha.

"Yours is simpler, I hope?"

"Yes, very boring in comparison: just one sister."

"Older or younger?"

"Two years younger. Parents still married, so really no family dramas."

I noticed Natasha's glass was nearly empty, so refilled it, then topped-up my own.

I did briefly do the music/books/films thing, but I was rather going through the motions – I'm always more interested in the juicier stuff. I told Natasha as much. She nodded.

"Oh god yes, life's far too short to chat about inanities."

I explained that I'd be in trouble with Helen.

"So my every word will be filed in your post-date report?" I felt I really should get lessons on that eyebrow thing.

I laughed: "Oh dear. No, it's not quite that bad, I promise."

"Have you been married?"

It seemed the chit-chat was indeed over. I gave the abbreviated version.

"And you?" I asked.

"I married very young."

"How young?"

"Nineteen."

"Ok, that is young."

"Yes. It wasn't a mistake, he was a lovely man, but your point about how much we change applies even more at that age; the marriage only lasted two years."

"Are you still in touch?"

"Our families know each other ..." She smiled. "It wasn't too far from an arranged marriage."

"And since then?" We seemed to have opened the door to this line of conversation, so ...

"One three-year relationship – one of those friendships that become something more and which really should have stayed as a friendship."

"Ah. Did the friendship survive the relationship?"

"It did. Well, after a bit of a bumpy patch, but he's fine about it now."

In the course of conversation, Natasha became Nat. Both conversation and wine flowed well, and it wasn't long before the bottle was empty.

"Dinner?" I suggested.

"You know, I'm quite comfortable here. Do they do bar-snacks?"

They did.

A second bottle of wine always feels like a very bad idea the following day, but often seems like a good idea at the time. We took the view that tomorrow was another day.

I was, I had to admit, getting somewhat squiffy, and perhaps sharing more than is wise on a first date, but the sharing was mutual, and sometimes you just feel comfortable with someone. Though quite how we got onto early sexual experiences, I have absolutely no idea.

It was one of those evenings where it was suddenly close to midnight, the hours having somehow zipped by unseen. I paid the bill and stood up, feeling slightly unsteady on my feet. Nat, somehow, seemed entirely poised.

"Thank you," she said, "it was an excellent evening."

"It was indeed," I said, trying hard not to slur the words. "Though I think more food to soak up the wine next time."

"My treat next time," announced Natasha. It appeared we had a second date.

"See?" asked Helen. "No dilemma. The only thing you need to know is whether you want to see her again, and you do."

"Well, we had had two bottles of wine by that point, so it was decision-making under the influence."

"In vino, veritas?"

"Well ..."

"What?"

"Well, yes, I liked her. We got on well. Very well, if I'm honest. But ... I still don't know if I'm ready for this."

"One day at a time."

"She seems like a lovely, genuine person and I don't want to mess her around. It's not fair to go on seeing someone if you're still thinking about someone else."

"Stephen, there's a difference between having designs on someone else, and missing them. You haven't changed your mind about the kid thing, I presume?"

"No."

"So. Eva is over. I know that's hard, and it's still a bit raw at the moment, but that is the way it is. You're not deceiving anyone, you're not going to suddenly run off with Eva, you simply have a history. Everyone has one of those."

Helen's voice softened. "Listen, it's clear breaking up with Eva hurt a lot more than you let on at the time. If you hadn't already met Natasha, then sure, I'd say at this point: go lick your wounds for a while, have some meaningless sex, whatever. I also know you've only had one date and it sounds like a fairly drunken one and maybe you'll meet her next time in the cold light of day and feel differently. But from the way you talked about the date, it's clear that there's at least a spark there, yes?"

I couldn't deny it.

"So do one of your famous cost-benefit analyses. What's the worst-case scenario if you continue dating her and it doesn't go anywhere?"

"We fall in love, something goes terribly wrong, we break up, I decide to give up on the whole relationship thing and become a Benedictine monk."

"Do those still exist?"

"They do, actually – I googled them."

"You googled them? I hadn't realised things had got that bad!"

"They haven't, quite. I think. There was just a piece on the BBC news website about them. Apparently they are so desperate for monks these days that they offer some kind of try-before-you-buy weekend. There was a reference to them still living by the Rules of St Benedict, written in 500-and-something AD. You know me and my aimless curiosity, so I googled the rules."

"I see. And did the rules meet with your approval?"

"Not really, no."

"So, on the whole, you don't see Benedictine monktitude as a likely future career path?"

"Well, no. But you did ask for the worst-case scenario."

"I did, didn't I. Now. Worst-case scenario of ceasing to date this woman with whom you feel a spark?"

"I decide to give up on the whole relationship thing and do in fact become a Benedictine monk."

"So there's nothing to lose, right?"

"I guess not."

"And the best-case scenario of dating her is sparks turning into fireworks and living happily ever after. Best-case of not dating her is you stay home and create some kind of dating analysis spreadsheet or something."

"You do make a good case."

"So."

"Hmmm."

"Let me know how the second date goes."

Chapter 15

Since I knew Nat's full name, and a few bits and pieces about her, I googled her. Her name plus 'health food shop', and telling google to restrict the search to the UK, turned out to be enough.

I guess I'd always thought of health food shops as rather hippyish backstreet endeavours with dusty shelves and obscure products served by vague staff in homemade clothing. Her shop was none of these things. It had a smart, modern-looking website with an ebay store attached. The photos of the physical shop showed a bright, clean, colourful interior that couldn't have looked more different to my stereotyped expectation.

The next hit was to a national association of health food shops; Natasha was its president. She was also on the national committee of the Federation of Small Businesses and had spoken at several conferences. My prejudices were now well & truly debunked.

We'd agreed on a Chinese restaurant behind Leicester Square that I'd first visited a couple of years ago and which always seemed full of Chinese people. It's funny the way we always assume that's a recommendation; I mean, McDonalds are always full of Brits ...

But it was indeed excellent, combining good food in absurd quantities with attentive and efficient service, so had become one of my regular haunts. They also did a passable job of pretending to recognise me, despite the fact that 'regular' to me meant once every couple of months.

It reminded me of a hotel in Hamburg. I stayed there a few times a year, and the receptionist always greeted me by name on arrival. I couldn't figure out how they did it: with 200+ rooms and god knows how many tens of thousands of guests each year, there wasn't the remotest possibility that it really was a feat of memory. Granted only 50-100 guests will be checking-in each day, they still can't memorise that many faces on a daily basis. I concluded in the end that they must have some kind of facial recognition system triggered by a hidden camera somewhere in the lobby; however they did it, it was a very neat trick.

The restaurant didn't quite run to greeting me by name, and I guess a generic "Lovely to see you again" can be done with anyone they vaguely recall has been there before, but it all helps the impression of friendly service.

I took the liberty of ordering a bottle of Merlot before Nat arrived, but it wasn't as presumptuous on my part as it might have appeared: they offered exactly three reds, only one of which was drinkable. The fact that I felt comfortable ordering the wine prior to her arrival did at least reassure me that I was confident there would be no replay of The Sumi Incident, as it was now known.

Nat was exactly on time, and looked stunning. She was wearing a dress I was pretty sure I recognised but couldn't immediately place. It was silk, mid-thigh, a sort of muted gold colour and had some ruffley bits that should have looked fussy but instead looked elegant.

My fashion photography isn't sufficiently elevated that it includes major designers, but I do flick through Vogue regularly to keep up to date with current looks, and I was fairly sure that's where I'd seen it.

I rose to greet her, and we did cheek kisses. Fortunately we'd both decided on one, so we avoided the awkward dance where one of you is going for one and the other for two.

"Love the dress," I said.

"Thanks," she smiled. "I decided to treat myself on Saturday. I don't indulge often, but every now and then ..."

"That's why we work," I smiled.

I poured her wine and she tasted it.

"It's drinkable rather than exceptional," I said, "but I seem to recall we agreed that the emphasis would be more on food this time."

"We did, didn't we? So, have you had any more young ladies from Soulmates seeking your company?"

I laughed. "I think I can only manage one at a time. And you – more gentlemen keen to make your acquaintance?"

"Many," she smiled.

"How many?" I asked.

"Oh, I get 40 or 50 emails a week."

"Really?"

"Really."

"I feel suddenly lacking in the sought-after department."

Nat laughed. "Oh, don't. It's a boy/girl thing. Girls always get lots of emails."

"Have you commissioned a survey?"

"I decided to compare notes with a few of the other sane-sounding women on the site: they all said the same thing." She found more sane-sounding ones? She apparently looked harder than I did.

"Seems women get the better deal in these things."

"Oh, I don't think so."

"40 or 50 men a week chasing you? How is that not a good thing on a dating site?"

"I'll show you my inbox sometime. A good 99% of them are cut-and-pasted emails that the no-hopers clearly send to just about every woman on the site. You'd think if they were going to use a 'one email fits all' approach, they'd at least take the trouble to write something witty or interesting, but no."

"Ah."

"Believe me, boys have by far the better deal – you don't have to wade through the crap we do."

We picked up our menus and I warned Nat about the portion sizes: "This isn't one of those Chinese places where you order three or four dishes between you: you'll be doing well if you manage to finish one."

It was also not a place to be adventurous in your choices, because if you found you weren't so keen on your experiment, there was a great deal of it to struggle through. We both took safe bets: shredded beef for me and won-ton soup for Nat.

"I like your photography," she said.

"Oh?" I asked. "Where did you see it."

"I have to confess to googling you. Is that terribly stalker-ish, do you think?"

I laughed. "I hope not, as I have to match your confession."

Nat giggled. "Well, if it is, mutual stalking must be slightly more socially acceptable."

"I suspect everyone does it these days, but I wasn't quite sure, so didn't know whether I should mention it."

"So what did you learn about me – anything worrying?"

"On the contrary, it was all most impressive. Your shop looks fantastic, and you seem rather active in your various professional associations."

"It does make dating something of a different experience, doesn't it? Being able to google your date, I mean."

"I still feel rather new to the whole grown-up dating thing, to be honest, so being able to google is just one of many new experiences. Dating when you're in your teens and in your 30s ... well, they are rather different experiences."

"Not to mention the fact that we seem to spend quite a lot of time on our dates discussing dating."

I laughed. "Oh dear. That's my analytical side again. Ok, other topics."

"It wasn't a complaint; I find it rather fun too."

"Still, we shall make a concerted effort to introduce some other topics of conversation into the mix! Tell me about the Federation of Small Businesses – you must think it worthwhile, to be on the committee."

"Well, I sort of got co-opted, but yes, it is one of the few organisations that has shown itself to be effective in communicating the realities and needs of small business to the government. You're not a member?"

"No, there are a number of photography-specific associations, but to be honest most of them are pure money-making operations appealing to the vanity of photographers who collect letters after their name and want to enter competitions to get pats on their back from other photographers. I collected a few competition wins, just so I can put 'award-winning' on my website, but gave them up after that."

"The FSB is pretty good. Aside from the lobbying aspects, there are discounts on all sorts of things, and an online forum that's a great source of advice." She paused. "Oh dear, I sound like I'm on a recruitment drive!"

I smiled. "And what sort of things do you like to do when not working or trying to sign up your dates to business associations?"

"Did your profile mention kites, or did I imagine that?"

"I think it did mention kite-flying, though I confess I haven't done it for a few years. It was more of a shorthand thing for someone who still has a playful attitude to life, really."

"I adore kites," she said. "Playful, as you say, but within a few minutes of launching one, I'm no longer stood on the ground, I'm up there darting around the sky. It's such a feeling of liberation and distance from the hassles of everyday life."

"We should have arranged that for our date."

"Next time." Her optimism remained undiminished, it seemed.

"Do you have a whole collection of kites?"

"Five, I think. My favourite is an old Peter Powell stunt-kite from the 80s. Rather basic by today's standards, but flies beautifully – and you don't have to be afraid to crash it, unlike the more exotic ones."

I grinned. "Then I needn't be afraid to admit that's what mine is! I was rather concerned a kite aficionado might look down their nose at it as some kind of prehistoric relic, and I'd be exposed as some kind of pretender unworthy of admission to the ranks of The Ancient and Noble Order of the Kite."

"Well, that may yet be the case – I have yet to see how you fly it."

"Ah, I'm on probation, am I?"

"You are if you expect to fly any of mine, at any rate!"

The waiter arrived with the food, and Nat did a double-take: "My! You weren't exaggerating about the portions. This isn't a bowl of soup, it's a veritable soup-lake."

"It is best to arrive hungry here!"

Nat took a sip of the soup, and nodded.

"Good?" I asked.

"Very."

"So ... kites – what else?"

"Cat shows take up a fair amount of time."

"Oh, what do you have?"

"Two Havanas, one Abyssinian, one Bengal and an Ocicat."

"Five cats?!"

Nat nodded: "It's the bare minimum, really."

"You're also going to have to excuse my ignorance on the topic of pedigree cats: I've always had rescue cats."

Nat nodded again: "I could tell you were a cat person. What do you have?"

"Oscar. A short-haired tabby. One of two brothers originally, but the other one died a couple of years ago."

"How old is he?"

"19."

"Wow, a good age for a cat!"

"Yes, and he stayed quite kitten-like for most of those years. It's only really in the last few months that he's slowed down noticeably. The vet gave him a clean bill of health, just old-age finally catching up with him. So tell me about yours. I'm not familiar with any of the breeds, I don't think, though Ocicat rings a vague bell."

"They're all orientals. The Ocicat is so-called because it looks somewhat like an Ocelot, though it's in fact an entirely domestic breed. The Havanas are basically brown Siamese cats. Rather dog-like in their behaviour: they tend to follow you around, and like to play fetch. Bengals are, technically, leopards. Despite them being entirely domestic in temperament, they still theoretically fall within the Dangerous Wild Animals Act, and you're supposed to have a licence to keep them."

"And do you?"

She grinned: "Fortunately even the government knows it's an anomaly, so it isn't ever enforced, and there's a DEFRA proposal in to exempt them."

"So you show them? Always having had moggies, it's not a world I know anything about."

I was slightly suspicious of cat shows. You hear stories of animals having ears docked or claws clipped or who knows what to make them meet some arbitrary standard of aesthetics, and the idea of cats being carted around the country in baskets to spend a day in some hall somewhere being picked up and prodded by judges didn't strike me as a particularly kind way to treat them, but I had learned something about this dating lark. I kept my thoughts to myself and listened to Nat explain how the shows worked.

She made a reasonable case – that cats that are used to it seem to enjoy it, or certainly don't complain about it, and most people don't take it terribly seriously: it was mostly, it seemed, an opportunity to talk cats with fellow addicts.

We again talked easily about anything and everything. I was enjoying myself. I felt comfortable with Nat. She was bright, witty, sparky ... all the right things. All the right things except one: she wasn't Eva.

How does that happen? I was too old to believe in there being just one The One, and if that were the case I'd already had mine and she'd ceased being it. There are multiple The Ones. So why did Eva feel like The One and Nat didn't? Looked at objectively, she had just as much going for her, and we were getting on just as easily. There was no reason at all she couldn't have the potential to be The One. No reason she couldn't be.

Except she wasn't Eva.

I realised that, of all the many topics of conversation we've managed to cover, the one I hadn't gone near, not even obliquely, was The Kid Thing.

Partly, of course, because I was behaving myself and trying to avoid questioning women about their ovary-related intentions within five minutes of meeting them. But more because it wasn't relevant.

"You seem distracted," said Nat.

"Sorry," I said. "Some things on my mind."

"Share them?"

I shook my head. "It's been a lovely evening, but I should think about heading home."

Nat studied me. "What changed?" she asked. "We seemed to be getting on really well. Did I misread things?"

"No. No, you didn't, and yes we are. It's just ... I need to figure something out, about me, not about you. Sorry, I didn't mean to spoil the evening."

Nat put a hand on mine, and smiled. "You haven't, don't worry. Sort out what you need to sort out and then give me a call when you're ready to, ok?"

Add grace and understanding to her virtues, I thought. Was I being a total idiot about this? Helen was right: Eva was history, and I needed to accept that. Why risk the beginnings of something promising for something I can't have?

"I will," I said. "And thank you."

"I'm screwed."

"You were?"

"No, I wasn't. I am."

"Tell me."

"Nat is great. If I'd never met Eva, I'd be excitedly telling you how well the date went, how much I like Nat and the plans I was making for our next date. But I just can't do it. I can't get Eva out of my head."

"You're in love with her."

"Yes."

"Did you know that before? You haven't ever used those words."

"No. Yes. Maybe. But I know it now."

"Enough to do the kid thing?"

"It's not about enough to do that, I just can't do it full-stop. I'd be a terrible father. I mean, I like kids in small doses. Controllable doses. Kids you can give back when you've had enough. But that life ... 24/7. The constant, unrelenting, all-encompassing nature of the relationship. You are a parent first, and everything else second. I really, really wish I could do that. Wish I wanted it. But I don't. Can't. It's just not who I am."

"You think you can change her mind about the kid thing?"

"No."

"So now what?"

"I'm screwed. I'm in love with a woman I can't have, and am messing things up with a woman I maybe can for no sane reason at all."

"Have you messed things up with her?"

"Maybe not yet, but if I don't call her soon, she's going to write me off as a flake, and move on. And rightly so. That's basically what I am right now where relationships are concerned. I've become the one thing I can't tolerate in others."

Helen said nothing.

"If I can't be happy dating someone like Nat," I continued, "how the hell am I ever going to find anyone I want to be with?"

"You found Isabel, and you found Eva, and – I respectfully suggest – it's way too early to decide things couldn't work with Nat. Give her a proper chance."

"Isabel ended in divorce, Eva wants the one thing I can't give her. And I don't know that I can give Nat a proper chance, given how I feel about Eva."

"Look," said Helen, carefully. "I know you did your experiment. I know we've been round this a hundred times. But are you sure? I mean, really sure? You're not the first man to be adamant he doesn't want kids until he has one of his own, and then turns into the most besotted father on the planet. I know It's different when it's your own kid is the biggest cliché out there, but things don't become clichés by accident, you know."

"You can't gamble on something like that, Helen. The chances are just infinitesimally slim, and then I've messed up three people's lives."

"Other men take that gamble."

"It's a crazy gamble. It's as close to a dead-cert as anything ever gets. It would be madness."

"Madder than walking away from the woman you're in love with?" asked Helen.

"What else can I do?"

"I don't know."

"Me neither."

We were both silent for a time.

Helen reached out for my hand. "Listen, Stephen. I know you hurt. But if it can't be, it can't be. And how often does a Nat come along?"

I smiled at her. "You're a good friend. And you're probably right. But I don't know that I can do it, and it wouldn't be fair to Nat to see her again when I feel like this."

"And is it fair on her to write her off because she's not Eva?"

"I'm not writing her off."

"You might be." Helen paused. "Listen, I can't tell you what to do here-" In a happier mood, I might have taken issue with her on that point. "- but think about it. Please?"

I squeezed her hand. "I will," I promised.

Chapter 16

I did think about it. A lot. It didn't help.

I'd once read a really good approach to making a tricky decision: you decide to flip a coin for it. Just before you flip the coin, you ask yourself which way up you want it to land: then you don't need to flip the coin. I'd tried it a few times, and stupid as it sounded, it really did work.

Ok, I told myself, heads I see Nat again, tails I won't. I dug a 10p coin out of my pocket and stared at it. Heads Nat, tails not. Which way up did I want it to land?

I wasn't sure.

Hmmm. My foolproof method was letting me down.

Ok, I thought, let's imagine it lands heads up: how would I feel about that?

I wasn't sure about that either.

Alright, if it lands tails up, how would I feel about that? Sad, I realised.

I still wasn't sure it was the right decision – I felt a hell of a lot more sad about Eva – but it was at least an end to the paralysis.

Texting Nat felt easier than calling her. I typed: *Fancy the cinema on Tuesday?*

She replied ten minutes later with *Sure – the Banksy film? Been meaning to see it. It's only on at the Curzon, and only one showing, at 6.45pm. Ok?*

I quickly replied with a *Perfect, see you then* before I could change my mind.

I didn't know anything about the Banksy film: if Nat was keen, I felt I should at least know something about it, so googled it. I read a couple of reviews, one of which made for an amusing read. I thought Nat might enjoy the review so emailed her the link with a quick *Look forward to enjoying it with you on Tues.*

She replied later with *Very assertive! I look forward to it too. Meet in the Curzon coffee-shop at 6.30-ish, then?*

I wasn't sure what the 'very assertive' bit meant, but was forming the view that attempting to understand everything women said or did was over-ambitious.

I got there early, and Nat and I approached the doors from opposite directions at exactly the same moment. We both laughed, and kissed. This was more like it was supposed to happen in the movies!

I joined the short queue for tickets while Nat went through to the coffee-shop to get drinks. Maybe this wouldn't be so bad after all, I told myself. I'd managed to (mostly) put Eva from my mind for most of the day. I hadn't spilled anything on myself. I hadn't made any small children cry. I hadn't yet said anything stupid. Ok, I thought, I hadn't yet had much opportunity to do that, but I was feeling confident.

I bought the tickets and turned away from the desk.

"Perfect timing!" she said with a smile. Which it would have been, had it been Nat with the drinks. It wasn't: it was Jane.

"Oh! Hi!" I said, trying to sound rather more pleased to see her than I felt. "What are you doing here? Uh, stupid question! You're here to see a film, of course. The Banksey one?"

Jane gave me a weird look. Ordinarily, I would have asked her about it, but right now I was starting to panic at the idea that Nat would be returning at any moment. Admittedly I wasn't double-dating any more because I'd decided not to see Jane again, but there was the tiny technicality of the fact that I hadn't actually yet mentioned this to her. If Nat returned while Jane was still standing there it would be awkward at least.

I tried to think about how to extract myself from the situation. I glanced over at the coffee shop. It looked quite crowded, but I still reckoned I had two minutes at best to extract myself from the conversation with Jane.

Jane looked at me: "Are you ok?"

One minute 55 seconds.

"Sorry," I replied, "bit of a long day. Tired, you know. Should have just gone home, really, but I'd arranged to see the film-" Well, that was a stupid tack. The obvious question for Jane to ask was who I'd arranged to see it with, and The other woman I'm dating, and who I've decided I prefer to you, so would you mind making yourself scarce before she returns? wasn't really going to be the ideal answer.

One minute 45 seconds.

"Anyway," I added, "I'd better let you go." Perhaps she was dating someone else, I thought! Yes, that would make life easier. Then we could both laugh about it and go our separate ways. But was there time for that conversation before Nat returned? Not really, I thought, and especially not if I was wrong. There definitely wasnt time for that conversation. Unless, of course, she'd reached the same conclusion as I had about the date, in which case there might be, just.

One minute 35 seconds.

But if she hadn't, then-

"Let me go?" Jane asked.

One minute 30 seconds.

"I mean your ... companion" - such a useful word - "must be wondering where you've got to."

One minute 25.

"My companion?"

"Oh ... you're here on your own?"

"Stephen, I'm here with you. You invited me here. The text." Jane looked at me like I was some kind on infant.

I stared at her. I couldn't have- I mean, I wouldn't have- Not even I, on my most stupid of days, could have possibly-

Oh. My. God.

The horrendous truth dawned. I'd somehow, by some monumental act of distracted idiocy I couldn't even comprehend, sent the text – the one inviting Nat to the cinema – to Jane instead of Nat.

No wonder Nat had replied to my email with that 'Very assertive' comment! I'd thought I was just commenting on a date already arranged, she'd thought I was arranging the date in some kind of macho 'You will be there' kind of manner.

I'd invited two different women to the same date.

Fuck!

Fuck, fuck, fuck!

One minute 15 seconds.

One minute 10 seconds.

I really ought to say something, I decided. But what? What does one say in the one minute and five seconds before date one arrives and finds you standing there chatting to inadverant date two?

Shit.

Ok, deep breath, calm thoughts. You're not her type anyway. You'll explain, she'll think it's funny, say that she couldn't really understand why you asked her out again given that you obviously weren't suited, and she only came along so she could let you down gently in person. Yes, that's how things will happen. That's how it will work. Everything will be fine. You'll somehow have this conversation in the remaining 60 seconds before Nat returns with the drinks, Jane will just have waved goodbye with a grin and everything will be just fine.

"Jane ..." I said.

I should probably say something more than that.

"Oh god, this is so embarrassing."

Yes. Yes it is. But you still need to say a bit more.

45 seconds.

"Um, I like you."

You are really planning to have that conversation in 40 seconds?

"The thing is ..."

Yes? What is the thing, exactly?

Jane was saying nothing, just looking at me with a bemused expression.

35 seconds.

"The thing is ..."

Yes, you said that. Now is the time to say something a little more concrete.

"Oh god, look, there's no sensible way to say this. I messed up. I liked you, I do like you. I hope we'll be friends, but I didn't think-"

30 seconds.

"Stephen."

"Yes?"

"Why did you ask me out on a date?"

"Um, the thing is, it was sort of an accident."

25 seconds.

Jane considered this for a moment. She didn't seem to appreciate the urgency of the situation. There really wasn't time for her to consider things for a moment.

"How," she asked, "do you accidentally ask someone out on a date?"

20 seconds.

"I meant to text someone else," I blurted. "I don't know how I texted you. It was ..." I tailed off. "Er, an accident."

15 seconds.

"I see."

"Yes, you see, what happ-"

"Sorry it took so long," said Nat, "bit of a queue."

Fuck! She was 15 seconds early. Not that the extra 15 seconds would have helped. Nor 15 minutes, for that matter. Right at that moment, I wasn't entirely convinced that 15 hours would have been sufficient to extract myself from this mess.

Nat at this point realised Jane was not just a random bystander, and raised her eyebrows in a kind of Well, aren't you going to introduce us? manner.

Just how did one introduce the woman one had accidentally invited to the woman you'd intended to invite to the date, I wondered?

Jane was quicker on the uptake than I was.

"Hello!" she said, brightly, addressing Nat. "I'm Jane. And you are ... ?"

"Natalie."

"Pleased to meet you, Natalie. You must be the other woman Stephen has invited on this date with him."

Oh god.

"The ... other woman?" enquired Nat.

"Yes, but don't worry, you, I think, are the woman he meant to invite, while I'm the one he's only dating accidentally."

This situation was never going to go well, I thought, but this did seem a particularly extreme version of not going well.

"I don't understand ... Stephen?"

This was my cue. I had to say something at this point. Something by way of explanation. And apology. And, ideally, something that would have us all relax and laugh at the silliness of it.

If I'd had any idea at all what that something might have been, I'd have been a very happy man.

"Um," I said.

On reflection, I thought, that probably wasn't quite going to do the trick.

"Oh dear," I said.

Nor was that.

"This is all terribly embarrassing," I added.

Nat was looking at me with a blank expression, Jane was developing distinct traces of an amused one.

I decided there was no alternative but to come clean and throw myself on the mercy of the court.

"You see, I had a date with Jane," I gave Jane what I hoped was an apologetic look, "but I think both of us had decided that we weren't suited-" I paused and looked at Jane, waiting for her to confirm this; instead, those traces of amusement were now fully-fledged.

"But somehow when I meant to text you," I gestured to Nat, "I seem to have ... um ... accidentally texted Jane instead. Then I emailed you, and, uh, that's why you're both here."

"Right," said Nat, expressionless.

"Could happen to anyone," commented Jane.

"I can only apologise to both of you," I said, my head swivelling between the two.

"Don't worry," said Jane, to Nat, "he was right: we're not suited. I'll leave the two of you to enjoy the film."

Nat looked at me. "I think, under the circumstances, I'll go home too."

"No, please, look, let me explain," I said.

Nat just looked through me. "I think not," she said.

The two of them then just turned and walked out together.

Fuck.

I wanted to go after Nat, but had no idea what I'd say. I mean, it was just a stupid mix-up. For one brief, idiotic moment I wondered whether I could use Jane's line that we hadn't even had a date anyway. Moron! Argh.

Ok, I thought, the moment is lost. You go home, phone Nat later and sort out the whole mess. You've fucked-up the evening, but not necessarily the whole deal.

My musings were interrupted by the sight of Nat and Jane, arm-in-arm, approaching me.

"The tickets, please," said Jane.

"What?"

"Why should we be the ones to go home alone when you're the one that messed-up?" she asked. "We had a little chat, your two dates, and decided that we would see the film and you could be the one to go home alone."

I was still trying to think of a response to this when Jane plucked the tickets from my hand and the two of them headed down the stairs to the screen.

It had not been one of my more successful dates.

Chapter 17

I devote one week a year to a charity project, and Nikolai, a friend in Kiev working for an orphanage there, needed some photography for a big fundraising push. He'd proposed that I spend a day taking photos at his orphanage, with the rest of the week doing the same with two others, a respite centre for severely disabled kids and some other local charities

I was happy to agree. As a bonus, it would keep me out of the UK for a week, which was a whole week during which I couldn't get myself into any further dating trouble.

Nikolai was an unnaturally tall and skinny 30-year-old Ukranian guy I'd met years ago when he was staying with a mutual friend in London. He'd been a charity worker since leaving university, mostly working with children, and had recently started a new job as deputy manager of an orphanage. When he'd emailed to outline his fundraising plans, and the photography he wanted to support them, there had been no question about what this year's charity project would be.

His idea was to tell the stories of real kids from the orphanage. Rather than selling the abstract idea of kids who need help, this would be specific kids, with names, faces, favourite toys, their drawings ... all the things that would make them real children you could relate to.

"The first child you will meet is Dima," he told me on the drive from the airport. "Short for Dmitriy. He is five years old. His mother died of cancer, his father became an alcoholic and couldn't care for him. It is unfortunately not a rare combination of circumstances."

"How long has he been in the orphanage?"

"A little more than a year."

"Are there no couple who want to adopt him? In the UK, I get the impression there are many more couples wanting children than there are children to adopt."

"It is a little different here. Not everyone can care for children. Some of the children we care for in our centres have a mother or father, but for various reasons cannot look after them. Dima is not a difficult child, but he is quite wary of strangers. And it is always easier to find a home for a baby or a very young child than for one even four or five."

I nodded.

"You have done photo projects like this before?" asked Nikolai.

"Not quite like this, but with children, yes."

"Do you have children of your own?"

If only he knew!

"No," I said. "I like kids in small doses."

"I think you will have quite a large dose by the end of the week!

I picked up my camera-bag from the back seat of the car and Nikolai showed me into an office just inside the main entrance. "I will find Oksana - she is the manager."

I looked around. The office was neat and tidy. The PC on the desk looked a little elderly, but the overall impression was of a very well-run operation. I unzipped my camera bag and took out two cameras, one with my favourite 24-70/2.8 lens - a versatile lens that could zoom quickly from a full-length shot to head-and-shoulders, and which worked well in low light. The second had a wide-angle lens for general interior shots. I also pulled out my lightmeter and checked the light levels: I had seen worse.

Oksana arrived. She was a matronesque woman in her 50s, and had the no-nonsense manner one associated with the stereotype.

"Hello Stephen," she said, "I'm Oksana. Welcome."

"Thanks – it's good to meet you."

"The children are just finishing a lesson, they will be just a few minutes, then we can take you through."

"They are schooled here?" I asked.

"The pre-school ones, and the most severely disabled, are educated here. The others go to local schools. We try to integrate them as much as possible, and one of the things we raise funds for is helping schools with the conversions needed for children in wheelchairs and so forth." She paused, then grinned. "Sorry, I'm giving you the sales-talk! Would you like some coffee?"

"Sales-talk is fine, "I smiled. "But do you have tea?"

"Sure."

"That would be lovely, thanks."

"We'll go through to the canteen." She led the way, while Nikolai and I followed.

The canteen would have put most UK ones to shame. Spotlessly clean, tidy and with brightly-coloured wall displays. Oksana saw me looking at them as she brought over three mugs of tea. "They are things the children have created. Paintings, colouring, collages, what have you."

"It looks great."

Oksana looked at Nikolai. "You have told Stephen a little about Dima?" He nodded. Oksana turned to me. "He is usually wary of strangers, but he loves having his photo taken, especially if you show him on the screen. That's why we chose him. Well, that and the fact that he is a very handsome chap! I think if you take things slowly, let him get used to you being here, then it should work out."

"No problem. Are there any particular aspects of his life we want to illustrate?"

"He will be in the main living-room when the lesson finishes, so I think the best plan is to take some photos there, and then we can see if a little tour will work – his bedroom, drinking some juice in the canteen and in the playground out the back. But don't worry if we don't manage all that, he may get a bit stressed by the attention, and even a few photos would be enough."

"Sounds like a plan!"

Nikolai had some errands to run, so said he would see me later. We finished our tea, and Oksana announced that the lesson should be over and we could go through to the living-room.

Dima looked a little younger than his age, and I was relieved to see that Oksana wasn't exaggerating: he was a very obviously photogenic kid. With these sorts of projects, you never know quite what you might face. Disabilities shouldn't matter, but the harsh truth is that there are some conditions that make people want to look away, which is not what you want to achieve with this type of photography. You want a cute kid that makes people go 'Awwww', and that's exactly what we had in Dima. Tussled black hair, very Slavic-looking bone structure and a huge grin. Perfect.

I have no idea how to relate to kids. The ones aged 7 or 8 plus, I just treat exactly like adults. Below that age, I generally rely on sitting on the floor to get myself down to their level, making eye-contact and smiling a lot. Despite my simplistic approaches, both generally do the trick, and Dima turned out to be quite possibly the smiliest kid I've ever known.

"Privet," I said, the casual Russian 'Hi' being one of the few words I knew.

"Hello," he said. Oksana laughed: "We told him you were English, but you are still very honoured at a greeting."

"Smart kid!" I said, belatedly realising I was talking about him rather than to him, and added: "Aren't you?" He smiled some more.

I picked up my main camera and raised it to my eye. He was still smiling. I took a couple of head-and-shoulder shots of him, then turned the camera around and held it out to him. He looked at himself on the screen and laughed. I lifted the camera again and fired off a succession of shots. He was beaming in every one.

I zoomed out, then turned to Oksana.

"Does he have a favourite toy? Something we can show him using?"

"If you want him holding something, this is probably best."

She reached over and picked up a soft toy tiger, handing it to Dima. He took it and immediately hugged it. I fired off some shots. This kid was making it all absurdly easy.

After a few minutes, I suggested we try the tour. Oksana held out her hand and asked Dima: "Would you like to show Stephen your racing car bed?" He took her hand and stood up. I followed.

Dima showed me his bed with the racing-car bed-spread and I made the appropriate 'Wow' noises. I asked him if he'd show me how he drove it, and he climbed up onto the bed pretending to steer and making vroom sounds. It was impossible to take a bad photo of him.

Oksana asked Dima if he wanted some juice. He shook his head and ran to a box in the corner. He extracted a red toy sports car – the sort of generic one that carefully avoided any resemblance to real makes in order to avoid licence fees – and proudly presented it to me.

Having already exhausted my repertoire of 'Wow' noises in regard to the bedspread, I mentally flicked through my 'small child' vocabulary to see whether I had any further options for expressing the appropriate degree of enthusiasm for a fresh toy. Nope: I had nothing. I made with the 'Wow' routine again; he didn't appear to notice it was a re-run.

Dima ran back to the box and returned with a second car, which he solemnly presented to me. I looked over at Oksana: "How are we doing for time?"

"No problem."

I found myself sitting on the floor alternately playing cars with Dima and taking photos of him. I was rather rusty on the 'playing cars' side of things, but we seemed to get along fine anyway.

If only parenting could be just about the fun bits, I thought. Play with the kids, take them to theme parks, enjoy the smiley times and then take out the batteries and put them in the cupboard until the next time you're in the mood. Or have some kind of kid rental service, where you choose your rental band: a Group A kid would play happily for a few hours and smile a bit, up to Group E, where the kid is guaranteed to smile and giggle and generally do cute things for a full weekend.

They would, of course, come complete with breakdown coverage: if the kid starts crying or acting-up in any way, you just call an 0800 number and a truck arrives within half an hour with a technician who either fixes the problem or gives you a replacement kid. As soon as you're bored, you return it to the depot and walk away whistling. There's definitely an untapped market there.

Once the required amount of car-playing was complete, we walked back to the canteen. Oksana asked Dima if he wanted some orange juice. "Stephen get it."

You see, that's cute. You'd get that with a Group C kid. (A Group D kid would do that the first time, just to make you smile, and thereafter fetch his own juice.)

Oksana got Dima's cup and handed me the juice from the fridge. I poured it and gave it to Dima. He smiled a Group D smile. I took photos of that.

"Would you like to show Stephen the swings?" Oksana asked.

Dima ran to the back door, then looked back to check that I was following. It seemed he would.

They had quite the playground: swings, a climbing frame, some kind of tented house that would have been called a Wendy House when I was a kid but was probably a Young Person's Dwelling Exploration Area these days.

Dima ran to the swings. He jumped on one and sat there looking at me expectantly. Even I could figure out the instructions for that one: I walked over and started pushing him.

"Sil'nee!" he called.

"Higher," translated Oksana.

"Higher," I repeated to him.

"Higher," he dutifully repeated. I wondered what all the fuss was about with this teacher-training lark: it's easy! I pushed him higher, and he rewarded me with some Group E giggling.

I asked Oksana if she would take over pushing duties while I took photos. I reached into my bag for a flashgun so I could use a slow shutter speed to blur the swing's motion, then a burst of flash at the end to freeze his laughing face.

I'm always looking for new angles on photos, and wondered whether motion-blur might work if I sat on the swing next to him and swung alongside him so he'd be static against a blurred background. After picking myself up off the ground and checking that my camera was undamaged, I decided the answer to that one was 'no'.

Swing photos done, a brief piece of negotiation was completed in which Dima would pose on the climbing frame in return for a little more pushing on the swing.

"You should be a dad," said Oksana.

"Um, no," I replied. "I'm really not parent material at all."

"The evidence is against you."

"I can do the easy bits and the short-duration stuff."

"You soon get used to the rest."

"I wish it were so."

We completed the playground shots and headed back inside. Oksana was about to introduce me to the next kid, when Dima said something to her in an excited tone.

It turned out he'd just been given a model aeroplane from a package of gifts sent by a local toy store, and wanted photos of him 'flying' it. "He's never had a model plane before, and is utterly fascinated by the idea. Could you take a few more photos of him playing with it?"

I grinned. It brought back memories of my first balsa-wood glider at about the same age. I too was completely fascinated by the concept of flight, and my battered glider must have been glued together after crashes a hundred times.

"You are smiling," said Oksana.

I explained. "I would just fly my glider for hours and hours. I was just amazed that this simple wooden thing that I'd built – well, watched while my dad built, really – could actually fly."

Oksana told Dima to fetch his plane, take it outside and we would meet him out there in a few minutes after she'd offered me some tea.

We walked out, just in time to see the plane hit the side of the climbing-frame with some force. Toy technology had clearly moved on a little since my childhood: my glider was made from unpainted balsa-wood that broke almost every time it hit the ground: Dima's glider looked like it was made from some kind of plastic, and it shrugged off the impact with no sign of damage. He picked it up and threw it again.

"Sil'nee!" I called, pleased to have a use for my 11th word of Russian. I'm hopeless at languages, so settle for the simple rule of learning 10 words of the language for each visit: Hello, Goodbye, Yes, No, Please, Thank-you, Taxi, Airport, Toilet and 'One of those' – the latter, twinned with 'please', allowing me to purchase anything I could point to. Brits having a terrible reputation for languages, even those ten words were appreciated.

Oksana laughed: "You remembered from the swings."

Dima laughed too, and rushed to pick up his plane. He then ran over to show it to me. It was some kind of cross between plastic and foam – slightly sponge-like to the touch, which is I guessed what gave it its crashproof properties. It was also incredibly light. I balanced it on my fingertips by the wings – the test of whether a model plane is properly weighted; it was. I launched it gently and it glided perfectly, making a smooth landing on the grass. I was very impressed.

Dima ran after it, picked it up and ran back to me with it. He held it up: "Sil'nee!" I went to take it from him to launch it higher, but he pulled his hand away. "Dima Sil'nee!"

I smiled, remembering my father lifting me high above his head so I could launch it from up high. I did the same with Dima, and he called out a gleeful "Da!". For a man and a child who had two words of Russian vocabulary in use at present, we seemed to be doing ok.

He threw it hard, but downward, and it dived straight into the ground at my feet. That would have pulverised my balsa-wood affair, but these things were obviously built tough! I put him down, picked up the glider and knelt down next to him. Having exhausted my Russian, I reverted to English:

"Watch," I said. I then held it carefully level, and launched it. It flew a short distance, gliding gently to the ground. Dima ran to pick it up, then ran back to me. He held it carefully up, but at an angle. He threw it, less hard than last time, but still with more enthusiasm than accuracy.

"Here," I said, as he returned it to me. "Straight ..." I tried to demonstrate ... "and gentle." I launched it forward. Dima watched, fetched it and came back to me.

He held the glider in his right hand, I lifted his hand, positioned it so it was straight, then pulled it back slowly until it was ready to launch. "Gently," I said, releasing his hand.

Dima launched the glider. It was still slightly wonky and a bit too hard, but a noticeable improvement, and it landed more softly. He laughed and said something in Russian. I looked to Oksana for a translation, then noticed she wasn't there. I guessed she'd been called away so returned to my job as flying instructor.

A few dozen flights later, Dima had really got the hang of it and the delight on his face was clear. It was that which reminded me, with a start, that I was supposed to be taking photos of him playing with the plane, not helping him to fly it!

I picked up my camera and started shooting. The obvious fascination and delight on his face made for fantastic photos, but also reminded me of when I was his age. All of us have a cutoff age below which we have few memories. Mine was somewhere around that age, and yet, watching Dima with the plane, memories of that rickety balsa-wood glider came flooding back.

As I watched Dima launch, fly, retrieve, launch, fly, retrieve, launch, fly retrieve ... I remembered my own childhood. That simple joy in the fact that a solid, heavier-than-air object could actually fly through the air. It seemed magical and impossible, and I could see in Dima's face that same fascination and delight.

Nikolai returned.

"Still on Dima?" he asked, in surprise.

I explained.

"Ah," he said with a smile. "But we should drag you away now and introduce you to Irena.

"Bye, Dima!" I called. He was engrossed in his flying and gave me a brief wave without looking up.

Irina was a lively 12 year old girl with the most amazing smile. I was beginning to suspect all the kids had been chosen on the basis of the quality and/or quantity of their smiles.

She was also a talented painter. A makeshift exhibition of her work had been set up in the lobby, and it really was impressive. Landscapes, woodland scenes, seascapes ... I wondered whether she could actually have seen all the things she had painted.

When Nikolai told me Irina's story, I was amazed both at that beaming smile and at her ability to see beauty in the world.

"Both her parents, and her younger brother, were killed in a car crash two years ago. She was the only survivor. For a long time, she wouldn't speak at all. Didn't take part in most of the activities. But she started to paint. Initially, very dark themes, but gradually she has blossomed."

Shooting her paintings, it amazed me the way she really seemed to understand light. All her paintings were credible and consistent in the direction and quality of the light. Perhaps she had just painted what she'd seen, or copied from photos, but there was something about the paintings that suggested a real eye.

We got out her paints and a canvas she had started. I was trying to avoid artificially posed shots, so suggested that she actually work on a painting instead of just pretending to. Within a couple of minutes, the concentration on her face generated some photos I really liked. This project was such a good decision, I thought. It had it all: an opportunity to really lose myself in something, a great cause and an opportunity to take some photographs which I felt sure would be among my favourites.

What struck me about both Dima and Irina was the way in which they immersed themselves 100% in what they were doing, whether it was flying a model plane or painting a sky. There seemed to be no part of them that wasn't fully engaged in the task in hand. No room for the kind of wondering and doubts and second-guessing that had become an unexpectedly familiar friend since I entered my Dating With Intent phase. That child-like engagement in the moment was, I realised, a space I fell into when behind the viewfinder, but which had been notable in its absence at other times.

Dima in particular really reminded me of myself at the same sort of age. Life was gloriously simple then. At that age, the future is a nebulous concept. 'Next week' is an idea with only the most tentative of meanings; 'next year' means nothing at all. Maybe spending a week hanging around kids would help me relearn the art of living in the moment, I thought.

When do we lose that, I wondered? I guessed school would do it. Suddenly our lives became structured around time. A lesson, and thus an activity, began and ended at fixed times. Right now, he's fascinated by flight, and can explore that fascination all day long (or at least until someone makes him come in to eat!). There are no deadlines, no schedules, no plans ... just him and something that has grabbed his attention.

Maybe his enthrallment will last as long as mine did, or maybe tomorrow or next week his attention will have turned to something else.

Later, much later, he'd have physics lessons. He'd learn about the structure of wings, and how they generate lift, and why airliners are fitted with those vertical winglets on the end of their wings, and the formulas for calculating coefficients of lift – and a hundred other things. But would any of them, I wondered, convey quite as much about the concept of flight as learning the angle and force with which to launch a simple toy glider to achieve the longest distance and gentlest landing?

That phrase about "the time to put away child-ish things" came to mind. Perhaps that time came too quickly, I thought.

I found myself smiling: if I had time for such philosophical musings, perhaps I really was achieving the kind of perspective I came here to find.

The final subject for the day was Leonid. He'd been selected for the project, Nikolai told me, mostly on the basis of the extent of his disabilities and the fact that he"d been abandoned by his parents because of them.

I'd discussed with Nikolai beforehand the overall tone they wanted to take with their case-studies, as that would determine the type of photography they needed. They'd talked of the dilemma they face in their fundraising: make things look too dreadful, and it's more than people want to face, so they will click away from the website or throw away the mailer; make the kids look too happy and well cared-for, and people think everything seems fine without their help.

The decision had been taken to major on happy photos, but to use Leonid to tell a more challenging story. He was eight years old, with short, spikey hair. I was brought face-to-face with my own prejudices about disability when I realised how surprised I was to see he wasn't in a wheelchair: when I'd been told he was one of the most severely disabled kids, I realised that had been my automatic assumption. Leonid looked outwardly perfectly healthy.

"Leonid is both blind and autistic," said Nikolai, simply. Such a short, matter-of-fact statement for such an unimaginable combination of disabilities. I supposed he'd seen it all before.

As Leonid's disabilities were not visible, my job was to portray them in other ways. His blindness was easy to convey through simple mechanisms like showing him reading a braille book. Nikolai told me that symptoms of his autism would become obvious at some point during my visit; he didn't elaborate.

I'd been photographing him for 10-15 minutes when he started rocking gently back and forth. The movements became more pronounced and he became visibly more distressed. Nikolai reached out to him and held his shoulder. The rocking just kept increasing. In the full flow of it, Nikolai had backed off and Leonid was crashing down on the sofa and then lifting himself back up, only to repeat the movement over and over, a look of anguish on his face.

There was no possible way to comprehend what might be going on in his head, but the feeling it suggested to me was an overwhelming sense of isolation. It was heartbreaking to watch. Not for the first time in this trip, I was grateful to have a viewfinder to hide behind.

It seemed like it would go on forever. I desperately wanted to do something, anything, to make him return from whatever horrible place he was in, and looked to Nikolai, somehow expecting him to be able to do something.

Nikolai just shook his head: "You just have to wait for him to calm down, then he can be held. But when he is gone like this, there is nothing to do."

I didn't doubt that this was the voice of experience, but it just felt impossible to me that there was nothing to do, no way he could be helped. The feeling of helplessness was almost unbearable.

To care for a blind child would be challenging, but I could get at least some vague sense of how the workers might cope. To care for an autistic child ... there I didn't know enough about autism to have a clue. But the combination of the two ... I literally could not comprehend how hard that must be. The idea of parents abandoning their child felt unspeakably cruel, but I found myself wondering what it must have been like for them when they learned of his condition.

It was a whole other aspect to the parenthood game, I thought. You could think you were signing-up to the life and sacrifices every parent makes (the ones I already couldn't cope with myself), and then have your whole life turned inside-out. You could essentially intend to become a parent and in fact become a 24/7 carer. The gamble was even greater than I had appreciated.

The void between me and those who want children had never seemed greater.

As suddenly as it had began, it ended. Leonid was suddenly still, and Nikolai took him in his arms. I was surprised to realise that I'd been photographing the whole thing: I hadn't even been aware of it at the time. I took more photos of Nikolai holding him.

The rest of the week flew by, shooting most of the day, processing back at the hotel at the end of each, and I returned to the orphanage on my final afternoon to do a quick run through of the photos and to get an idea of which ones they were likely to use.

Afterwards, Oksana took me through to the canteen for tea.

"Nikolai has to go to the airport later to collect a trainer, but he doesn't leave here for an hour – what time is your flight?"

"It's not until six, so an hour's time will be fine."

"Dima has been asking when he can see his photos!"

"He can see them now, if he's free?"

"He is in an English lesson, but I think if he is talking with you, we can call that an informal lesson."

Dima came bounding through. Where do kids get all that energy, I wondered? They always seem to be running and jumping.

"Hi Dima."

"Hello, Stephen." He climbed up on the chair next to me.

"What were you learning in your English lesson today?" I asked.

"Counting."

"So can you count to ten?"

He nodded in that very exaggerated way young kids do when they are pleased with themselves.

"Show me."

"One, two, thuree-"

"Three," I said. "Not thuree, just three."

"Three."

"That's it."

He hesitated, and I guessed he'd lost his flow. "Start again from one," I suggested.

"One, two, three-" he looked at me and gave a big grin- "four, five, six, seven, eight, nine, ten."

"Excellent!" I didn't add that I wasn't able to do the same in Russian.

I opened my laptop. The software I use lets me add keywords to each batch of photos as I transfer them, so displaying Dima's photos took just a few seconds. I was a little surprised to see there were 168 of them. I'm usually quite an economical shooter, and it hadn't seemed that many when we'd run through them in the meeting.

I set the software in slideshow mode and slid the laptop over so it was in front of him. Dima smiled, giggled, pointed, clapped and laughed all the way through. He seemed thrilled to see so many photos of him. I generally had happy clients, but I had to admit to myself that this was possibly the most gratifying reaction I'd ever had to a set of photos.

When we'd finished, Dima climbed down and went to whisper something in Oksana's ear.

"He would like to hold your camera," she explained.

I grimaced. My cameras and lenses are expensive pieces of kit, and while I don't baby them, I am rather wary of allowing other people to hold them. To hand one to a boisterous four year old didn't seem the best of plans. No, I decided, it wasn't a good idea.

"Sorry," I said. "They are expensive."

I am a grown man. A rational one. One who does not allow small children to play with thousands of pounds worth of camera equipment. I took one look at Dima's crestfallen face and got out five and a half grand's worth of camera and lens for him to play with. He beamed.

It was too heavy for him to hold, so I dug out a small table-top tripod, set the camera on that, set and checked the exposure, then stood him on a chair and showed him how to look through the viewfinder. I turned the camera to point at a painting on the wall, then showed him how the zoom ring worked. He zoomed in and out, giggling.

I put his finger on the shutter button and gestured for him to press it very, very gently. He did so, and I heard it focus. I motioned for him to keep pressing, then showed him the photo he'd just taken on the rear viewfinder. He laughed and clapped his hands together.

In the next ten minutes, with me as tripod-operator and Dima as zoomer and button-pusher, he took photos of the wall, the door, the fridge, various toys, Oksana and me. It was clear he was having a great time.

I copied his photos to the laptop so he could see them full size. When I ran a slideshow of his photos, he gave a huge smile, looking from the screen to me to Oksana and laughing aloud.

It seemed Dima and I had another shared childhood fascination. Though in the days of film, I'd had to use my camera sparingly: in these digital days, he could fill his boots. With point-and-shoot digitals almost costing pennies these days, I asked Dima: "Would you like to have your own camera? A small one?"

Dima's whole face lit up.

Oksana quickly intervened: "To be shared with all the children," she said. She gave me a sharp look that told me I'd made a faux pas: clearly in an orphanage, one did not offer a present to a single child. Come to think of it, I realised, you couldn't do that with any family with more than one kid: even if something was clearly aimed at a particular child's interests, you either had to make it a shared present or buy them something each. The realisation of what ought to have been the bleeding obvious made me realise that, however much I seemed to have hit it off with Dima, I was still essentially rubbish at this kid stuff.

"Yes," I agreed. "For you and the other children to use." Dima clearly saw such distinctions as irrelevant: he was still making those excited-sounding noises that only young kids can do and which I have no clue how to describe.

Oksana drew me aside and said quietly: "It's very kind of you, but you must understand that promises are very important to these children. Most of them are slowly learning to trust again, and sometimes visitors can say things casually and then not follow-through."

She was right, of course. I had, naturally, fully intended to make good on my promise – but it would have been added to a to-do list that can sometimes grow lengthy, and even a short delay is a very long time to a child of Dima's age. I got out my phone and made a diary note: "I'll order it as soon as I get home," I promised.

"Thank you," she smiled. "I hope you don't think I was being rude."

"Not at all. It was a useful reminder – it might have taken me a few weeks without your prompting. I'm a bit of an amateur where kids are concerned."

"We all are, even the professionals!"

I put the camera away while Dima watched his slideshow. I may have been uncharacteristically soppy when it came to that disappointed face, but he was now happily engrossed in looking at his photos and I was relieved to put away my kit.

Nikolai came in. "Privet Dima!"

Dima smiled and replied in Russian. Nikolai crouched down by him and the two of them had an animated conversation. Nikolia then grabbed a coffee then returned to the table. "We'll be leaving in a few minutes, if that's ok?"

Had that really been an hour, I wondered?

"Sure, I just need to put my laptop away and I'm ready to roll."

Oksana said: "Then I think we will return Dima to his classes."

"If I can drag him away from his photos!" I replied. "Actually," I added, "I have an idea." I carried a few promotional USB keys in my bag. I plugged one into the laptop, set Lightroom to export JPEGs to it and presented it to Oksana when it was complete. "Now he can look at them on your PC anytime."

Oksana turned to Dima: "Say goodbye to Stephen, Dima."

I turned to him and smiled: "Poka, Dima."

Unexpectedly, Dima gave me a hug. I returned it, and lifted him up, throwing him up in the air slightly and catching him. I'm not generally demonstrative with kids, but I realised that, brief acquaintance notwithstanding, I was actually going to miss him. Maybe that kid rental scheme should have some kind of once-a-month deal for the same kid.

Chapter 18

"Come in, make yourself at home, wine's on the table – I'm just having a minor kitchen crisis," I said, dashing back to the kitchen as Helen arrived for a catch-up dinner at my place.

Helen glanced into the kitchen, and spotted my laptop, open next to the hob. "Does your cooking normally involve a laptop as an ingredient?"

"Shoo! Go drink wine. Glasses are on the table too."

I was cooking red wine and mushroom sauce for steaks, and my minor crisis was that I had been paying rather more attention to my musings than to my cooking. There may be times when one can get away with mixing musing and cooking, but while adding salt to a sauce is not one of those times.

Not wanting to make matters worse by burning anything while I searched for a solution to this, I'd quickly grabbed my laptop and placed it next to the cooker where I could keep an eye on things while typing 'too much salt in sauce' into google.

I'd learned that adding a skinned, quartered potato or two and simmering for 15 mins would absorb some of the salt, so was busy peeling a couple of extra potatoes for the purpose. The article said that there was a limit to how much salt the potatoes could absorb but didn't get specific. Not that it would have helped if it had, as I had no idea how much salt I'd added, only that I'd caught myself standing over the pan with a salt-grinder in my hand while absolutely miles away.

Potatoes added, I set it to minimum heat, put a timer on for 15 mins (yes, I'm mathematical about my cooking too) and decided that my backup plan was to offer Helen sufficient wine that she wouldn't notice what the sauce tasted like.

"Is it safe to talk to you yet?" asked Helen, leaning round from the doorway with just her head visible.

"Yes. Well, I think so. That is: I'm ok now, dinner may or may not be."

"Shall we save time by phoning for the pizza now?"

That was a reference to a previous cooking disaster that had taken place several years earlier and which I had still not been allowed to forget.

"Pass me wine."

She did so.

"So, how was the trip?"

"Memorable would be the one-word summary."

"We have three or four hours, I think you can afford a slightly less summarised summary."

I told her about it, mentioning along the way my idea for a kid rental agency.

"Are you getting broody, Mr Adams?"

"Don't be silly. I still only want the good bits, in small doses, when I'm in the mood. But I would go for maybe every fourth Sunday afternoon with a kid like him."

"I don't think I've ever heard you actively enthuse about a kid like that, though."

"Well, he reminded me a lot of me at that age. The glider thing, and playing with the camera. If parenting could be just those bits, I'd be signing-up like a shot."

"You sent the camera?"

"I sent two – my sneaky way of trying to give him his own camera while the others have one to share too."

The timer bleeped. "Stand by with the pizza menu," I said, as I went into the kitchen to check on the sauce.

I tasted it. It was borderline now: still tasted salty, but probably wouldn't actually shrivel up our tongues on contact. The article had suggested a second solution was to dilute the salt with additional liquid. Since the main liquid was red wine, this seemed a plan with no flaws: I splashed in another half a glass.

While I was waiting for the sauce to reduce, I heated a frying-pan ready for the steaks and boiled a kettle to provide water for the green beans. When the sauce looked almost there, I put some butter in the frying-pan, slapped in the steaks and set a timer for two minutes. I then poured the boiling water into a saucepan and tipped in the beans. At the end of two minutes, I flipped the steaks. Two minutes after that, I put the steaks on the warmed plates.

The saving grace about steak sauces is that, if they go horribly wrong, you can always abandon the sauce and eat the steaks au naturelle, as it were. I tasted the sauce. I tasted some more. It seemed the combination of the potato trick and sufficient wine had saved the day. I poured the sauce over the steaks, drained the green beans in a colander sprayed them with a little olive-oil and tipped them onto the plates. Job done.

I carried the plates through to the dining table and sat down. Helen raised a glass to me: "To the chef."

"You may want to taste it first ..."

She did, and nodded: "Either the crisis was solved, or you've blanketed it with enough wine to disguise it."

"That obvious, eh?"

"It wasn't a complaint."

We ate in companionable silence for a while before Helen looked at me: "Should I ask?"

"Tell me the question and I'll let you know whether you should ask."

"Whether the break worked – gave you some perspective."

"Perspective, yes. Hard to remain too self-obsessed when you see some of that stuff."

Helen looked at me. "You've still been thinking about her, haven't you." It wasn't a question.

"Every day."

"So what now?"

"Time out from dating, for sure."

"And Nat?"

"I just have to hope she's still around when I finally pull myself together."

We finished our meals and took our wine over to the sofa.

"So listen," said Helen, "I know I teased you about the broody bit, and I know we can't go on having this same conversation, but are you absolutely certain? I haven't ever seen you like this about a woman before, and you really did talk about Dima in a way that suggested something might have changed."

I paused. "Truthfully, I became very fond of Dima in a short time, but why wouldn't I? I just experienced exactly what I joke about with the kid rental thing. I saw him in his happy, smiling times when he was enjoying new stuff. What's not to love about that? What I didn't see was any of the tantrums, the frustrations, the waking up in the middle of the night and the sheer 24/7 relentlessness that is the reality of parenthood."

"It's not just that, though. Something did change."

"I suppose what changed was I got something about it that I hadn't got before. Because he was so similar to me as a kid, at least in a couple of ways, I suppose I got a tiny glimpse of that It's different when it's your own mindset. I don't think that would change all the stuff I don't like about it, but I did get to understand some tiny part of that argument. So yes, something changed. But not enough."

"We've been friends a long time."

"We have."

"I know who you are, and you know who I am."

"I think so, yes."

"Sometimes a close friend can see something we can't."

"All the bloody time, lately!"

"I know everything you've said about the kid thing. It makes complete sense, and you convinced me."

"But?"

"But you love her. You really do. It's obvious. And while you might see the shift that took place with Dima as a small one, I'm not so sure it was. I don't have any answers for you, any logical solution, but my every gut instinct says talk to her. Go see her. Maybe you're right, and it's hopeless, and nothing can change, but I think you should see her."

"And say what? Nothing has changed. Ok, I met a lovely kid for a short time and got a bit soppy over him. But that's just a matter of degree. I've always liked kids in small doses. It's nothing new, really – just somewhat more than usual."

"Ok, two questions. No, two-and-a-half questions."

"Ok."

"If Eva didn't want kids, we wouldn't be having this conversation, right."

"God no."

"And if she somehow found out tomorrow that she was infertile, and couldn't have kids, same deal, right?"

"I- yes. Well, I don't know. I mean, she might want to adopt or something."

"But if kids weren't an option full-stop, you'd be together."

"Yes. Well, I hope so, anyway."

"Ok, that's the one-and-a-half questions."

"What's the other one?"

"It's a multi-part one. And I know you're going to see where this is going, and you'll want to head it off, but just answer it one step at a time honestly, ok?"

"Do I have a choice?"

"And no flippancy, ok?"

"Ok."

"Suppose Dima's orphanage weren't a three-hour flight away. Suppose it were a mile from here. You'd see him again, right?"

"Sure. But that's very different-"

"Sssh. One step at a time."

"Ok."

"And if you did, and you continued to feel the same way about him, maybe most weekends?"

"I don't know."

Helen said nothing.

"It's possible. I mean, I like him, the staff are fantastic there, but I guess a kind of godfather role, I guess I could see that."

"And if he weren't a mile away, if the orphanage were next door, do you think you'd only see him once a week then?"

Helen had been right: I could see exactly where this was headed. It was how you steal a salami: slice by slice. But I'd agreed to go with it, and to answer each question honestly, so I did.

"Ok, sure, I'd probably pop in on my way home."

"Each day."

"Each day when I was in the UK, and when he was awake at whatever time I happened to get back, and when I wasn't too tired, and when I didn't have other things to do, sure. But that's the whole point: those are the qualifications I can apply to your idealised god-child scenario that can't be applied to parenthood. It's the difference between a hobby and a job. It's the old line about ham and eggs: the chicken was involved but the pig was committed."

"You love your job."

"Yes."

"Not all of the time."

"No, obviously there are some aspects that drive you nuts, but that's true of anything."

It was hard not to jump in. It was obvious where Helen was going with this, and it really wasn't going to change the way I thought about it. Yes, anything you love has good stuff and bad stuff. Fascinating aspects and tedious aspects. The parts you love and the parts you hate. And yes, a kid would be no different, but we'd already established that I couldn't do it. Twenty-four hours had been enough to show that.

"Helen-"

"Stephen."

"You know I know all that. You know that it's not about logic. You know I just can't do it."

"I know what you think you know. I do know it's not about logic. And I know what you think you can and can't do."

"It's not about thinking it, though, is it? I have, thanks to you and your bloody thought experiments, been there, done that and got the raspberry jam stains on the t-shirt."

"With someone else's kids, for 24 hours. Like I say, I don't know that you could do it, and I don't claim to have any answers, but the stakes here are as high as they get, and I think you need to be willing to at least explore outside your comfort-zone."

"Isn't that what I've been doing?"

"Maybe."

I looked at her blankly. "Maybe? Maybe? The winging it experiment. The 24-hour kid thing. The-" I stopped. Well, that and a bit of thinking it over had been it, really. But it had certainly felt like a definite rather than a maybe.

"I know. But somehow, you still did all of that from within your existing perspective." She saw me starting to object, and held up a hand. "I don't mean you didn't make a genuine attempt – you really did, I know. But – and I don't know if I can explain this very well – but there was still some sense of it all being done from within your model of the world, if that makes any sense?"

I thought about it for a moment. "But surely that's all any of us can do? It's not like my model of the world was plucked randomly from the air: it's a reflection of who I am."

"Who we are isn't a static thing."

"No, but this is the age thing we've talked about: we change a hell of a lot less, or a lot more gradually, anyway, as we get older."

Helen looked thoughtful.

"You remember when you were married – the good times, I mean. You remember that feeling of being able to do anything together, to take on the world. That sense that, no matter what each of you might have found difficult before, there's nothing you can't achieve between you."

I did. "I guess I thought of that as a function of age too."

"Conquering the world, possibly. Taking on some medium-sized challenges, however ..."

"I have never viewed parenting as a 'medium-sized' challenge."

"I know. But really, it is. Millions of people manage it, you know."

"Rather badly, in many cases, from what I can see."

Helen said nothing.

"Ok, but that's not an entirely flippant remark. I really do fear I'd make a terrible father."

Helen smiled.

"What?" I asked.

"All that conscious experimenting, and really nothing changed. A week away supposedly not even thinking about the issue and you've shifted ground significantly."

"I have? How?"

"You just said you feared you'd make a terrible father. You were previously rather definite on that point."

I considered that for a moment. It didn't feel to me like my position had changed.

"I don't know, Helen. I'm really not convinced anything substantive has changed."

"But you're not certain it hasn't."

"Truth be told, I don't feel certain about very much at the moment. Other than it's time for pudding. I made Lemon Mousse."

I cleared away the plates and retrieved the mousse from the fridge.

"Call her."

"I still don't know what to say."

"That you love her, that you want to be with her, that you want to find some way to make it work."

"That simple, eh?"

"Simple? Yes. Easy? No."

"She might have moved on by now. It's been three months since that last night together, and we haven't spoken or even emailed since then."

"She might, yes. Some chance vs no chance. You're supposed to be able to do simple maths."

I decided I should get Tom's take too, for balance.

"Jeez, dude, Eva still?"

"Eva still."

"But the kid thing."

I told him what Helen had said; that she thought my position was softening.

"Is it?" He asked.

"I honestly don't know any more."

"Jeez."

"Yeah."

"You really love her, don't you?"

"Yes."

"Then do it. Call her. Work it out."

It seemed Tom thought it was simple too.

Chapter 19

"Hi, Eva."

It was late – just after midnight – by the time Helen left, but I was afraid that if I didn't do this now, I never would.

There was about a fortnight's silence at the other end of the phone. I probably ought to have planned what I intended to say to her a little further ahead than 'Hi'.

"Stephen. Sorry, I'd deleted you from my phone, so your name didn't come up."

Oh fuck! She's in a relationship. That's when you delete exes from your phone. Fuck, fuck, fuck.

"Fuck."

"Isn't that a bit sudden, given we haven't even spoken for three months?" The joke was light-hearted, but the tone had some bite to it.

"Sorry. I meant- Well, it doesn't matter. You're seeing someone, I take it?"

"Why do you think that?"

"You deleted me from your phone."

"I did a lot of things. I need to know why you're calling now."

Simple but not easy. I spoke quickly, before logic or mathematics got the chance to intervene.

"I'm calling because I love you. Because I was stupid to walk away. Because I think of you every day. Because, somehow, in some way, I want to find a way to make it work."

Silence. Then more silence.

"Are you still there?"

"Yes."

"Say something."

"I don't know what to say."

"Say yes. Say no. Say 'go to hell', but please say something."

"What do you want me to say, Stephen? You made it very clear you didn't love me enough. You said goodbye. And since then, nothing. No calls. No emails. Nothing. Gone. Now three months later you're on the phone telling me you love me."

I hadn't known what to expect. Rationally, I hadn't held out much hope. But I realised as she spoke that there must have been some part of me that expected her to just metaphorically fall into my arms. That if it really were meant to be, she'd feel the same way. That she'd tell me she too had been thinking of us every day. That she loved me.

I'd expected some caution, but not this. Not coldness. Not this hard tone.

"It was never that I didn't love you enough, Eva."

"What was it, Stephen?"

"That I didn't know how to get past the kid thing."

"And you do now?"

That was the question, wasn't it? The one question I should have had an answer to before we began the conversation. The question I still couldn't answer now.

"I don't know."

Was that it? Was that my answer to the key question? Three months later, countless hours spent thinking and wondering about it, endless rehashed conversations with Helen, and that's where I'd got to with it?

"You don't know?"

"No."

"You've phoned me, three months later, to tell me that."

I didn't know what to say. What could I say? I was where I was with it, no matter how hard I might wish that the issue was resolved for me.

"I love you, Eva."

"I believe you mentioned that already."

Whatever fond illusions I may have harboured for this conversation were gone.

"No, Stephen, it's not enough."

Not enough, I thought? I was willing to reconsider one of the most fundamental decisions we ever make in our lives, one that had been an absolute for me, and that wasn't enough for her? What the hell more did she expect from me?

It truly was hopeless.

There were a hundred things I wanted to say, but I didn't have the words for any of them. I said the only thing I could think of to say: "Ok."

"Bye, Stephen." <Click>

In the movies, the hero would pause for a moment, then grab his jacket, run through the pouring rain to her apartment, stand outside, dripping wet, calling up to her window. She'd throw open the window, ask him what the hell he was doing and they'd have a shouted argument while the neighbours twitched their curtains. She'd finally tell him to go to hell, and he'd start walking slowly away. There would be a pause, then her door would open, she'd be standing there quietly, then she'd call his name. He'd turn, look at her. She'd incline her head. He'd walk slowly towards her, the music would build and finally they'd fall into each other's arms as the camera panned slowly back to a helicopter view of the city, the two of them hugging and kissing on her doorstep.

But this wasn't a movie. It was real-life. And a conversation that cold, that final, leaves absolutely no room for doubt:. Her goodbye left no room for romantic gestures. That was it. Done. Over.

Chapter 20

"Damn you!"

I'm never at my most alert when woken suddenly by a ringing phone. It was a moment before I could summon any kind of response. I looked at my watch as I did so: ten past three in the morning.

"Eva ..."

"I was not going to let you do this. I'd talked it over with my friends, and we'd all agreed, I was going to mope for a bit then move on. We'd discussed what I'd do if you called. We had a pact. And I was so good, did exactly what I'd promised myself I'd do."

That sounded familiar.

I sat up in bed. "Did your friends set a time-limit on the moping? Mine did."

"Two weeks."

"I got about the same. Maybe they read the same Cosmo column."

"They obviously didn't get it from what's-her-name in Sex and the City. Didn't she reckon it took half as long to get over a break-up as the relationship lasted??"

"Charlotte. Yeah, I think so."

"How the hell do you know that, anyway? Boys don't watch Sex and the City."

I didn't know whether to admit that it had been a Sunday ritual with my wife.

"I collect useless information."

We were both silent for a while.

"So," I said.

"So," she said.

We were silent again.

Except inside my head: there, it was very noisy, as my hopes and fears did battle. My hopes told me there was no reason for her to be making this call if not to say she wanted us to give it another chance. My fears still remembered the finality in her voice a few hours earlier, and pointed out that we were in any case no closer to resolving the issue that separated us. My hopes denied this, pointing out that there was a big difference between a firm deci-

"No promises, Stephen."

"There never are, are there?"

"What?"

"Promises. Well, there are promises, sometimes kept, sometimes broken, but there are never any guarantees."

"No, there aren't."

Perhaps I was wrong before, when I concluded that love is not enough. Perhaps that's the secret after all, and the rest of the stuff you do finally figure out if you love each other enough?

"Do you love me?" I asked. I was aware my earlier declaration had been far from reciprocated.

"Of course I fucking love you, you freaking moron! Why the hell do you think I was so angry with you?"

"Oh."

More silence.

"So what happens now?" I asked.

"You'd better be in a taxi, Adams, when asking a question that dumb."

"Oh."

It wasn't even raining.

THE END

Afterword

If you've enjoyed this book, a review on Amazon is very much appreciated. Reviews help visibility, and qualify the book for promotions.

If you'd like to be one of the first to know about upcoming titles, and be offered access to special launch pricing, please subscribe to my occasional newsletter at benlovejoyauthor.com.

Thank you!

Ben